The

Horror

in the **Museum**

Other titles by H. P. Lovecraft
available from Carroll & Graf

The Loved Dead

The Lurker at the Threshold
(with August Derleth)

The Watchers Out of Time
(with August Derleth)

The Horror in the Museum

and Other Revisions

H. P. Lovecraft

CARROLL & GRAF PUBLISHERS
NEW YORK

THE HORROR IN THE MUSEUM
And Other Revisions

Carroll & Graf Publishers
An Imprint of Avalon Publishing Group Inc.
161 William Street, 16th Floor
New York, NY 10038

First Carroll & Graf trade paperback edition 2002

Library of Congress Cataloging-in-Publication Data is available.

ISBN: 0-7867-0964-2

Printed in the United States of America
Distributed by Publishers Group West

Contents

The Horror in the Museum

Translated by Elizabeth Neville Berkeley
and Lewis Theobald, Jun.

The Green Meadow

INTRODUCTORY NOTE: The following very singular narrative or record of impressions was discovered under circumstances
so extraordinary that they deserve careful description. On the evening of Wednesday, August 27, 1913, at about 8:30 o'clock, the
population of the small seaside village of Potowonket, Maine,
U.S.A., was aroused by a thunderous report accompanied by a
blinding flash; and persons near the shore beheld a mammoth ball
of fire dart from the heavens into the sea but a short distance out,
sending up a prodigious column of water. The following Sunday a
fishing party composed of John Richmond, Peter B. Carr, and
Simon Canfield caught in their trawl and dragged ashore a mass
of metallic rock, weighing 360 pounds, and looking (as Mr. Canfield said) like a piece of slag. Most of the inhabitants agreed that
this heavy body was none other than the fireball which had fallen
from the sky four days before; and Dr. Richmond M. Jones, the
local scientific authority, allowed that it must be an aerolite or
meteoric stone. In chipping off specimens to send to an expert
Boston analyst, Dr. Jones discovered imbedded in the semi-
metallic mass the strange book containing the ensuing tale, which
is still in his possession.

In form the discovery resembles an ordinary notebook, about
5 × 3 inches in size, and containing thirty leaves. In material,
however, it presents marked peculiarities. The covers are ap-

parently of some dark stony substance unknown to geologists, and unbreakable by any mechanical means. No chemical reagent seems to act upon them. The leaves are much the same, save that they are lighter in colour, and so infinitely thin as to be quite flexible. The whole is bound by some process not very clear to those who have observed it; a process involving the adhesion of the leaf substance to the cover substance. These substances cannot now be separated, nor can the leaves be torn by any amount of force. The writing is *Greek of the purest classical quality,* and several students of palaeography declare that the characters are in a cursive hand used about the second century B. C. There is little in the text to determine the date. The mechanical mode of writing cannot be deduced beyond the fact that it must have resembled that of the modern slate and slate-pencil. During the course of analytical efforts made by the late Prof. Chambers of Harvard, several pages, mostly at the conclusion of the narrative, were blurred to the point of utter effacement before being read; a circumstance forming a well-nigh irreparable loss. What remains of the contents was done into modern Greek letters by the palaeographer Rutherford and in this form submitted to the translators.

Prof. Mayfield of the Massachusetts Institute of Technology, who examined samples of the strange stone, declares it a true meteorite; an opinion in which Dr. von Winterfeldt of Heidelberg (interned in 1918 as a dangerous enemy alien) does not concur. Prof. Bradley of Columbia College adopts a less dogmatic ground; pointing out that certain utterly unknown ingredients are present in large quantities, and warning that no classification is as yet possible.

The presence, nature, and message of the strange book form so momentous a problem, that no explanation can even be attempted. The text, as far as preserved, is here rendered as literally as our language permits, in the hope that some reader may eventually hit upon an interpretation and solve one of the greatest scientific mysteries of recent years.

—E.N.B.—L.T., Jun.

(THE STORY)

It was a narrow place, and I was alone. On one side, beyond a margin of vivid waving green, was the sea; blue, bright, and billowy, and sending up vaporous exhalations which intoxicated me. So profuse, indeed, were these exhalations, that they gave me an odd impression of a coalescence of sea and sky; for the heavens were likewise bright and blue. On the other side was the forest, ancient almost as the sea itself, and stretching infinitely inland. It was very dark, for the trees were grotesquely huge and luxuriant, and incredibly numerous. Their giant trunks were of a horrible green which blended weirdly with the narrow green tract whereon I stood. At some distance away, on either side of me, the strange forest extended down to the water's edge; obliterating the shore line and completely hemming in the narrow tract. Some of the trees, I observed, stood in the water itself; as though impatient of any barrier to their progress.

I saw no living thing, nor sign that any living thing save myself had ever existed. The sea and the sky and the wood encircled me, and reached off into regions beyond my imagination. Nor was there any sound save of the wind-tossed wood and of the sea.

As I stood in this silent place, I suddenly commenced to tremble; for though I knew not how I came there, and could scarce remember what my name and rank had been, I felt that I should go mad if I could understand what lurked about me. I recalled things I had learned, things I had dreamed, things I had imagined and yearned for in some other distant life. I thought of long nights when I had gazed up at the stars of heaven and cursed the gods that my free soul could not traverse the vast abysses which were inaccessible to my body. I conjured up ancient blasphemies, and terrible delvings into the papyri of Democritus; but as memories appeared, I shuddered in deeper fear, for I knew that I was alone—horribly alone. Alone, yet close to sentient impulses of vast, vague kind; which I prayed never to comprehend nor encounter. In the voice of the swaying green branches I fancied I could detect a kind of malignant hatred and daemoniac triumph. Sometimes they struck me as being in horrible colloquy with ghastly and unthinkable things which the scaly green bodies of the trees half hid; hid from sight but not from consciousness. The most oppressive of my sensations was a sinister feeling of alienage. Though I saw about me objects which I could name—trees, grass, sea, and sky; I felt that their relation to me was not the same as that of the trees, grass, sea, and sky I knew in another and dimly remembered life. The nature of the difference I could not tell, yet I shook in stark fright as it impressed itself upon me.

And then, in a spot where I had before discerned nothing but the misty sea, I beheld the Green Meadow; separated from me by a vast expanse of blue rippling water with sun-tipped wavelets, yet strangely near. Often I would peep fearfully over my right shoulder at the trees, but I preferred to look at the Green Meadow, which affected me oddly.

It was while my eyes were fixed upon this singular tract, that I first felt the ground in motion beneath me. Beginning with a kind of throbbing agitation which held a fiendish suggestion of conscious action, the bit of bank on which I stood detached itself from the grassy shore and commenced to float away; borne slowly onward as if by some current of resistless force. I did not move, astonished and startled as I was by the unprecedented phenomenon; but stood rigidly still until a wide lane of water yawned betwixt me and the land of trees. Then I sat down in a sort of daze, and again looked at the sun-tipped water and the Green Meadow.

Behind me the trees and the things they may have been hiding seemed to radiate infinite menace. This I knew without turning to view them, for as I grew more used to the scene I became less and less dependent upon the five senses that once had been my sole reliance. I knew the green scaly forest hated me, yet now I was safe from it, for my bit of bank had drifted far from the shore.

But though one peril was past, another loomed up before me. Pieces of earth were constantly crumbling from the floating isle which held me, so that death could not be far distant in any event. Yet even then I seemed to sense that death would be death to me no more, for I turned again to watch the Green Meadow, imbued with a curious feeling of security in strange contrast to my general horror.

Then it was that I heard, at a distance immeasurable, the sound of falling water. Not that of any trivial cascade such as I had known, but that which might be heard in the far Scythian lands if all the Mediterranean were poured down an unfathomable abyss. It was toward this sound that my shrinking island was drifting, yet I was content.

Far in the rear were happening weird and terrible things; things which I turned to view, yet shivered to behold. For in the sky dark vaporous forms hovered fantastically, brooding over trees and seeming to answer the challenge of the waving green branches. Then a thick mist arose from the sea to join the sky-forms, and the shore was erased from my sight. Though the sun—what sun I knew not—shone brightly on the water around me, the land I had left seemed involved in a daemoniac tempest where clashed the will of the hellish trees and what they hid, with that of the sky and the sea.

And when the mist vanished, I saw only the blue sky and the blue sea, for the land and the trees were no more.

It was at this point that my attention was arrested by the *singing* in the Green Meadow. Hitherto, as I have said, I had encountered no sign of human life; but now there arose to my ears a dull chant whose origin and nature were apparently unmistakable. While the words were utterly undistinguishable, the chant awaked in me a peculiar train of associations; and I was reminded of some vaguely disquieting lines I had once translated out of an Egyptian book, which in turn were taken from a papyrus of ancient Meroë. Through my brain ran lines that I fear to repeat; lines telling of very antique things and forms of life in the days when our earth was exceeding young. Of things which thought and moved and were alive, yet which gods and men would not consider alive. It was a strange book.

As I listened, I became gradually conscious of a circumstance which had before puzzled me only subconsciously. At no time had my sight distinguished any definite objects in the Green Meadow, an impression of vivid homogeneous verdure being the sum total of my perception. Now, however, I saw that the current would cause my island to pass the shore at but a little distance; so that I might learn more of the land and of the singing thereon. My curiosity to behold the singers had mounted high, though it was mingled with apprehension.

Bits of sod continued to break away from the tiny tract which carried me, but I heeded not their loss; for I felt that I was not to die with the body (or appearance of a body) which I seemed to possess. That everything about me, even life and death, was illusory; that I had overleaped the bounds of mortality and corporeal entity, becoming a free, detached thing; impressed me as almost certain. Of my location I knew nothing, save that I felt I could not be on the earth-planet once so familiar to me. My sensations, apart from a kind of haunting terror, were those of a traveller just embarked upon an unending voyage of discovery. For a moment I thought of the lands and persons I had left behind; and of strange ways whereby I might some day tell them of my adventurings, even though I might never return.

I had now floated very near the Green Meadow, so that the voices were clear and distinct; but though I knew many languages I could not quite interpret the words of the chanting. Familiar they indeed were, as I had subtly felt when at a greater distance, but beyond a sensation of vague and awesome remembrance I could make nothing of them. A most extraordinary *quality* in the voices —a quality which I cannot describe—at once frightened and fascinated me. My eyes could now discern several things amidst the omnipresent verdure—rocks, covered with bright green moss, shrubs of considerable height, and less definable shapes of great magnitude which seemed to move or vibrate amidst the shrubbery in a peculiar way. The chanting, whose authors I was so anxious to glimpse, seemed loudest at points where these shapes were most numerous and most vigorously in motion.

And then, as my island drifted closer and the sound of the distant waterfall grew louder, I saw clearly the *source* of the chanting, and in one horrible instant remembered everything. Of such things I cannot, dare not tell, for therein was revealed the hideous solution of all which had puzzled me; and that solution would drive you mad, even as it almost drove me. . . . I knew now the change through which I had passed, and through which certain others who once were men had passed! and I knew the endless cycle of the future which none like me may escape. . . . I shall live forever, be conscious forever, though my soul cries out to the gods for the boon of death and oblivion. . . . All is before me: beyond the deafening torrent lies the land of Stethelos, where young men are infinitely old. . . . The Green Meadow . . . I will send a message across the horrible immeasurable abyss. . . .

[*At this point the text becomes illegible.*]

Elizabeth Berkeley and Lewis Theobald, Jun.

The Crawling Chaos

Of the pleasures and pains of opium much has been written. The ecstasies and horrors of De Quincey and the *paradis artificiels* of Baudelaire are preserved and interpreted with an art which makes them immortal, and the world knows well the beauty, the terror, and the mystery of those obscure realms into which the inspired dreamer is transported. But much as has been told, no man has yet dared intimate the *nature* of the phantasms thus unfolded to the mind, or hint at the *direction* of the unheard-of roads along whose ornate and exotic course the partaker of the drug is so irresistibly borne. De Quincey was drawn back into Asia, that teeming land of nebulous shadows whose hideous antiquity is so impressive that "the vast age of the race and name overpowers the sense of youth in the individual", but farther than that he dared not go. Those who *have* gone farther seldom returned; and even when they have, they have been either silent or quite mad. I took opium but once—in the year of the plague, when doctors sought to deaden the agonies they could not cure. There was an overdose—my physician was worn out with horror and exertion—and I travelled very far indeed. In the end I returned and lived, but my nights are filled with strange memories, nor have I ever permitted a doctor to give me opium again.

The pain and pounding in my head had been quite unendurable when the drug was administered. Of the future I had no heed; to escape, whether by cure, unconsciousness, or death, was all that concerned me. I was partly delirious, so that it is hard to place the exact moment of transition, but I think the effect must have begun shortly before the pounding ceased to be painful. As I have said, there was an overdose; so my reactions were probably far from normal. The sensation of falling, curiously dissociated from the idea of gravity or direction, was paramount; though there was a subsidiary impression of unseen throngs in incalculable profusion, throngs of infinitely diverse nature, but all more or less related to me. Sometimes it seemed less as though I were falling, than as though the universe or the ages were falling past me. Suddenly my pain ceased, and I began to associate the pounding with an external rather than internal force. The falling has ceased also, giving place to a sensation of uneasy, temporary rest; and when I listened closely, I fancied the pounding was that of the vast, inscrutable sea as its sinister, colossal breakers lacerated some desolate shore after a storm of titanic magnitude. Then I opened my eyes.

For a moment my surroundings seemed confused, like a projected image hopelessly out of focus, but gradually I realised my solitary presence in a strange and beautiful room lighted by many windows. Of the exact nature of the apartment I could form no idea, for my thoughts were still far from settled; but I noticed varicoloured rugs and draperies, elaborately fashioned tables, chairs, ottomans, and divans, and delicate vases and ornaments which conveyed a suggestion of the exotic without being actually alien. These things I noticed, yet they were not long uppermost in my mind. Slowly but inexorably crawling upon my consciousness, and rising above every other impression, came a dizzying fear of the unknown; a fear all the greater because I could not analyse it, and seeming to concern a stealthily approaching menace—not death, but some nameless, unheard-of thing inexpressibly more ghastly and abhorrent.

Presently I realised that the direct symbol and excitant of my fear was the hideous pounding whose incessant reverberations throbbed maddeningly against my exhausted brain. It seemed to come from a point outside and below the edifice in which I stood, and to associate itself with the most terrifying mental images. I felt that some horrible scene or object lurked beyond the silk-hung walls, and shrank from glancing through the arched, latticed windows that opened so bewilderingly on every hand. Perceiving shutters attached to these windows, I closed them all, averting my eyes from the exterior as I did so. Then, employing a flint and steel which I found on one of the small tables, I lit the many candles reposing about the walls in Arabesque sconces. The added sense of security brought by closed shutters and artificial light calmed my nerves to some degree, but I could not shut out the monotonous pounding. Now that I was calmer, the sound became as fascinating as it was fearful, and I felt a contradictory desire to seek out its source despite my still powerful shrinking. Opening a portiere at the side of the room nearest the pounding, I beheld a small and richly draped corridor ending in a carven door and large oriel window. To this window I was irresistibly drawn, though my ill-defined apprehensions seemed almost equally bent on holding me back. As I approached it I could see a chaotic whirl of waters in the distance. Then, as I attained it and glanced out on all sides, the stupendous picture of my surroundings burst upon me with full and devastating force.

I beheld such a sight as I had never beheld before, and which no living person can have seen save in the delirium of fever or the inferno of opium. The building stood on a narrow point of land—or what was *now* a narrow point of land—fully 300 feet above what must lately have been a seething vortex of mad waters. On either side of the house there fell a newly washed-out precipice of red earth, whilst ahead of me the hideous waves were still rolling in frightfully, eating away the land with ghastly monotony and deliberation. Out a mile or more there rose and fell menacing breakers at least fifty feet in height, and on the far horizon ghoulish black clouds of grotesque contour were resting and brooding like unwholesome vultures. The waves were dark and purplish, almost black, and clutched at the yielding red mud of the bank as if with uncouth, greedy hands. I could not but feel that some noxious marine mind had declared a war of extermination upon all the solid ground, perhaps abetted by the angry sky.

Recovering at length from the stupor into which this unnatural spectacle had thrown me, I realised that my actual physical danger was acute. Even whilst I gazed the bank had lost many feet, and it could not be long before the house would fall undermined into the awful pit of lashing waves. Accordingly I hastened to the opposite side of the edifice, and finding a door, emerged at once, locking it after me with a curious key which had hung inside. I now beheld more of the strange region about me, and marked a singular division which seemed to exist in the hostile ocean and firmament. On each side of the jutting promontory different conditions held sway. At my left as I faced inland was a gently heaving sea with great green waves rolling peacefully in under a brightly shining sun. Something about that sun's nature and position made me shudder, but I could not then tell, and cannot tell now, what it was. At my right also was the sea, but it was blue, calm, and only gently undulating, while the sky above it was darker and the washed-out bank more nearly white than reddish.

I now turned my attention to the land, and found occasion for fresh surprise; for the vegetation resembled nothing I had ever seen or read about. It was apparently tropical or at least sub-tropical—a conclusion borne out by the intense heat of the air. Sometimes I thought I could trace strange analogies with the flora of my native land, fancying that the well-known plants and shrubs might assume such forms under a radical change of climate; but the gigantic and omnipresent palm trees were plainly foreign. The house I had just left was very small—hardly more than a cottage—but its material was evidently marble, and its architecture was weird and composite, involving a quaint fusion of Western and Eastern forms. At the corners were Corinthian columns, but the red tile roof was like that of a Chinese pagoda. From the door inland there stretched a path of singularly white sand, about four feet wide, and lined on either side with stately palms and unidentifiable flowering shrubs and plants. It lay toward the side of the promontory where the sea was blue and the bank rather whitish. Down this path I felt impelled to flee, as if pursued by some malignant spirit from the pounding ocean. At first it was slightly uphill, then I reached a gentle crest. Behind me I saw the scene I had left; the entire point with the cottage and the black water, with the green sea on one side and the blue sea on the other, and a curse unnamed and unnamable lowering over all. I never saw it again, and often wonder. . . . After this last look I strode ahead and surveyed the inland panorama before me.

The path, as I have intimated, ran along the right-hand shore as one went inland. Ahead and to the left I now viewed a magnificent valley comprising thousands of acres, and covered with a swaying growth of tropical grass higher than my head. Almost at the limit of vision was a colossal palm tree which seemed to fascinate and beckon me. By this time wonder and escape from the imperilled peninsula had largely dissipated my fear, but as I paused and sank fatigued to the path, idly digging with my hands into the warm, whitish-golden sand, a new and acute sense of danger seized me. Some terror in the swishing tall grass seemed added to that of the diabolically pounding sea, and I started up crying aloud and disjointedly, "Tiger? Tiger? Is it Tiger? Beast? Beast? Is it a Beast that I am afraid of?" My mind wandered back to an ancient and classical story of tigers which I had read; I strove to recall the author, but had difficulty. Then in the midst of my fear I remembered that the tale was by Rudyard Kipling; nor did the grotesqueness of deeming him an ancient author occur to me. I wished for the volume containing this story, and had almost started back toward the doomed cottage to procure it when my better sense and the lure of the palm prevented me.

Whether or not I could have resisted the backward beckoning without the counter-fascination of the vast palm tree, I do not know. This attraction was now dominant, and I left the path and crawled on hands and knees down the valley's slope despite my fear of the grass and of the serpents it might contain. I resolved to fight for life and reason as long as possible against all menaces of sea or land, though I sometimes feared defeat as the maddening swish of the uncanny grasses joined the still audible and irritating pounding of the distant breakers. I would frequently pause and put my hands to my ears for relief, but could never quite shut out the detestable sound. It was, as it seemed to me, only after ages that I finally dragged myself to the beckoning palm tree and lay quiet beneath its protecting shade.

There now ensued a series of incidents which transported me to the opposite extremes of ecstasy and horror; incidents which I tremble to recall and dare not seek to interpret. No sooner had I crawled beneath the overhanging foliage of the palm, than there dropped from its branches a young child of such beauty as I never beheld before. Though ragged and dusty, this being bore the features of a faun or demigod, and seemed almost to diffuse a radiance in the dense shadow of the tree. It smiled and extended its hand, but before I could arise and speak I heard in the upper air the exquisite melody of singing; notes high and low blent with a sublime and ethereal harmoniousness. The sun had by this time sunk below the horizon, and in the twilight I saw that an aureola of lambent light encircled the child's head. Then in a tone of silver it addressed me: "It is the end. They have come down through the gloaming from the stars. Now all is over, and beyond the Arinurian streams we shall dwell blissfully in Teloe." As the child spoke, I beheld a soft radiance through the leaves of the palm tree, and rising greeted a pair whom I knew to be the chief singers among those I had heard. A god and goddess they must have been, for such beauty is not mortal; and they took my hands, saying, "Come, child, you have heard the voices, and all is well. In Teloe beyond the Milky Way and the Arinurian streams are cities all of amber and chalcedony. And upon their domes of many facets glisten the images of strange and beautiful stars. Under the ivory bridges of Teloe flow rivers of liquid gold bearing pleasure-barges bound for blossomy Cytharion of the Seven Suns. And in Teloe and Cytharion abide only youth, beauty, and pleasure, nor are any sounds heard, save of laughter, song, and the lute. Only the gods dwell in Teloe of the golden rivers, but among them shalt thou dwell."

As I listened, enchanted, I suddenly became aware of a change in my surroundings. The palm tree, so lately overshadowing my exhausted form, was now some distance to my left and considerably below me. I was obviously floating in the atmosphere; companioned not only by the strange child and the radiant pair, but by a constantly increasing throng of half-luminous, vine-crowned youths and maidens with wind-blown hair and joyful countenance. We slowly ascended together, as if borne on a fragrant breeze which blew not from the earth but from the golden nebulae, and the child whispered in my ear that I must look always upward to the pathways of light, and never backward to the sphere I had just left. The youths and maidens now chaunted mellifluous choriambics to the accompaniment of lutes, and I felt enveloped in a peace and happiness more profound than any I had in life imagined, when the intrusion of a single sound altered my destiny and shattered my soul. Through the ravishing strains of the singers and the lutanists, as if in mocking, daemoniac concord, throbbed from gulfs below the damnable, the detestable pounding of that hideous ocean. And as those black breakers beat their message into my ears I forgot the words of the child and looked back, down upon the doomed scene from which I thought I had escaped.

Down through the aether I saw the accursed earth turning, ever turning, with angry and tempestuous seas gnawing at wild desolate shores and dashing foam against the tottering towers of deserted cities. And under a ghastly moon there gleamed sights I can never describe, sights I can never forget; deserts of corpse-like clay and jungles of ruin and decadence where once stretched the populous plains and villages of my native land, and maelstroms of frothing ocean where once rose the mighty temples of my forefathers. Around the northern pole steamed a morass of noisome growths and miasmal vapours, hissing before the onslaught of the ever-mounting waves that curled and fretted from the shuddering deep. Then a rending report clave the night, and athwart the desert of deserts appeared a smoking rift. Still the black ocean foamed and gnawed, eating away the desert on either side as the rift in the centre widened and widened.

There was now no land left but the desert, and still the fuming ocean ate and ate. All at once I thought even the pounding sea seemed afraid of something, afraid of dark gods of the inner earth that are greater than the evil god of waters, but even if it was it could not turn back; and the desert had suffered too much from those nightmare waves to help them now. So the ocean ate the last of the land and poured into the smoking gulf, thereby giving up all it had ever conquered. From the new-flooded lands it flowed again, uncovering death and decay; and from its ancient and immemorial bed it trickled loathsomely, uncovering nighted secrets of the years when Time was young and the gods unborn. Above the waves rose weedy, remembered spires. The moon laid pale lilies of light on dead London, and Paris stood up from its damp grave to be sanctified with star-dust. Then rose spires and monoliths that were weedy but not remembered; terrible spires and monoliths of lands that men never knew were lands.

There was not any pounding now, but only the unearthly roaring and hissing of waters tumbling into the rift. The smoke of that rift had changed to steam, and almost hid the world as it grew denser and denser. It seared my face and hands, and when I looked to see how it affected my companions I found they had all disappeared. Then very suddenly it ended, and I knew no more till I awaked upon a bed of convalescence. As the cloud of steam from the Plutonic gulf finally concealed the entire surface from my sight, all the firmament shrieked at a sudden agony of mad reverberations which shook the trembling aether. In one delirious flash and burst it happened; one blinding, deafening holocaust of fire, smoke, and thunder that dissolved the wan moon as it sped outward to the void.

And when the smoke cleared away, and I sought to look upon the earth, I beheld against the background of cold, humorous stars only the dying sun and the pale mournful planets searching for their sister.

Adolphe de Castro

The Electric Executioner

For one who has never faced the danger of legal execution, I have a rather queer horror of the electric chair as a subject. Indeed, I think the topic gives me more of a shudder than it gives many a man who has been on trial for his life. The reason is that I associate the thing with an incident of forty years ago—a very strange incident which brought me close to the edge of the unknown's black abyss.

In 1889 I was an auditor and investigator connected with the Tlaxcala Mining Company of San Francisco, which operated several small silver and copper properties in the San Mateo Mountains in Mexico. There had been some trouble at Mine No. 3, which had a surly, furtive assistant superintendent named Arthur Feldon; and on August 6th the firm received a telegram saying that Feldon had decamped, taking with him all the stock records, securities, and private papers, and leaving the whole clerical and financial situation in dire confusion.

This development was a severe blow to the company, and late in the afternoon President McComb called me into his office to give orders for the recovery of the papers at any cost. There were, he knew, grave drawbacks. I had never seen Feldon, and there were only very indifferent photographs to go by. Moreover, my own wedding was set for Thursday of the following week—only nine days ahead—so that I was naturally not eager to be hurried off to Mexico on a man-hunt of indefinite length. The need, however, was so great that McComb felt justified in asking me to go at once; and I for my part decided that the effect on my status with the company would make ready acquiescence eminently worth while.

I was to start that night, using the president's private car as far as Mexico City, after which I would have to take a narrow-gauge railway to the mines. Jackson, the superintendent of No. 3, would give me all details and any possible clues upon my arrival; and then the search would begin in earnest—through the mountains, down to the coast, or among the byways of Mexico City, as the case might be. I set out with a grim determination to get the matter done —and successfully done—as swiftly as possible; and tempered my discontent with pictures of an early return with papers and culprit, and of a wedding which would be almost a triumphal ceremony.

Having notified my family, fiancée, and principal friends, and made hasty preparations for the trip, I met President McComb at eight p.m. at the Southern Pacific depot, received from him some written instructions and a check-book, and left in his car attached to the 8:15 eastbound transcontinental train. The journey that followed seemed destined for uneventfulness, and after a good night's sleep I revelled in the ease of the private car so thoughtfully assigned me; reading my instructions with care, and formulating plans for the capture of Feldon and the recovery of the documents. I knew the Tlaxcala country quite well—probably much better than the missing man—hence had a certain amount of advantage in my search unless he had already used the railway.

According to the instructions, Feldon had been a subject of worry to Superintendent Jackson for some time; acting secretively, and working unaccountably in the company's laboratory at odd hours. That he was implicated with a Mexican boss and several peons in some thefts of ore was strongly suspected; but though the natives had been discharged, there was not enough evidence to warrant any positive step regarding the subtle official. Indeed, despite his furtiveness, there seemed to be more of defiance than of guilt in the man's bearing. He wore a chip on his shoulder, and talked as if the company were cheating him instead of his cheating the company. The obvious surveillance of his colleagues, Jackson wrote, appeared to irritate him increasingly; and now he had gone with everything of importance in the office. Of his possible whereabouts no guess could be made; though Jackson's final telegram suggested the wild slopes of the Sierra de Malinche, that tall, myth-sur-rounded peak with the corpse-shaped silhouette, from whose neighbourhood the thieving natives were said to have come.

At El Paso, which we reached at two a.m. of the night following our start, my private car was detached from the transcontinental train and joined to an engine specially ordered by telegraph to take it southward to Mexico City. I continued to drowse till dawn, and all the next day grew bored on the flat, desert Chihuahua land-scape. The crew had told me we were due in Mexico City at noon Friday, but I soon saw that countless delays were wasting precious hours. There were waits on sidings all along the single-tracked route, and now and then a hot-box or other difficulty would fur-ther complicate the schedule.

At Torreón we were six hours late, and it was almost eight o'clock on Friday evening—fully twelve hours behind schedule—when the conductor consented to do some speeding in an effort to make up time. My nerves were on edge, and I could do nothing but pace the car in desperation. In the end I found that the speeding had been purchased at a high cost indeed, for within a half-hour the symptoms of a hot-box had developed in my car itself; so that after a maddening wait the crew decided that all the bearings would have to be overhauled after a quarter-speed limp ahead to the next sta-tion with shops—the factory town of Querétaro. This was the last straw, and I almost stamped like a child. Actually I sometimes caught myself pushing at my chair-arm as if trying to urge the train forward at a less snail-like pace.

It was almost ten in the evening when we drew into Querétaro, and I spent a fretful hour on the station platform while my car was sidetracked and tinkered at by a dozen native mechanics. At last they told me the job was too much for them, since the forward truck needed new parts which could not be obtained nearer than Mexico City. Everything indeed seemed against me, and I gritted my teeth when I thought of Feldon getting farther and farther away —perhaps to the easy cover of Vera Cruz with its shipping or Mex-ico City with its varied rail facilities—while fresh delays kept me tied and helpless. Of course Jackson had notified the police in all the cities around, but I knew with sorrow what their efficiency amounted to.

The best I could do, I soon found out, was to take the regular night express for Mexico City, which ran from Aguas Calientes and made a five-minute stop at Querétaro. It would be along at one a.m. if on time, and was due in Mexico City at five o'clock Saturday morning. When I purchased my ticket I found that the train would be made up of European compartment carriages instead of long American cars with rows of two-seat chairs. These had been much used in the early days of Mexican railroading, owing to the European construction interests back of the first lines; and in 1889 the Mexican Central was still running a fair number of them on its shorter trips. Ordinarily I prefer the American coaches, since I hate to have people facing me; but for this once I was glad of the foreign carriage. At such a time of night I stood a good chance of having a whole compartment to myself, and in my tired, nervously hypersensitive state I welcomed the solitude—as well as the comfortably upholstered seat with soft arm-rests and head-cushion, running the whole width of the vehicle. I bought a first-class ticket, obtained my valise from the sidetracked private car, telegraphed both President McComb and Jackson of what had happened, and settled down in the station to wait for the night express as patiently as my strained nerves would let me.

For a wonder, the train was only half an hour late; though even so, the solitary station vigil had about finished my endurance. The conductor, shewing me into a compartment, told me he expected to make up the delay and reach the capital on time; and I stretched myself comfortably on the forward-facing seat in the expectation of a quiet three-and-a-half-hour run. The light from the overhead oil lamp was soothingly dim, and I wondered whether I could snatch some much-needed sleep in spite of my anxiety and nerve-tension. It seemed, as the train jolted into motion, that I was alone; and I was heartily glad of it. My thoughts leaped ahead to my quest, and I nodded with the accelerating rhythm of the speeding string of carriages.

Then suddenly I perceived that I was not alone after all. In the corner diagonally opposite me, slumped down so that his face was invisible, sat a roughly clad man of unusual size, whom the feeble light had failed to reveal before. Beside him on the seat was a huge valise, battered and bulging, and tightly gripped even in his sleep by one of his incongruously slender hands. As the engine whistled sharply at some curve or crossing, the sleeper started nervously into a kind of watchful half-awakening; raising his head and disclosing a handsome face, bearded and clearly Anglo-Saxon, with dark, lustrous eyes. At sight of me his wakefulness became complete, and I wondered at the rather hostile wildness of his glance. No doubt, I thought, he resented my presence when he had hoped to have the compartment alone all the way; just as I was myself disappointed to find strange company in the half-lighted carriage. The best we could do, however, was to accept the situation gracefully; so I began apologising to the man for my intrusion. He seemed to be a fellow-American, and we could both feel more at ease after a few civilities. Then we could leave each other in peace for the balance of the journey.

To my surprise, the stranger did not respond to my courtesies with so much as a word. Instead, he kept staring at me fiercely and almost appraisingly, and brushed aside my embarrassed proffer of a cigar with a nervous lateral movement of his disengaged hand. His other hand still tensely clutched the great, worn valise, and his whole person seemed to radiate some obscure malignity. After a time he abruptly turned his face toward the window, though there was nothing to see in the dense blackness outside. Oddly, he appeared to be looking at something as intently as if there really were something to look at. I decided to leave him to his own curious devices and meditations without further annoyance; so settled back in my seat, drew the brim of my soft hat over my face, and closed my eyes in an effort to snatch the sleep I had half counted on.

I could not have dozed very long or very fully when my eyes fell open as if in response to some external force. Closing them again with some determination, I renewed my quest of a nap, yet wholly without avail. An intangible influence seemed bent on keeping me awake; so raising my head, I looked about the dimly lighted compartment to see if anything were amiss. All appeared normal, but I noticed that the stranger in the opposite corner was looking at me very intently—intently, though without any of the geniality or friendliness which would have implied a change from his former surly attitude. I did not attempt conversation this time, but leaned back in my previous sleepy posture; half closing my eyes if I had dozed off once more, yet continuing to watch him curiously from beneath my down-turned hat brim.

As the train rattled onward through the night I saw a subtle and gradual metamorphosis come over the expression of the staring man. Evidently satisfied that I was asleep, he allowed his face to reflect a curious jumble of emotions, the nature of which seemed anything but reassuring. Hatred, fear, triumph, and fanaticism flickered compositely over the lines of his lips and the angles of his eyes, while his gaze became a glare of really alarming greed and ferocity. Suddenly it dawned upon me that this man was mad, and dangerously so.

I will not pretend that I was anything but deeply and thoroughly frightened when I saw how things stood. Perspiration started out all over me, and I had hard work to maintain my attitude of relaxation and slumber. Life had many attractions for me just then, and the thought of dealing with a homicidal maniac—possibly armed and certainly powerful to a marvellous degree—was a dismaying and terrifying one. My disadvantage in any sort of struggle was enormous; for the man was a virtual giant, evidently in the best of athletic trim, while I have always been rather frail, and was then almost worn out with anxiety, sleeplessness, and nervous tension. It was undeniably a bad moment for me, and I felt pretty close to a horrible death as I recognised the fury of madness in the stranger's eyes. Events from the past came up into my consciousness as if for a farewell—just as a drowning man's whole life is said to resurrect itself before him at the last moment.

Of course I had my revolver in my coat pocket, but any motion of mine to reach and draw it would be instantly obvious. Moreover, if I did secure it, there was no telling what effect it would have on the maniac. Even if I shot him once or twice he might have enough remaining strength to get the gun from me and deal with me in his own way; or if he were armed himself he might shoot or stab without trying to disarm me. One can cow a sane man by covering him with a pistol, but an insane man's complete indifference to consequences gives him a strength and menace quite superhuman for the time being. Even in those pre-Freudian days I had a common-sense realisation of the dangerous power of a person without normal inhibitions. That the stranger in the corner was indeed about to start some murderous action, his burning eyes and twitching facial muscles did not permit me to doubt for a moment.

Suddenly I heard his breath begin to come in excited gasps, and saw his chest heaving with mounting excitement. The time for a showdown was close, and I tried desperately to think of the best thing to do. Without interrupting my pretence of sleep, I began to slide my right hand gradually and inconspicuously toward the pocket containing my pistol; watching the madman closely as I did so, to see if he would detect any move. Unfortunately he did—almost before he had time to register the fact in his expression. With a bound so agile and abrupt as to be almost incredible in a man of his size, he was upon me before I knew what had happened; looming up and swaying forward like a giant ogre of legend, and pinioning me with one powerful hand while with the other he forestalled me in reaching the revolver. Taking it from my pocket and placing it in his own, he released me contemptuously, well knowing how fully his physique placed me at his mercy. Then he stood up at his full height—his head almost touching the roof of the carriage—and stared down at me with eyes whose fury had quickly turned to a look of pitying scorn and ghoulish calculation.

I did not move, and after a moment the man resumed his seat opposite me; smiling a ghastly smile as he opened his great bulging valise and extracted an article of peculiar appearance—a rather large cage of semi-flexible wire, woven somewhat like a baseball catcher's mask, but shaped more like the helmet of a diving-suit. Its top was connected with a cord whose other end remained in the valise. This device he fondled with obvious affection, cradling it in his lap as he looked at me afresh and licked his bearded lips with an almost feline motion of the tongue. Then, for the first time, he spoke—in a deep, mellow voice of softness and cultivation startlingly at variance with his rough corduroy clothes and unkempt aspect.

"You are fortunate, sir. I shall use you first of all. You shall go into history as the first fruits of a remarkable invention. Vast sociological consequences—I shall let my light shine, as it were. I'm radiating all the time, but nobody knows it. Now you shall know. Intelligent guinea-pig. Cats and burros—it worked even with a burro. . . ."

He paused, while his bearded features underwent a convulsive motion closely synchronised with a vigorous gyratory shaking of the whole head. It was as though he were shaking clear of some nebulous obstructing medium, for the gesture was followed by a clarification or subtilisation of expression which hid the more obvious madness in a look of suave composure through which the craftiness gleamed only dimly. I glimpsed the difference at once, and put in a word to see if I could lead his mind into harmless channels.

"You seem to have a marvellously fine instrument, if I'm any judge. Won't you tell me how you came to invent it?"

He nodded.

"Mere logical reflection, dear sir. I consulted the needs of the age and acted upon them. Others might have done the same had their minds been as powerful—that is, as capable of sustained concentration—as mine. I had the sense of conviction—the available will power—that is all. I realised, as no one else has yet realised, how imperative it is to remove everybody from the earth before Quetzalcoatl comes back, and realised also that it must be done elegantly. I hate butchery of any kind, and hanging is barbarously crude. You know last year the New York legislature voted to adopt electric execution for condemned men—but all the apparatus they have in mind is as primitive as Stephenson's 'Rocket' or Davenport's first electric engine. I knew of a better way, and told them so, but they paid no attention to me. God, the fools! As if I didn't know all there is to know about men and death and electricity—student, man, and boy—technologist and engineer—soldier of fortune. . . ."

He leaned back and narrowed his eyes.

"I was in Maximilian's army twenty years and more ago. They were going to make me a nobleman. Then those damned greasers killed him and I had to go home. But I came back—back and forth, back and forth. I live in Rochester, N.Y. . . ."

His eyes grew deeply crafty, and he leaned forward, touching me on the knee with the fingers of a paradoxically delicate hand.

"I came back, I say, and I went deeper than any of them. I hate greasers, but I like Mexicans! A puzzle? Listen to me, young fellow —you don't think Mexico is really Spanish, do you? God, if you knew the tribes I know! In the mountains—in the mountains— Anahuac—Tenochtitlan—the old ones. . . ."

His voice changed to a chanting and not unmelodious howl.

"Iä! Huitzilopotchli! . . . Nahuatlacatl! Seven, seven, seven . . . Xochimilca, Chalca, Tepaneca, Acolhua, Tlahuica, Tlascalteca, Azteca! . . . Iä! Iä! I have been to the Seven Caves of Chicomoztoc, but no one shall ever know! I tell you *because you will never repeat it*. . . ."

He subsided, and resumed a conversational tone.

"It would surprise you to know what things are told in the mountains. Huitzilopotchli is coming back . . . of that there can be no doubt. Any peon south of Mexico City can tell you that. But I meant to do nothing about it. I went home, as I tell you, again and again, and was going to benefit society with my electric executioner when that cursed Albany legislature adopted the other way. A joke, sir, a joke! Grandfather's chair—sit by the fireside—Hawthorne—"

The man was chuckling with a morbid parody of good nature.

"Why, sir, I'd like to be the first man to sit in their damned chair and feel their little two-bit battery current! It wouldn't make a frog's legs dance! And they expect to kill murderers with it—reward of merit—everything! But then, young man, I saw the uselessness—the pointless illogicality, as it were—of killing just a few. Everybody is a murderer—they murder ideas—steal inventions—stole mine by watching, and watching, and watching—"

The man choked and paused, and I spoke soothingly.

"I'm sure your invention was much the better, and probably they'll come to use it in the end."

Evidently my tact was not great enough, for his response shewed fresh irritation.

"'Sure,' are you? Nice, mild, conservative assurance! Cursed lot you care—*but you'll soon know!* Why, damn you, all the good there ever will be in that electric chair will have been stolen from me. The ghost of Nezahualpilli told me that on the sacred mountain. They watched, and watched, and watched—"

He choked again, then gave another of those gestures in which he seemed to shake both his head and his facial expression. That seemed temporarily to steady him.

"What my invention needs is testing. That is it—here. The wire hood or head-net is flexible, and slips on easily. Neckpiece binds but doesn't choke. Electrodes touch forehead and base of cerebellum—all that's necessary. Stop the head, and what else can go? The fools up at Albany, with their carved oak easy-chair, think they've got to make it a head-to-foot affair. Idiots!—don't they know that you don't need to shoot a man through the body after you've plugged him through the brain? I've seen men die in battle—I know better. And then their silly high-power circuit—dynamos—all that. Why didn't they see what I've done with the storage-battery? Not a hearing—nobody knows—I alone have the secret—that's why I and Quetzalcoatl and Huitzilopotchli will rule the world alone—I and they, if I choose to let them. . . . But I must have experimental subjects—subjects—*do you know whom I've chosen for the first?*"

I tried jocoseness, quickly merging into friendly seriousness, as a sedative. Quick thought and apt words might save me yet.

"Well, there are lots of fine subjects among the politicians of San Francisco, where I come from! They need your treatment, and I'd like to help you introduce it! But really, I think I can help you in all truth. I have some influence in Sacramento, and if you'll go back to the States with me after I'm through with my business in Mexico, I'll see that you get a hearing."

He answered soberly and civilly.

"No—I can't go back. I swore not to when those criminals at Albany turned down my invention and set spies to watch me and steal from me. But I must have American subjects. Those greasers are under a curse, and would be too easy; and the full-blood Indians—the real children of the feathered serpent—are sacred and inviolate except for proper sacrificial victims . . . and even those must be slain according to ceremony. I must have Americans without going back—and the first man I choose will be signally honoured. Do you know who he is?"

I temporised desperately.

"Oh, if that's all the trouble, I'll find you a dozen first-rate Yankee specimens as soon as we get to Mexico City! I know where there are lots of small mining men who wouldn't be missed for days—"

But he cut me short with a new and sudden air of authority which had a touch of real dignity in it.

"That'll do—we've trifled long enough. Get up and stand erect like a man. You're the subject I've chosen, and you'll thank me for the honour in the other world, just as the sacrificial victim thanks the priest for transferring him to eternal glory. A new principle—no other man alive has dreamed of such a battery, and it might never again be hit on if the world experimented a thousand years. Do you know that atoms aren't what they seem? Fools! A century after this some dolt would be guessing if I were to let the world live!"

As I arose at his command, he drew additional feet of cord from the valise and stood erect beside me; the wire helmet outstretched toward me in both hands, and a look of real exaltation on his tanned and bearded face. For an instant he seemed like a radiant Hellenic mystagogue or hierophant.

"Here, O Youth—a libation! Wine of the cosmos—nectar of the starry spaces—Linos—Iacchus—Ialmenos—Zagreus—Dionysos—Atys—Hylas—sprung from Apollo and slain by the hounds of Argos—seed of Psamathë—child of the sun—Evoë! Evoë!"

He was chanting again, and this time his mind seemed far back amongst the classic memories of his college days. In my erect posture I noticed the nearness of the signal cord· overhead, and wondered whether I could reach it through some gesture of ostensible response to his ceremonial mood. It was worth trying, so with an antiphonal cry of "Evoë!" I put my arms forward and upward toward him in a ritualistic fashion, hoping to give the cord a tug before he could notice the act. But it was useless. He saw my purpose, and moved one hand toward the right-hand coat pocket where my revolver lay. No words were needed, and we stood for a moment like carven figures. Then he quietly said, "Make haste!"

Again my mind rushed frantically about seeking avenues of escape. The doors, I knew, were not locked on Mexican trains; but my companion could easily forestall me if I tried to unlatch one and jump out. Besides, our speed was so great that success in that direction would probably be as fatal as failure. The only thing to do was to play for time. Of the three-and-a-half-hour trip a good slice was already worn away, and once we got to Mexico City the guards and police in the station would provide instant safety.

There would, I thought, be two distinct times for diplomatic stalling. If I could get him to postpone the slipping on of the hood, that much time would be gained. Of course I had no belief that the thing was really deadly; but I knew enough of madmen to understand what would happen when it failed to work. To his disappointment would be added a mad sense of my responsibility for the failure, and the result would be a red chaos of murderous rage. Therefore the experiment must be postponed as long as possible. Yet the second opportunity did exist, for if I planned cleverly I might devise explanations for the failure which would hold his attention and lead him into more or less extended searches for corrective influences. I wondered just how far his credulity went, and whether I could prepare in advance a prophecy of failure which would make the failure itself stamp me as a seer or initiate, or perhaps a god. I had enough of a smattering of Mexican mythology to make it worth trying; though I would try other delaying influences first and let the prophecy come as a sudden revelation. Would he spare me in the end if I could make him think me a prophet or divinity? Could I "get by" as Quetzalcoatl or Huitzilopotchli? Anything to drag matters out till five o'clock, when we were due in Mexico City.

But my opening "stall" was the veteran will-making ruse. As the maniac repeated his command for haste, I told him of my family and intended marriage, and asked for the privilege of leaving a message and disposing of my money and effects. If, I said, he would lend me some paper and agree to mail what I should write, I could die more peacefully and willingly. After some cogitation he gave a favourable verdict and fished in his valise for a pad, which he handed me solemnly as I resumed my seat. I produced a pencil, artfully breaking the point at the outset and causing some delay while he searched for one of his own. When he gave me this, he took my broken pencil and proceeded to sharpen it with a large, horn-handled knife which had been in his belt under his coat. Evidently a second pencil-breaking would not profit me greatly.

What I wrote, I can hardly recall at this date. It was largely gibberish, and composed of random scraps of memorised literature when I could think of nothing else to set down. I made my handwriting as illegible as I could without destroying its nature as writing; for I knew he would be likely to look at the result before commencing his experiment, and realised how he would react to the sight of obvious nonsense. The ordeal was a terrible one, and I chafed each second at the slowness of the train. In the past I had often whistled a brisk gallop to the sprightly "tac" of wheels on rails, but now the tempo seemed slowed down to that of a funeral march—my funeral march, I grimly reflected.

My ruse worked till I had covered over four pages, six by nine; when at last the madman drew out his watch and told me I could have but five minutes more. What should I do next? I was hastily going through the form of concluding the will when a new idea struck me. Ending with a flourish and handing him the finished sheets, which he thrust carelessly into his left-hand coat pocket, I reminded him of my influential Sacramento friends who would be so much interested in his invention.

"Oughtn't I to give you a letter of introduction to them?" I said. "Oughtn't I to make a signed sketch and description of your executioner so that they'll grant you a cordial hearing? They can make you famous, you know—and there's no question at all but that they'll adopt your method for the state of California if they hear of it through someone like me, whom they know and trust."

I was taking this tack on the chance that his thoughts as a disappointed inventor would let him forget the Aztec-religious side of his mania for a while. When he veered to the latter again, I reflected, I would spring the "revelation" and "prophecy". The scheme worked, for his eyes glowed an eager assent, though he brusquely told me to be quick. He further emptied the valise, lifting out a queer-looking congeries of glass cells and coils to which the wire from the helmet was attached, and delivering a fire of running comment too technical for me to follow yet apparently quite plausible and straightforward. I pretended to note down all he said, wondering as I did so whether the queer apparatus was really a battery after all. Would I get a slight shock when he applied the device? The man surely talked as if he were a genuine electrician. Description of his own invention was clearly a congenial task for him, and I saw he was not as impatient as before. The hopeful grey of dawn glimmered red through the windows before he wound up, and I felt at last that my chance of escape had really become tangible.

But he, too, saw the dawn, and began glaring wildly again. He knew the train was due in Mexico City at five, and would certainly force quick action unless I could override all his judgment with engrossing ideas. As he rose with a determined air, setting the battery on the seat beside the open valise, I reminded him that I had not made the needed sketch; and asked him to hold the headpiece so that I could draw it near the battery. He complied and resumed his seat, with many admonitions to me to hurry. After another moment I paused for some information, asking him how the victim was placed for execution, and how his presumable struggles were overcome.

"Why," he replied, "the criminal is securely strapped to a post. It does not matter how much he tosses his head, for the helmet fits tightly and draws even closer when the current comes on. We turn the switch gradually—you see it here, a carefully arranged affair with a rheostat."

A new idea for delay occurred to me as the tilled fields and increasingly frequent houses in the dawnlight outside told of our approach to the capital at last.

"But," I said, "I must draw the helmet in place on a human head as well as beside the battery. Can't you slip it on yourself a moment so that I can sketch you with it? The papers as well as the officials will want all this, and they are strong on completeness."

I had, by chance, made a better shot than I had planned; for at my mention of the press the madman's eyes lit up afresh.

"The papers? Yes—damn them, you can make even the papers give me a hearing! They all laughed at me and wouldn't print a word. Here, you, hurry up! We've not a second to lose!"

He had slipped the headpiece on and was watching my flying pencil avidly. The wire mesh gave him a grotesque, comic look as he sat there with nervously twitching hands.

"Now, curse 'em, they'll print pictures! I'll revise your sketch if you make any blunders—must be accurate at any cost. Police will find you afterward—they'll tell how it works. Associated Press item —back up your letter—immortal fame. . . . Hurry, I say—hurry, confound you!"

The train was lurching over the poorer roadbed near the city, and we swayed disconcertingly now and then. With this excuse I managed to break the pencil again, but of course the maniac at once handed me my own which he had sharpened. My first batch of ruses was about used up, and I felt that I should have to submit to the headpiece in a moment. We were still a good quarter-hour from the terminal, and it was about time for me to divert my companion to his religious side and spring the divine prophecy.

Mustering up my scraps of Nahuan-Aztec mythology, I suddenly threw down pencil and paper and commenced to chant.

"Iä! Iä! Tloquenahuaque, Thou Who Art All In Thyself! Thou, too, Ipalnemoan, By Whom We Live! I hear, I hear! I see, I see! Serpent-bearing Eagle, hail! A message! A message! Huitzilopotchli, in my soul echoes thy thunder!"

At my intonations the maniac stared incredulously through his odd mask, his handsome face shewn in a surprise and perplexity which quickly changed to alarm. His mind seemed to go blank a moment, and then to recrystallise in another pattern. Raising his hands aloft, he chanted as if in a dream.

"Mictlanteuctli, Great Lord, a sign! A sign from within thy black cave! Iä! Tonatiuh-Metztli! Cthulhutl! Command, and I serve!"

Now in all this responsive gibberish there was one word which struck an odd chord in my memory. Odd, because it never occurs in any printed account of Mexican mythology, yet had been overheard by me more than once as an awestruck whisper amongst the peons in my own firm's Tlaxcala mines. It seemed to be part of an exceedingly secret and ancient ritual; for there were characteristic whispered responses which I had caught now and then, and which were as unknown as itself to academic scholarship. This maniac must have spent considerable time with the hill peons and Indians, just as he had said; for surely such unrecorded lore could have come from no mere book-learning. Realising the importance he must attach to this doubly esoteric jargon, I determined to strike at his most vulnerable spot and give him the gibberish responses the natives used.

"Ya-R'lyeh! Ya-R'lyeh!" I shouted. "Cthulhutl fhtaghn! Niguratl-Yig! Yog-Sototl—"

But I never had a chance to finish. Galvanised into a religious epilepsy by the exact response which his subconscious mind had probably not really expected, the madman scrambled down to a kneeling posture on the floor, bowing his wire-helmeted head again and again, and turning it to the right and left as he did so. With each turn his obeisances became more profound, and I could hear his foaming lips repeating the syllable "kill, kill, kill," in a rapidly swelling monotone. It occurred to me that I had overreached myself, and that my response had unloosed a mounting mania which would rouse him to the slaying-point before the train reached the station.

As the arc of the madman's turnings gradually increased, the slack in the cord from his headpiece to the battery had naturally been taken up more and more. Now, in an all-forgetting delirium of ecstasy, he began to magnify his turns to complete circles, so that the cord wound round his neck and began to tug at its moorings to the battery on the seat. I wondered what he would do when the inevitable would happen, and the battery would be dragged to presumable destruction on the floor.

Then came the sudden cataclysm. The battery, yanked over the seat's edge by the maniac's last gesture of orgiastic frenzy, did indeed fall; but it did not seem to have wholly broken. Instead, as my eye caught the spectacle in one too-fleeting instant, the actual impact was borne by the rheostat, so that the switch was jerked over instantly to full current. And the marvellous thing is that there *was* a current. The invention was no mere dream of insanity.

I saw a blinding blue auroral coruscation, heard an ululating shriek more hideous than any of the previous cries of that mad, horrible journey, and smelled the nauseous odour of burning flesh. That was all my overwrought consciousness could bear, and I sank instantly into oblivion.

When the train guard at Mexico City revived me, I found a crowd on the station platform around my compartment door. At my involuntary cry the pressing faces became curious and dubious, and I was glad when the guard shut out all but the trim doctor who had pushed his way through to me. My cry was a very natural thing, but it had been prompted by something more than the shocking sight on the carriage floor which I had expected to see. Or should say, by something *less,* because in truth there was not anything on the floor at all.

Nor, said the guard, had there been when he opened the door and found me unconscious within. My ticket was the only one sold for that compartment, and I was the only person found within it. Just myself and my valise, nothing more. I had been alone all the way from Querétaro. Guard, doctor, and spectators alike tapped their foreheads significantly at my frantic and insistent questions.

Had it all been a dream, or was I indeed mad? I recalled my anxiety and overwrought nerves, and shuddered. Thanking the guard and doctor, and shaking free of the curious crowd, I staggered into a cab and was taken to the Fonda Nacional, where, after telegraphing Jackson at the mine, I slept till afternoon in an effort to get a fresh grip on myself. I had myself called at one o'clock, in time to catch the narrow-gauge for the mining country, but when I got up I found a telegram under the door. It was from Jackson, and said that Feldon had been found dead in the mountains that morning, the news reaching the mine about ten o'clock. The papers were all safe, and the San Francisco office had been duly notified. So the whole trip, with its nervous haste and harrowing mental ordeal, had been for nothing!

Knowing that McComb would expect a personal report despite the course of events, I sent another wire ahead and took the narrow-gauge after all. Four hours later I was rattled and jolted into the station of Mine No. 3, where Jackson was waiting to give a cordial greeting. He was so full of the affair at the mine that he did not notice my still shaken and seedy appearance.

The superintendent's story was brief, and he told me it as he led me toward the shack up the hillside above the *arrastre,* where Feldon's body lay. Feldon, he said, had always been a queer, sullen character, ever since he was hired the year before; working at some secret mechanical device and complaining of constant espionage, and being disgustingly familiar with the native workmen. But he certainly knew the work, the country, and the people. He used to make long trips into the hills where the peons lived, and even to take part in some of their ancient, heathenish ceremonies. He hinted at odd secrets and strange powers as often as he boasted of his mechanical skill. Of late he had disintegrated rapidly; growing morbidly suspicious of his colleagues, and undoubtedly joining his native friends in ore-thieving after his cash got low. He needed unholy amounts of money for something or other—was always having boxes come from laboratories and machine shops in Mexico City or the States.

As for the final absconding with all the papers—it was only a crazy gesture of revenge for what he called "spying". He was certainly stark mad, for he had gone across country to a hidden cave on the wild slope of the haunted Sierra de Malinche, where no white men live, and had done some amazingly queer things. The cave, which would never have been found but for the final tragedy, was full of hideous old Aztec idols and altars; the latter covered with the charred bones of recent burnt-offerings of doubtful nature. The natives would tell nothing—indeed, they swore they knew nothing—but it was easy to see that the cave was an old rendezvous of theirs, and that Feldon had shared their practices to the fullest extent.

The searchers had found the place only because of the chanting and the final cry. It had been close to five that morning, and after an all-night encampment the party had begun to pack up for its empty-handed return to the mines. Then somebody had heard faint rhythms in the distance, and knew that one of the noxious old native rituals was being howled from some lonely spot up the slope of the corpse-shaped mountain. They heard the same old names— Mictlanteuctli, Tonatiuh-Metzli, Cthulhutl, Ya-R'lyeh, and all the rest—but the queer thing was that some English words were mixed with them. Real white man's English, and no greaser patter. Guided by the sound, they had hastened up the weed-entangled mountainside toward it, when after a spell of quiet the shriek had burst upon them. It was a terrible thing—a worse thing than any of them had ever heard before. There seemed to be some smoke, too, and a morbid acrid smell.

Then they stumbled on the cave, its entrance screened by scrub mesquites, but now emitting clouds of foetid smoke. It was lighted within, the horrible altars and grotesque images revealed flickeringly by candles which must have been changed less than a half-hour before; and on the gravelly floor lay the horror that made all the crowd reel backward. It was Feldon, head burned to a crisp by some odd device he had slipped over it—a kind of wire cage connected with a rather shaken-up battery which had evidently fallen to the floor from a nearby altar-pot. When the men saw it they exchanged glances, thinking of the "electric executioner" Feldon had always boasted of inventing—the thing which everyone had rejected, but had tried to steal and copy. The papers were safe in Feldon's open portmanteau which stood close by, and an hour later the column of searchers started back for No. 3 with a grisly burden on an improvised stretcher.

That was all, but it was enough to make me turn pale and falter as Jackson led me up past the *arrastre* to the shed where he said the body lay. For I was not without imagination, and knew only too well into what hellish nightmare this tragedy somehow supernaturally dovetailed. I knew what I should see inside that gaping door around which the curious miners clustered, and did not flinch when my eyes took in the giant form, the rough corduroy clothes, the oddly delicate hands, the wisps of burnt beard, and the hellish machine itself—battery slightly broken, and headpiece blackened by the charring of what was inside. The great, bulging portmanteau did not surprise me, and I quailed only at two things—the folded sheets of paper sticking out of the left-hand pocket, and the queer sagging of the corresponding right-hand pocket. In a moment when no one was looking I reached out and seized the too familiar sheets, crushing them in my hand without daring to look at their penmanship. I ought to be sorry now that a kind of panic fear made me burn them that night with averted eyes. They would have been a positive proof or disproof of something—but for that matter I could still have had proof by asking about the revolver the coroner afterward took from that sagging right-hand coat pocket. I never had the courage to ask about that—because my own revolver was missing after the night on the train. My pocket pencil, too, shewed signs of a crude and hasty sharpening unlike the precise pointing I had given it Friday afternoon on the machine in President McComb's private car.

So in the end I went home still puzzled—mercifully puzzled, perhaps. The private car was repaired when I got back to Querétaro, but my greatest relief was crossing the Rio Grande into El Paso and the States. By the next Friday I was in San Francisco again, and the postponed wedding came off the following week.

As to what really happened that night—as I've said, I simply don't dare to speculate. That chap Feldon was insane to start with, and on top of his insanity he had piled a lot of prehistoric Aztec witch-lore that nobody has any right to know. He was really an inventive genius, and that battery must have been the genuine stuff. I heard later how he had been brushed aside in former years by press, public, and potentates alike. Too much disappointment isn't good for men of a certain kind. Anyhow, some unholy combination of influences was at work. He had really, by the way, been a soldier of Maximilian's.

When I tell my story most people call me a plain liar. Others lay it to abnormal psychology—and heaven knows I *was* overwrought

—while still others talk of "astral projection" of some sort. My zeal to catch Feldon certainly sent my thoughts ahead toward him, and with all his Indian magic he'd be about the first one to recognise and meet them. Was he in the railway carriage or was I in the cave on the corpse-shaped haunted mountain? What would have happened to me, had I not delayed him as I did? I'll confess I don't know, and I'm not sure that I want to know. I've never been in Mexico since—and as I said at the start, I don't enjoy hearing about electric executions.

Zealia Bishop

The Curse of Yig

In 1925 I went into Oklahoma looking for snake lore, and I came out with a fear of snakes that will last me the rest of my life. I admit it is foolish, since there are natural explanations for everything I saw and heard, but it masters me none the less. If the old story had been all there was to it, I would not have been so badly shaken. My work as an American Indian ethnologist has hardened me to all kinds of extravagant legendry, and I know that simple white people can beat the redskins at their own game when it comes to fanciful inventions. But I can't forget what I saw with my own eyes at the insane asylum in Guthrie.

I called at that asylum because a few of the oldest settlers told me I would find something important there. Neither Indians nor white men would discuss the snake-god legends I had come to trace. The oil-boom newcomers, of course, knew nothing of such matters, and the red men and old pioneers were plainly frightened when I spoke of them. Not more than six or seven people mentioned the asylum, and those who did were careful to talk in whispers. But the whisperers said that Dr. McNeill could shew me a very terrible relic and tell me all I wanted to know. He could explain why Yig, the half-human father of serpents, is a shunned and feared object in central Oklahoma, and why old settlers shiver at the secret Indian orgies which make the autumn days and nights hideous with the ceaseless beating of tom-toms in lonely places.

It was with the scent of a hound on the trail that I went to Guthrie, for I had spent many years collecting data on the evolution of serpent-worship among the Indians. I had always felt, from well-defined undertones of legend and archaeology, that great Quetzal-coatl—benign snake-god of the Mexicans—had had an older and darker prototype; and during recent months I had well-nigh proved it in a series of researches stretching from Guatemala to the Oklahoma plains. But everything was tantalising and incomplete, for above the border the cult of the snake was hedged about by fear and furtiveness.

Now it appeared that a new and copious source of data was about to dawn, and I sought the head of the asylum with an eagerness I did not try to cloak. Dr. McNeill was a small, clean-shaven man of somewhat advanced years, and I saw at once from his speech and manner that he was a scholar of no mean attainments in many branches outside his profession. Grave and doubtful when I first made known my errand, his face grew thoughtful as he carefully scanned my credentials and the letter of introduction which a kindly old ex–Indian agent had given me.

"So you've been studying the Yig legend, eh?" he reflected sententiously. "I know that many of our Oklahoma ethnologists have tried to connect it with Quetzalcoatl, but I don't think any of them have traced the intermediate steps so well. You've done remarkable work for a man as young as you seem to be, and you certainly deserve all the data we can give.

"I don't suppose old Major Moore or any of the others told you what it is I have here. They don't like to talk about it, and neither do I. It is very tragic and very horrible, but that is all. I refuse to consider it anything supernatural. There's a story about it that I'll tell you after you see it—a devilish sad story, but one that I won't call magic. It merely shews the potency that belief has over some people. I'll admit there are times when I feel a shiver that's more than physical, but in daylight I set all that down to nerves. I'm not a young fellow any more, alas!

"To come to the point, the thing I have is what you might call a victim of Yig's curse—a physically living victim. We don't let the bulk of the nurses see it, although most of them know it's here. There are just two steady old chaps whom I let feed it and clean out its quarters—used to be three, but good old Stevens passed on a few years ago. I suppose I'll have to break in a new group pretty soon; for the thing doesn't seem to age or change much, and we old boys can't last forever. Maybe the ethics of the near future will let us give it a merciful release, but it's hard to tell.

"Did you see that single ground-glass basement window over in the east wing when you came up the drive? That's where it is. I'll take you there myself now. You needn't make any comment. Just look through the moveable panel in the door and thank God the light isn't any stronger. Then I'll tell you the story—or as much as I've been able to piece together."

We walked downstairs very quietly, and did not talk as we threaded the corridors of the seemingly deserted basement. Dr. McNeill unlocked a grey-painted steel door, but it was only a bulkhead leading to a further stretch of hallway. At length he paused before a door marked B 116, opened a small observation panel which he could use only by standing on tiptoe, and pounded several times upon the painted metal, as if to arouse the occupant, whatever it might be.

A faint stench came from the aperture as the doctor unclosed it, and I fancied his pounding elicited a kind of low, hissing response. Finally he motioned me to replace him at the peep-hole, and I did so with a causeless and increasing tremor. The barred, ground-glass window, close to the earth outside, admitted only a feeble and uncertain pallor; and I had to look into the malodorous den for several seconds before I could see what was crawling and wriggling about on the straw-covered floor, emitting every now and then a weak and vacuous hiss. Then the shadowed outlines began to take shape, and I perceived that the squirming entity bore some remote resemblance to a human form laid flat on its belly. I clutched at the door-handle for support as I tried to keep from fainting.

The moving object was almost of human size, and entirely devoid of clothing. It was absolutely hairless, and its tawny-looking back seemed subtly squamous in the dim, ghoulish light. Around the shoulders it was rather speckled and brownish, and the head was very curiously flat. As it looked up to hiss at me I saw that the beady little black eyes were damnably anthropoid, but I could not bear to study them long. They fastened themselves on me with a horrible persistence, so that I closed the panel gaspingly and left the creature to wriggle about unseen in its matted straw and spectral twilight. I must have reeled a bit, for I saw that the doctor was gently holding my arm as he guided me away. I was stuttering over and over again: "B-but for God's sake, *what is it?*"

Dr. McNeill told me the story in his private office as I sprawled opposite him in an easy-chair. The gold and crimson of late afternoon changed to the violet of early dusk, but still I sat awed and motionless. I resented every ring of the telephone and every whir of the buzzer, and I could have cursed the nurses and internes whose knocks now and then summoned the doctor briefly to the outer office. Night came, and I was glad my host switched on all the lights. Scientist though I was, my zeal for research was half forgotten amidst such breathless ecstasies of fright as a small boy might feel when whispered witch-tales go the rounds of the chimney-corner.

It seems that Yig, the snake-god of the central plains tribes—presumably the primal source of the more southerly Quetzalcoatl or Kukulcan—was an odd, half-anthropomorphic devil of highly arbitrary and capricious nature. He was not wholly evil, and was usually quite well-disposed toward those who gave proper respect to him and his children, the serpents; but in the autumn he became abnormally ravenous, and had to be driven away by means of suitable rites. That was why the tom-toms in the Pawnee, Wichita, and Caddo country pounded ceaselessly week in and week out in August, September, and October; and why the medicine-men made strange noises with rattles and whistles curiously like those of the Aztecs and Mayas.

Yig's chief trait was a relentless devotion to his children—a devotion so great that the redskins almost feared to protect themselves from the venomous rattlesnakes which thronged the region. Frightful clandestine tales hinted of his vengeance upon mortals who flouted him or wreaked harm upon his wriggling progeny; his chosen method being to turn his victim, after suitable tortures, to a spotted snake.

In the old days of the Indian Territory, the doctor went on, there was not quite so much secrecy about Yig. The plains tribes, less cautious than the desert nomads and Pueblos, talked quite freely of their legends and autumn ceremonies with the first Indian agents, and let considerable of the lore spread out through the neighbouring regions of white settlement. The great fear came in the land-rush days of '89, when some extraordinary incidents had been rumoured, and the rumours sustained, by what seemed to be hideously tangible proofs. Indians said that the new white men did not know how to get on with Yig, and afterward the settlers came to take that theory at face value. Now no old-timer in middle Oklahoma, white or red, could be induced to breathe a word about the snake-god except in vague hints. Yet after all, the doctor added with almost needless emphasis, the only truly authenticated horror had been a thing of pitiful tragedy rather than of bewitchment. It was all very material and cruel—even that last phase which had caused so much dispute.

Dr. McNeill paused and cleared his throat before getting down to his special story, and I felt a tingling sensation as when a theatre curtain rises. The thing had begun when Walker Davis and his wife Audrey left Arkansas to settle in the newly opened public lands in the spring of 1889, and the end had come in the country of the Wichitas—north of the Wichita River, in what is at present Caddo County. There is a small village called Binger there now, and the railway goes through; but otherwise the place is less changed than other parts of Oklahoma. It is still a section of farms and ranches—quite productive in these days—since the great oil-fields do not come very close.

Walker and Audrey had come from Franklin County in the Ozarks with a canvas-topped wagon, two mules, an ancient and useless dog called "Wolf", and all their household goods. They were typical hill-folk, youngish and perhaps a little more ambitious than most, and looked forward to a life of better returns for their hard work than they had had in Arkansas. Both were lean, raw-boned specimens; the man tall, sandy, and grey-eyed, and the woman short and rather dark, with a black straightness of hair suggesting a slight Indian admixture.

In general, there was very little of distinction about them, and but for one thing their annals might not have differed from those of thousands of other pioneers who flocked into the new country at that time. That thing was Walker's almost epileptic fear of snakes, which some laid to prenatal causes, and some said came from a dark prophecy about his end with which an old Indian squaw had tried to scare him when he was small. Whatever the cause, the effect was marked indeed; for despite his strong general courage the very mention of a snake would cause him to grow faint and pale, while the sight of even a tiny specimen would produce a shock sometimes bordering on a convulsion seizure.

The Davises started out early in the year, in the hope of being on their new land for the spring ploughing. Travel was slow; for the roads were bad in Arkansas, while in the Territory there were great stretches of rolling hills and red, sandy barrens without any roads whatever. As the terrain grew flatter, the change from their native mountains depressed them more, perhaps, than they realised; but they found the people at the Indian agencies very affable, while most of the settled Indians seemed friendly and civil. Now and then they encountered a fellow-pioneer, with whom crude pleasantries and expressions of amiable rivalry were generally exchanged.

Owing to the season, there were not many snakes in evidence, so Walker did not suffer from his special temperamental weakness. In the earlier stages of the journey, too, there were no Indian snake-legends to trouble him; for the transplanted tribes from the south-east do not share the wilder beliefs of their western neighbours. As fate would have it, it was a white man at Okmulgee in the Creek country who gave the Davises the first hint of Yig beliefs; a hint which had a curiously fascinating effect on Walker, and caused him to ask questions very freely after that.

Before long Walker's fascination had developed into a bad case of fright. He took the most extraordinary precautions at each of the nightly camps, always clearing away whatever vegetation he found, and avoiding stony places whenever he could. Every clump of stunted bushes and every cleft in the great, slab-like rocks seemed to him now to hide malevolent serpents, while every human figure not obviously part of a settlement or emigrant train seemed to him a potential snake-god till nearness had proved the contrary. Fortunately no troublesome encounters came at this stage to shake his nerves still further.

As they approached the Kickapoo country they found it harder and harder to avoid camping near rocks. Finally it was no longer possible, and poor Walker was reduced to the puerile expedient of droning some of the rustic anti-snake charms he had learned in his boyhood. Two or three times a snake was really glimpsed, and these sights did not help the sufferer in his efforts to preserve composure.

On the twenty-second evening of the journey a savage wind made it imperative, for the sake of the mules, to camp in as sheltered a spot as possible; and Audrey persuaded her husband to take advantage of a cliff which rose uncommonly high above the dried bed of a former tributary of the Canadian River. He did not like the rocky cast of the place, but allowed himself to be overruled this once; leading the animals sullenly toward the protecting slope, which the nature of the ground would not allow the wagon to approach.

Audrey, examining the rocks near the wagon, meanwhile noticed a singular sniffing on the part of the feeble old dog. Seizing a rifle, she followed his lead, and presently thanked her stars that she had forestalled Walker in her discovery. For there, snugly nested in the gap between two boulders, was a sight it would have done him no good to see. Visible only as one convoluted expanse, but perhaps comprising as many as three or four separate units, was a mass of lazy wriggling which could not be other than a brood of new-born rattlesnakes.

Anxious to save Walker from a trying shock, Audrey did not hesitate to act, but took the gun firmly by the barrel and brought the butt down again and again upon the writhing objects. Her own sense of loathing was great, but it did not amount to a real fear. Finally she saw that her task was done, and turned to cleanse the improvised bludgeon in the red sand and dry, dead grass near by. She must, she reflected, cover the nest up before Walker got back from tethering the mules. Old Wolf, tottering relic of mixed shepherd and coyote ancestry that he was, had vanished, and she feared he had gone to fetch his master.

Footsteps at that instant proved her fear well founded. A second more, and Walker had seen everything. Audrey made a move to catch him if he should faint, but he did no more than sway. Then the look of pure fright on his bloodless face turned slowly to something like mingled awe and anger, and he began to upbraid his wife in trembling tones.

"Gawd's sake, Aud, but why'd ye go for to do that? Hain't ye heerd all the things they've been tellin' about this snake-devil Yig? Ye'd ought to a told me, and we'd a moved on. Don't ye know they's a devil-god what gets even if ye hurts his children? What for d'ye think the Injuns all dances and beats their drums in the fall about? This land's under a curse, I tell ye—nigh every soul we've a-talked to sence we come in's said the same. Yig rules here, an' he comes out every fall for to git his victims and turn 'em into snakes. Why, Aud, they won't none of them Injuns acrost the Canayjin kill a snake for love nor money!

"Gawd knows what ye done to yourself, gal, a-stompin' out a hull brood o' Yig's chillen. He'll git ye, sure, sooner or later, unlessen I kin buy a charm offen some o' the Injun medicine-men. He'll git ye, Aud, as sure's they's a Gawd in heaven—he'll come outa the night and turn ye into a crawlin' spotted snake!"

All the rest of the journey Walker kept up the frightened reproofs and prophecies. They crossed the Canadian near Newcastle, and soon afterward met with the first of the real plains Indians they had seen—a party of blanketed Wichitas, whose leader talked freely under the spell of the whiskey offered him, and taught poor Walker a long-winded protective charm against Yig in exchange for a quart bottle of the same inspiring fluid. By the end of the week the chosen site in the Wichita country was reached, and the Davises made haste to trace their boundaries and perform the spring ploughing before even beginning the construction of a cabin.

The region was flat, drearily windy, and sparse of natural vegetation, but promised great fertility under cultivation. Occasional outcroppings of granite diversified a soil of decomposed red sandstone, and here and there a great flat rock would stretch along the surface of the ground like a man-made floor. There seemed to be a very few snakes, or possible dens for them; so Audrey at last persuaded Walker to build the one-room cabin over a vast, smooth slab of exposed stone. With such a flooring and with a good-sized fireplace the wettest weather might be defied—though it soon became evident that dampness was no salient quality of the district. Logs were hauled in the wagon from the nearest belt of woods, many miles toward the Wichita Mountains.

Walker built his wide-chimneyed cabin and crude barn with the aid of some of the other settlers, though the nearest one was over a mile away. In turn, he helped his helpers at similar house-raisings, so that many ties of friendship sprang up between the new neighbours. There was no town worthy the name nearer than El Reno, on the railway thirty miles or more to the northeast; and before many weeks had passed, the people of the section had become very cohesive despite the wideness of their scattering. The Indians, a few of whom had begun to settle down on ranches, were for the most part harmless, though somewhat quarrelsome when fired by the liquid stimulation which found its way to them despite all government bans.

Of all the neighbours the Davises found Joe and Sally Compton, who likewise hailed from Arkansas, the most helpful and congenial. Sally is still alive, known now as Grandma Compton; and her son Clyde, then an infant in arms, has become one of the leading men of the state. Sally and Audrey used to visit each other often, for their cabins were only two miles apart; and in the long spring and summer afternoons they exchanged many a tale of old Arkansas and many a rumour about the new country.

Sally was very sympathetic about Walker's weakness regarding snakes, but perhaps did more to aggravate than cure the parallel nervousness which Audrey was acquiring through his incessant praying and prophesying about the curse of Yig. She was uncommonly full of gruesome snake stories, and produced a direfully strong impression with her acknowledged masterpiece—the tale of a man in Scott County who had been bitten by a whole horde of rattlers at once, and had swelled so monstrously from poison that his body had finally burst with a pop. Needless to say, Audrey did not repeat this anecdote to her husband, and she implored the Comptons to beware of starting it on the rounds of the countryside. It is to Joe's and Sally's credit that they heeded this plea with the utmost fidelity.

Walker did his corn-planting early, and in midsummer improved his time by harvesting a fair crop of the native grass of the region. With the help of Joe Compton he dug a well which gave a moderate supply of very good water, though he planned to sink an artesian later on. He did not run into many serious snake scares, and made his land as inhospitable as possible for wriggling visitors. Every now and then he rode over to the cluster of thatched, conical huts which formed the main village of the Wichitas, and talked long with the old men and shamans about the snake-god and how to nullify his wrath. Charms were always ready in exchange for whiskey, but much of the information he got was far from reassuring.

Yig was a great god. He was bad medicine. He did not forget things. In the autumn his children were hungry and wild, and Yig was hungry and wild, too. All the tribes made medicine against Yig when the corn harvest came. They gave him some corn, and danced in proper regalia to the sound of whistle, rattle, and drum. They kept the drums pounding to drive Yig away, and called down the aid of Tiráwa, whose children men are, even as the snakes are Yig's children. It was bad that the squaw of Davis killed the children of Yig. Let Davis say the charms many times when the corn harvest comes. Yig is Yig. Yig is a great god.

By the time the corn harvest did come, Walker had succeeded in getting his wife into a deplorably jumpy state. His prayers and borrowed incantations came to be a nuisance; and when the autumn rites of the Indians began, there was always a distant wind-borne pounding of tom-toms to lend an added background of the sinister. It was maddening to have the muffled clatter always stealing over the wide red plains. Why would it never stop? Day and night, week on week, it was always going in exhaustless relays, as persistently as the red dusty winds that carried it. Audrey loathed it more than her husband did, for he saw in it a compensating element of protection. It was with this sense of a mighty, intangible bulwark against evil that he got in his corn crop and prepared cabin and stable for the coming winter.

The autumn was abnormally warm, and except for their primitive cookery the Davises found scant use for the stone fireplace Walker had built with such care. Something in the unnaturalness of the hot dust-clouds preyed on the nerves of all the settlers, but most of all on Audrey's and Walker's. The notions of a hovering snake-curse and the weird, endless rhythm of the distant Indian drums formed a bad combination which any added element of the bizarre went far to render utterly unendurable.

Notwithstanding this strain, several festive gatherings were held at one or another of the cabins after the crops were reaped; keeping naively alive in modernity those curious rites of the harvest-home which are as old as human agriculture itself. Lafayette Smith, who came from southern Missouri and had a cabin about three miles east of Walker's, was a very passable fiddler; and his tunes did much to make the celebrants forget the monotonous beating of the distant tom-toms. Then Hallowe'en drew near, and the settlers planned another frolic—this time, had they but known it, of a lineage older than even agriculture; the dread Witch-Sabbath of the primal pre-Aryans, kept alive through ages in the midnight blackness of secret woods, and still hinting at vague terrors under its latter-day mask of comedy and lightness. Hallowe'en was to fall on a Thursday, and the neighbours agreed to gather for their first revel at the Davis cabin.

It was on that thirty-first of October that the warm spell broke. The morning was grey and leaden, and by noon the incessant winds had changed from searingness to rawness. People shivered all the more because they were not prepared for the chill, and Walker Davis' old dog Wolf dragged himself wearily indoors to a place beside the hearth. But the distant drums still thumped on, nor were the white citizenry less inclined to pursue their chosen rites. As early as four in the afternoon the wagons began to arrive at Walker's cabin; and in the evening, after a memorable barbecue, Lafayette Smith's fiddle inspired a very fair-sized company to great feats of saltatory grotesqueness in the one good-sized but crowded room. The younger folk indulged in the amiable inanities proper to the season, and now and then old Wolf would howl with doleful and spine-tickling ominousness at some especially spectral strain from Lafayette's squeaky violin—a device he had never heard before. Mostly, though, this battered veteran slept through the merriment; for he was past the age of active interests and lived largely in his dreams. Tom and Jennie Rigby had brought their collie Zeke along, but the canines did not fraternise. Zeke seemed strangely uneasy over something, and nosed around curiously all the evening.

Audrey and Walker made a fine couple on the floor, and Grandma Compton still likes to recall her impression of their dancing that night. Their worries seemed forgotten for the nonce, and Walker was shaved and trimmed into a surprising degree of spruceness. By ten o'clock all hands were healthily tired, and the guests began to depart family by family with many handshakings and bluff assurances of what a fine time everybody had had. Tom and Jennie thought Zeke's eerie howls as he followed them to their wagon were marks of regret at having to go home; though Audrey said it must be the far-away tom-toms which annoyed him, for the distant thumping was surely ghastly enough after the merriment within.

The night was bitterly cold, and for the first time Walker put a great log in the fireplace and banked it with ashes to keep it smouldering till morning. Old Wolf dragged himself within the ruddy glow and lapsed into his customary coma. Audrey and Walker, too tired to think of charms or curses, tumbled into the rough pine bed and were asleep before the cheap alarm-clock on the mantel had ticked out three minutes. And from far away, the rhythmic pounding of those hellish tom-toms still pulsed on the chill night-wind.

Dr. McNeill paused here and removed his glasses, as if a blurring of the objective world might make the reminiscent vision clearer.

"You'll soon appreciate," he said, "that I had a great deal of difficulty in piecing out all that happened after the guests left. There were times, though—at first—when I was able to make a try at it." After a moment of silence he went on with the tale.

Audrey had terrible dreams of Yig, who appeared to her in the guise of Satan as depicted in cheap engravings she had seen. It was, indeed, from an absolute ecstasy of nightmare that she started suddenly awake to find Walker already conscious and sitting up in bed. He seemed to be listening intently to something, and silenced her with a whisper when she began to ask what had roused him.

"Hark, Aud!" he breathed. "Don't ye hear somethin' a-singin' and buzzin' and rustlin'? D'ye reckon it's the fall crickets?"

Certainly, there was distinctly audible within the cabin such a sound as he had described. Audrey tried to analyse it, and was impressed with some element at once horrible and familiar, which hovered just outside the rim of her memory. And beyond it all, waking a hideous thought, the monotonous beating of the distant tom-toms came incessantly across the black plains on which a cloudy half-moon had set.

"Walker—s'pose it's—the—the—curse o' Yig?"

She could feel him tremble.

"No, gal, I don't reckon he comes that away. He's shapen like a man, except ye look at him clost. That's what Chief Grey Eagle says. This here's some varmints come in outen the cold—not crickets, I calc'late, but summat like 'em. I'd orter git up and stomp 'em out afore they make much headway or git at the cupboard."

He rose, felt for the lantern that hung within easy reach, and rattled the tin match-box nailed to the wall beside it. Audrey sat up in bed and watched the flare of the match grow into the steady glow of the lantern. Then, as their eyes began to take in the whole of the room, the crude rafters shook with the frenzy of their simultaneous shriek. For the flat, rocky floor, revealed in the new-born illumination, was one seething, brown-speckled mass of wriggling rattlesnakes, slithering toward the fire, and even now turning their loathsome heads to menace the fright-blasted lantern-bearer.

It was only for an instant that Audrey saw the things. The reptiles were of every size, of uncountable numbers, and apparently of several varieties; and even as she looked, two or three of them reared their heads as if to strike at Walker. She did not faint—it was Walker's crash to the floor that extinguished the lantern and plunged her into blackness. He had not screamed a second time— fright had paralysed him, and he fell as if shot by a silent arrow from no mortal's bow. To Audrey the entire world seemed to whirl about fantastically, mingling with the nightmare from which she had started.

Voluntary motion of any sort was impossible, for will and the sense of reality had left her. She fell back inertly on her pillow, hoping that she would wake soon. No actual sense of what had happened penetrated her mind for some time. Then, little by little, the suspicion that she was really awake began to dawn on her; and she was convulsed with a mounting blend of panic and grief which made her long to shriek out despite the inhibiting spell which kept her mute.

Walker was gone, and she had not been able to help him. He had died of snakes, just as the old witch-woman had predicted when he was a little boy. Poor Wolf had not been able to help, either—probably he had not even awaked from his senile stupor. And now the crawling things must be coming for her, writhing closer and closer every moment in the dark, perhaps even now twining slipperily about the bedposts and oozing up over the coarse woollen blankets. Unconsciously she crept under the clothes and trembled.

It must be the curse of Yig. He had sent his monstrous children on All-Hallows' Night, and they had taken Walker first. Why was that—wasn't he innocent enough? Why not come straight for her—hadn't she killed those little rattlers alone? Then she thought of the curse's form as told by the Indians. She wouldn't be killed—just turned to a spotted snake. Ugh! So she would be like those things she had glimpsed on the floor—those things which Yig had sent to get her and enroll her among their number! She tried to mumble a charm that Walker had taught her, but found she could not utter a single sound.

The noisy ticking of the alarm-clock sounded above the maddening beat of the distant tom-toms. The snakes were taking a long time—did they mean to delay on purpose to play on her nerves? Every now and then she thought she felt a steady, insidious pressure on the bedclothes, but each time it turned out to be only the automatic twitchings of her overwrought nerves. The clock ticked on in the dark, and a change came slowly over her thoughts.

Those snakes *couldn't* have taken so long! They couldn't be Yig's messengers after all, but just natural rattlers that were nested below the rock and had been drawn there by the fire. They weren't coming for her, perhaps—perhaps they had sated themselves on poor Walker. Where were they now? Gone? Coiled by the fire? Still crawling over the prone corpse of their victim? The clock ticked, and the distant drums throbbed on.

At the thought of her husband's body lying there in the pitch blackness a thrill of purely physical horror passed over Audrey. That story of Sally Compton's about the man back in Scott County! He, too, had been bitten by a whole bunch of rattlesnakes, and what had happened to him? The poison had rotted the flesh and swelled the whole corpse, and in the end the bloated thing had *burst* horribly—burst horribly with a detestable *popping* noise. Was that what was happening to Walker down there on the rock floor? Instinctively she felt she had begun to *listen* for something too terrible even to name to herself.

The clock ticked on, keeping a kind of mocking, sardonic time with the far-off drumming that the night-wind brought. She wished it were a striking clock, so that she could know how long this eldritch vigil must last. She cursed the toughness of fibre that kept her from fainting, and wondered what sort of relief the dawn could bring, after all. Probably neighbours would pass—no doubt somebody would call—would they find her still sane? Was she still sane now?

Morbidly listening, Audrey all at once became aware of something which she had to verify with every effort of her will before she could believe it; and which, once verified, she did not know whether to welcome or dread. *The distant beating of the Indian tom-toms had ceased.* They had always maddened her—but had not Walker regarded them as a bulwark against nameless evil from outside the universe? What were some of those things he had repeated to her in whispers after talking with Grey Eagle and the Wichita medicine-men?

She did not relish this new and sudden silence, after all! There was something sinister about it. The loud-ticking clock seemed abnormal in its new loneliness. Capable at last of conscious motion, she shook the covers from her face and looked into the darkness toward the window. It must have cleared after the moon set, for she saw the square aperture distinctly against the background of stars.

Then without warning came that shocking, unutterable sound—ugh!—that dull, putrid *pop* of cleft skin and escaping poison in the dark. God!—Sally's story—that obscene stench, and this gnawing, clawing silence! It was too much. The bonds of muteness snapped, and the black night waxed reverberant with Audrey's screams of stark, unbridled frenzy.

Consciousness did not pass away with the shock. How merciful if only it had! Amidst the echoes of her shrieking Audrey still saw the star-sprinkled square of window ahead, and heard the doomboding ticking of that frightful clock. Did she hear another sound? Was that square window still a perfect square? She was in no condition to weigh the evidence of her senses or distinguish between fact and hallucination.

No—that window was *not* a perfect square. *Something had encroached on the lower edge.* Nor was the ticking of the clock the only sound in the room. There was, beyond dispute, a heavy breathing neither her own nor poor Wolf's. Wolf slept very silently, and his wakeful wheezing was unmistakable. Then Audrey saw against the stars the black, daemoniac silhouette of something anthropoid—the undulant bulk of a gigantic head and shoulders fumbling slowly toward her.

"Y'aaaah! Y'aaaah! Go away! Go away! Go away, snake-devil! Go 'way, Yig! I didn't mean to kill 'em—I was feared he'd be scairt of 'em. Don't, Yig, don't! I didn't go for to hurt yore chillen—don't come nigh me—don't change me into no spotted snake!"

But the half-formless head and shoulders only lurched onward toward the bed, very silently.

Everything snapped at once inside Audrey's head, and in a second she had turned from a cowering child to a raging madwoman. She knew where the axe was—hung against the wall on those pegs near the lantern. It was within easy reach, and she could find it in the dark. Before she was conscious of anything further it was in her hands, and she was creeping toward the foot of the bed—toward the monstrous head and shoulders that every moment groped their way nearer. Had there been any light, the look on her face would not have been pleasant to see.

"Take *that,* you! And *that,* and *that,* and *that!*"

She was laughing shrilly now, and her cackles mounted higher as she saw that the starlight beyond the window was yielding to the dim prophetic pallor of coming dawn.

Dr. McNeill wiped the perspiration from his forehead and put on his glasses again. I waited for him to resume, and as he kept silent I spoke softly.

"She lived? She was found? Was it ever explained?"

The doctor cleared his throat.

"Yes—she lived, in a way. And it was explained. I told you there was no bewitchment—only cruel, pitiful, material horror."

It was Sally Compton who had made the discovery. She had ridden over to the Davis cabin the next afternoon to talk over the party with Audrey, and had seen no smoke from the chimney. That was queer. It had turned very warm again, yet Audrey was usually cooking something at that hour. The mules were making hungry-sounding noises in the barn, and there was no sign of old Wolf sunning himself in the accustomed spot by the door.

Altogether, Sally did not like the look of the place, so was very timid and hesitant as she dismounted and knocked. She got no answer but waited some time before trying the crude door of split logs. The lock, it appeared, was unfastened; and she slowly pushed her way in. Then, perceiving what was there, she reeled back, gasped, and clung to the jamb to preserve her balance.

A terrible odour had welled out as she opened the door, but that was not what had stunned her. It was what she had seen. For within that shadowy cabin monstrous things had happened and three shocking objects remained on the floor to awe and baffle the beholder.

Near the burned-out fireplace was the great dog—purple decay on the skin left bare by mange and old age, and the whole carcass burst by the puffing effect of rattlesnake poison. It must have been bitten by a veritable legion of the reptiles.

To the right of the door was the axe-hacked remnant of what had been a man—clad in a nightshirt, and with the shattered bulk of a lantern clenched in one hand. *He was totally free from any sign of snake-bite.* Near him lay the ensanguined axe, carelessly discarded.

And wriggling flat on the floor was a loathsome, vacant-eyed thing that had been a woman, but was now only a mute mad caricature. All that this thing could do was to hiss, and hiss, and hiss.

Both the doctor and I were brushing cold drops from our foreheads by this time. He poured something from a flask on his desk, took a nip, and handed another glass to me. I could only suggest tremulously and stupidly:

"So Walker had only fainted that first time—the screams roused him, and the axe did the rest?"

"Yes." Dr. McNeill's voice was low. "But he met his death from snakes just the same. It was his fear working in two ways—it made him faint, and it made him fill his wife with the wild stories that caused her to strike out when she thought she saw the snake-devil."

I thought for a moment.

"And Audrey—wasn't it queer how the curse of Yig seemed to work itself out on her? I suppose the impression of hissing snakes had been fairly ground into her."

"Yes. There were lucid spells at first, but they got to be fewer and fewer. Her hair came white at the roots as it grew, and later began to fall out. The skin grew blotchy, and when she died—"

I interrupted with a start.

"*Died?* Then what was that—that thing downstairs?"

McNeill spoke gravely.

"*That* is what was born to her three-quarters of a year afterward. There were three more of them—two were even worse—but this is the only one that lived."

Zealia Bishop

The Mound

I.

It is only within the last few years that most people have stopped thinking of the West as a *new* land. I suppose the idea gained ground because our own especial civilisation happens to be new there; but nowadays explorers are digging beneath the surface and bringing up whole chapters of life that rose and fell among these plains and mountains before recorded history began. We think nothing of a Pueblo village 2500 years old, and it hardly jolts us when archaeologists put the sub-pedregal culture of Mexico back to 17,000 or 18,000 B. C. We hear rumours of still older things, too—of primitive man contemporaneous with extinct animals and known today only through a few fragmentary bones and artifacts—so that the idea of newness is fading out pretty rapidly. Europeans usually catch the sense of immemorial ancientness and deep deposits from successive life-streams better than we do. Only a couple of years ago a British author spoke of Arizona as a "moon-dim region, very lovely in its way, and stark and old—an ancient, lonely land".

Yet I believe I have a deeper sense of the stupefying—almost horrible—ancientness of the West than any European. It all comes from an incident that happened in 1928; an incident which I'd greatly like to dismiss as three-quarters hallucination, but which has left such a frightfully firm impression on my memory that I can't put it off very easily. It was in Oklahoma, where my work as an American Indian ethnologist constantly takes me and where I had come upon some devilishly strange and disconcerting matters before. Make no mistake—Oklahoma is a lot more than a mere pioneers' and promoters' frontier. There are old, old tribes with old, old memories there; and when the tom-toms beat ceaselessly over brooding plains in the autumn the spirits of men are brought dangerously close to primal, whispered things. I am white and Eastern enough myself, but anybody is welcome to know that the rites of Yig, Father of Snakes, can get a real shudder out of me any day. I have heard and seen too much to be "sophisticated" in such matters. And so it is with this incident of 1928. I'd like to laugh it off—but I can't.

I had gone into Oklahoma to track down and correlate one of the many ghost tales which were current among the white settlers, but which had strong Indian corroboration, and—I felt sure—an ultimate Indian source. They were very curious, these open-air ghost tales; and though they sounded flat and prosaic in the mouths of the white people, they had earmarks of linkage with some of the richest and obscurest phases of native mythology. All of them were woven around the vast, lonely, artificial-looking mounds in the western part of the state, and all of them involved apparitions of exceedingly strange aspect and equipment.

The commonest, and among the oldest, became quite famous in 1892, when a government marshal named John Willis went into the mound region after horse-thieves and came out with a wild yarn of nocturnal cavalry horses in the air between great armies of invisible spectres—battles that involved the rush of hooves and feet, the thud of blows, the clank of metal on metal, the muffled cries of warriors, and the fall of human and equine bodies. These things happened by moonlight, and frightened his horse as well as himself. The sounds persisted an hour at a time; vivid, but subdued as if brought from a distance by a wind, and unaccompanied by any glimpse of the armies themselves. Later on Willis learned that the seat of the sounds was a notoriously haunted spot, shunned by settlers and Indians alike. Many had seen, or half seen, the warring horsemen in the sky, and had furnished dim, ambiguous descriptions. The settlers described the ghostly fighters as Indians, though of no familiar tribe, and having the most singular costumes and weapons. They even went so far as to say that they could not be sure the horses were really horses.

The Indians, on the other hand, did not seem to claim the spec-

THE HORROR IN THE MUSEUM 53

tres as kinsfolk. They referred to them as "those people", "the old people", or "they who dwell below", and appeared to hold them in too great a frightened veneration to talk much about them. No ethnologist had been able to pin any tale-teller down to a specific description of the beings, and apparently nobody had ever had a very clear look at them. The Indians had one or two old proverbs about these phenomena, saying that "men very old, make very big spirit; not so old, not so big; older than all time, then spirit he so big he near flesh; those old people and spirits they mix up—get all the same".

Now all of this, of course, is "old stuff" to an ethnologist—of a piece with the persistent legends of rich hidden cities and buried races which abound among the Pueblo and plains Indians, and which lured Coronado centuries ago on his vain search for the fabled Quivira. What took me into western Oklahoma was something far more definite and tangible—a local and distinctive tale which, though really old, was wholly new to the outside world of research, and which involved the first clear descriptions of the ghosts which it treated of. There was an added thrill in the fact that it came from the remote town of Binger, in Caddo County, a place I had long known as the scene of a very terrible and partly inexplicable occurrence connected with the snake-god myth.

The tale, outwardly, was an extremely naive and simple one, and centred in a huge, lone mound or small hill that rose above the plain about a third of a mile west of the village—a mound which some thought a product of Nature, but which others believed to be a burial-place or ceremonial dais constructed by prehistoric tribes. This mound, the villagers said, was constantly haunted by two Indian figures which appeared in alternation; an old man who paced back and forth along the top from dawn till dusk, regardless of the weather and with only brief intervals of disappearance, and a squaw who took his place at night with a blue-flamed torch that glimmered quite continuously till morning. When the moon was bright the squaw's peculiar figure could be seen fairly plainly, and over half the villagers agreed that the apparition was headless.

Local opinion was divided as to the motives and relative ghostliness of the two visions. Some held that the man was not a ghost at all, but a living Indian who had killed and beheaded a squaw for gold and buried her somewhere on the mound. According to these theorists he was pacing the eminence through sheer remorse, bound by the spirit of his victim which took visible shape after dark. But other theorists, more uniform in their spectral beliefs, held that both man and woman were ghosts; the man having killed the squaw and himself as well at some very distant period. These and minor variant versions seemed to have been current ever since the settlement of the Wichita country in 1889, and were, I was told, sustained to an astonishing degree by still-existing phenomena which anyone might observe for himself. Not many ghost tales offer such free and open proof, and I was very eager to see what bizarre wonders might be lurking in this small, obscure village so far from the beaten path of crowds and from the ruthless search-light of scientific knowledge. So, in the late summer of 1928 I took a train for Binger and brooded on strange mysteries as the cars rattled timidly along their single track through a lonelier and lonelier landscape.

Binger is a modest cluster of frame houses and stores in the midst of a flat windy region full of clouds of red dust. There are about 500 inhabitants besides the Indians on a neighbouring reservation; the principal occupation seeming to be agriculture. The soil is decently fertile, and the oil boom has not reached this part of the state. My train drew in at twilight, and I felt rather lost and uneasy —cut off from wholesome and every-day things—as it puffed away to the southward without me. The station platform was filled with curious loafers, all of whom seemed eager to direct me when I asked for the man to whom I had letters of introduction. I was ushered along a commonplace main street whose rutted surface was red with the sandstone soil of the country, and finally delivered at the door of my prospective host. Those who had arranged things for me had done well; for Mr. Compton was a man of high intelligence and local responsibility, while his mother—who lived with him and was familiarly known as "Grandma Compton"—was one of the first pioneer generation, and a veritable mine of anecdote and folklore.

That evening the Comptons summed up for me all the legends current among the villagers, proving that the phenomenon I had come to study was indeed a baffling and important one. The ghosts, it seems, were accepted almost as a matter of course by everyone in Binger. Two generations had been born and grown up within sight of that queer, lone tumulus and its restless figures. The neighbourhood of the mound was naturally feared and shunned, so that the village and the farms had not spread toward it in all four decades of settlement; yet venturesome individuals had several times visited it. Some had come back to report that they saw no ghosts at all when they neared the dreaded hill; that somehow the lone sentinel had stepped out of sight before they reached the spot, leaving them free to climb the steep slope and explore the flat summit. There was nothing up there, they said—merely a rough expanse of underbrush. Where the Indian watcher could have vanished to, they had no idea. He must, they reflected, have descended the slope and somehow managed to escape unseen along the plain; although there was no convenient cover within sight. At any rate, there did not appear to be any opening into the mound; a conclusion which was reached after considerable exploration of the shrubbery and tall grass on all sides. In a few cases some of the more sensitive searchers declared that they felt a sort of invisible restraining presence; but they could describe nothing more definite than that. It was simply as if the air thickened against them in the direction they wished to move. It is needless to mention that all these daring surveys were conducted by day. Nothing in the universe could have induced any human being, white or red, to approach that sinister elevation after dark; and indeed, no Indian would have thought of going near it even in the brightest sunlight.

But it was not from the tales of these sane, observant seekers that the chief terror of the ghost-mound sprang; indeed, had their experience been typical, the phenomenon would have bulked far less prominently in the local legendry. The most evil thing was the fact that many other seekers had come back strangely impaired in mind and body, or had not come back at all. The first of these cases had occurred in 1891, when a young man named Heaton had gone with a shovel to see what hidden secrets he could unearth. He had heard curious tales from the Indians, and had laughed at the barren report of another youth who had been out to the mound and had found nothing. Heaton had watched the mound with a spy glass from the village while the other youth made his trip; and as the explorer neared the spot, he saw the sentinel Indian walk deliberately down into the tumulus as if a trap-door and staircase existed on the top. The other youth had not noticed how the Indian disappeared, but had merely found him gone upon arriving at the mound.

When Heaton made his own trip he resolved to get to the bottom of the mystery, and watchers from the village saw him hacking diligently at the shrubbery atop the mound. Then they saw his figure melt slowly into invisibility; not to reappear for long hours, till after the dusk drew on, and the torch of the headless squaw glimmered ghoulishly on the distant elevation. About two hours after nightfall he staggered into the village minus his spade and other belongings, and burst into a shrieking monologue of disconnected ravings. He howled of shocking abysses and monsters, of terrible carvings and statues, of inhuman captors and grotesque tortures, and of other fantastic abnormalities too complex and chimerical even to remember. "Old! Old! Old!" he would moan over and over again, "great God, they are older than the earth, and came here from somewhere else—they know what you think, and make you know what they think—they're half-man, half-ghost—crossed the line—melt and take shape again—getting more and more so, yet we're all descended from them in the beginning—children of Tulu—everything made of gold—monstrous animals, half-human—dead slaves—madness—Iä! Shub-Niggurath!—*that white man—oh, my God, what they did to him! . . .*"

Heaton was the village idiot for about eight years, after which he died in an epileptic fit. Since his ordeal there had been two more cases of mound-madness, and eight of total disappearance. Immediately after Heaton's mad return, three desperate and determined men had gone out to the lone hill together; heavily armed, and with spades and pickaxes. Watching villagers saw the Indian ghost melt away as the explorers drew near, and afterward saw the men climb the mound and begin scouting around through the underbrush. All at once they faded into nothingness, and were never seen again. One watcher, with an especially powerful telescope, thought he saw other forms dimly materialise beside the hapless men and drag them down into the mound; but this account remained uncorroborated. It is needless to say that no searching-party went out after the lost ones, and that for many years the mound was wholly unvisited. Only when the incidents of 1891 were largely forgotten did anybody dare to think of further explorations. Then, about 1910, a fellow too young to recall the old horrors made a trip to the shunned spot and found nothing at all.

By 1915 the acute dread and wild legendry of '91 had largely faded into the commonplace and unimaginative ghost-tales at present surviving—that is, had so faded among the white people. On the nearby reservation were old Indians who thought much and kept their own counsel. About this time a second wave of active curiosity and adventuring developed, and several bold searchers made the trip to the mound and returned. Then came a trip of two Eastern visitors with spades and other apparatus—a pair of amateur archaeologists connected with a small college, who had been making studies among the Indians. No one watched this trip from the village, but they never came back. The searching-party that went out after them—among whom was my host Clyde Compton—found nothing whatsoever amiss at the mound.

The next trip was the solitary venture of old Capt. Lawton, a grizzled pioneer who had helped to open up the region in 1889, but who had never been there since. He had recalled the mound and its fascination all through the years; and being now in comfortable retirement, resolved to have a try at solving the ancient riddle. Long familiarity with Indian myth had given him ideas rather stranger than those of the simple villagers, and he had made preparations for some extensive delving. He ascended the mound on the morning of Thursday, May 11, 1916, watched through spy glasses by more than twenty people in the village and on the adjacent plain. His disappearance was very sudden, and occurred as he was hacking at the shrubbery with a brush-cutter. No one could say more than that he was there one moment and absent the next. For over a week no tidings of him reached Binger, and then—in the middle of the night—there dragged itself into the village the object about which dispute still rages.

It said it was—or had been—Capt. Lawton, but it was definitely *younger* by as much as forty years than the old man who had climbed the mound. Its hair was jet black, and its face—now distorted with nameless fright—free from wrinkles. But it did remind Grandma Compton most uncannily of the captain as he had looked back in '89. Its feet were cut off neatly at the ankles, and the stumps were smoothly healed to an extent almost incredible if the being really were the man who had walked upright a week before. It babbled of incomprehensible things, and kept repeating the name "George Lawton, George E. Lawton" as if trying to reassure itself of its own identity. The things it babbled of, Grandma Compton thought, were curiously like the hallucinations of poor young Heaton in '91; though there were minor differences. "The blue light!—the blue light! . . ." muttered the object, "always down there, before there were any living things—older than the dinosaurs—always the same, only weaker—never death—brooding and brooding and brooding—*the same people, half-man and half-gas*— the dead that walk and work—oh, those beasts, those half-human unicorns—houses and cities of gold—old, old, old, older than time

—came down from the stars—Great Tulu—Azathoth—Nyarlath-
otep—waiting, waiting. . . ." The object died before dawn.

Of course there was an investigation, and the Indians at the reservation were grilled unmercifully. But they knew nothing, and had
nothing to say. At least, none of them had anything to say except
old Grey Eagle, a Wichita chieftain whose more than a century of
age put him above common fears. He alone deigned to grunt some
advice.

"You let um 'lone, white man. No good—those people. All under
here, all under there, them old ones. Yig, big father of snakes, he
there. Yig is Yig. Tiráwa, big father of men, he there. Tiráwa is
Tiráwa. No die. No get old. Just same like air. Just live and wait.
One time they come out here, live and fight. Build um dirt tepee.
Bring up gold—they got plenty. Go off and make new lodges. Me
them. You them. Then big waters come. All change. Nobody come
out, let nobody in. Get in, no get out. You let um 'lone, you have
no bad medicine. Red man know, he no get catch. White man med-
dle, he no come back. Keep 'way little hills. No good. Grey Eagle
say this."

If Joe Norton and Rance Wheelock had taken the old chief's advice, they would probably be here today; but they didn't. They
were great readers and materialists, and feared nothing in heaven
or earth; and they thought that some Indian fiends had a secret
headquarters inside the mound. They had been to the mound
before, and now they went again to avenge old Capt. Lawton—
boasting that they'd do it if they had to tear the mound down
altogether. Clyde Compton watched them with a pair of prism
binoculars and saw them round the base of the sinister hill. Evidently they meant to survey their territory very gradually and
minutely. Minutes passed, and they did not reappear. Nor were
they ever seen again.

Once more the mound was a thing of panic fright, and only the
excitement of the Great War served to restore it to the farther
background of Binger folklore. It was unvisited from 1916 to 1919,
and would have remained so but for the daredeviltry of some of the
youths back from service in France. From 1919 to 1920, however,
there was a veritable epidemic of mound-visiting among the pre-
maturely hardened young veterans—an epidemic that waxed as one
youth after another returned unhurt and contemptuous. By
1920—so short is human memory—the mound was almost a joke;

and the tame story of the murdered squaw began to displace darker whispers on everybody's tongues. Then two reckless young brothers —the especially unimaginative and hard-boiled Clay boys—decided to go and dig up the buried squaw and the gold for which the old Indian had murdered her.

They went out on a September afternoon—about the time the Indian tom-toms begin their incessant annual beating over the flat, red-dusty plains. Nobody watched them, and their parents did not become worried at their non-return for several hours. Then came an alarm and a searching-party, and another resignation to the mystery of silence and doubt.

But one of them came back after all. It was Ed, the elder, and his straw-coloured hair and beard had turned an albino white for two inches from the roots. On his forehead was a queer scar like a branded hieroglyph. Three months after he and his brother Walker had vanished he skulked into his house at night, wearing nothing but a queerly patterned blanket which he thrust into the fire as soon as he had got into a suit of his own clothes. He told his parents that he and Walker had been captured by some strange Indians—not Wichitas or Caddos—and held prisoners somewhere toward the west. Walker had died under torture, but he himself had managed to escape at a high cost. The experience had been particularly terrible, and he could not talk about it just then. He must rest—and anyway, it would do no good to give an alarm and try to find and punish the Indians. They were not of a sort that could be caught or punished, and it was especially important for the good of Binger— for the good of the world—that they be not pursued into their secret lair. As a matter of fact, they were not altogether what one could call real Indians—he would explain about that later. Meanwhile he must rest. Better not to rouse the village with the news of his return—he would go upstairs and sleep. Before he climbed the rickety flight to his room he took a pad and pencil from the living-room table, and an automatic pistol from his father's desk drawer.

Three hours later the shot rang out. Ed Clay had put a bullet neatly through his temples with a pistol clutched in his left hand, leaving a sparsely written sheet of paper on the rickety table near his bed. He had, it later appeared from the whittled pencil-stub and stove full of charred paper, originally written much more; but had finally decided not to tell what he knew beyond vague hints. The surviving fragment was only a mad warning scrawled in a curiously backhanded script—the ravings of a mind obviously deranged by hardships—and it read thus; rather surprisingly for the utterance of one who had always been stolid and matter-of-fact:

> For gods sake never go nere that mound it is part of some kind of a world so devilish and old it cannot be spoke about me and Walker went and was took into the thing just melted at times and made up agen and the whole world outside is helpless alongside of what they can do—they what live forever young as they like and you cant tell if they are really men or just gostes—and what they do cant be spoke about and this is only 1 entrance—you cant tell how big the whole thing is—after what we seen I dont want to live aney more France was nothing besides this—and see that people always keep away o god they wood if they see poor walker like he was in the end.
>
> Yrs truely
> Ed Clay

At the autopsy it was found that all of young Clay's organs were transposed from right to left within his body, as if he had been turned inside out. Whether they had always been so, no one could say at the time, but it was later learned from army records that Ed had been perfectly normal when mustered out of the service in May, 1919. Whether there was a mistake somewhere, or whether some unprecedented metamorphosis had indeed occurred, is still an unsettled question, as is also the origin of the hieroglyph-like scar on the forehead.

That was the end of the explorations of the mound. In the eight intervening years no one had been near the place, and few indeed had even cared to level a spy glass at it. From time to time people continued to glance nervously at the lone hill as it rose starkly from the plain against the western sky, and to shudder at the small dark speck that paraded by day and the glimmering will-o'-the-wisp that danced by night. The thing was accepted at face value as a mystery not to be probed, and by common consent the village shunned the subject. It was, after all, quite easy to avoid the hill; for space was unlimited in every direction, and community life always follows beaten trails. The mound side of the village was simply kept trail-less, as if it had been water or swampland or desert. And it is a curious commentary on the stolidity and imaginative sterility of the human animal that the whispers with which children and strangers were warned away from the mound quickly sank once more into the flat tale of a murderous Indian ghost and his squaw victim. Only the tribesmen on the reservation, and thoughtful old-timers like Grandma Compton, remembered the overtones of unholy vistas and deep cosmic menace which clustered around the ravings of those who had come back changed and shattered.

It was very late, and Grandma Compton had long since gone upstairs to bed, when Clyde finished telling me this. I hardly knew what to think of the frightful puzzle, yet rebelled at any notion to conflict with sane materialism. What influence had brought madness, or the impulse of flight and wandering, to so many who had visited the mound? Though vastly impressed, I was spurred on rather than deterred. Surely I must get to the bottom of this matter, as well I might if I kept a cool head and an unbroken determination. Compton saw my mood and shook his head worriedly. Then he motioned me to follow him outdoors.

We stepped from the frame house to the quiet side street or lane, and walked a few paces in the light of a waning August moon to where the houses were thinner. The half-moon was still low, and had not blotted many stars from the sky; so that I could see not only the westering gleams of Altair and Vega, but the mystic shimmering of the Milky Way, as I looked out over the vast expanse of earth and sky in the direction that Compton pointed. Then all at once I saw a spark that was not a star—a bluish spark that moved and glimmered against the Milky Way near the horizon, and that seemed in a vague way more evil and malevolent than anything in the vault above. In another moment it was clear that this spark came from the top of a long distant rise in the outspread and faintly litten plain; and I turned to Compton with a question.

"Yes," he answered, "it's the blue ghost-light—and that is the mound. There's not a night in history that we haven't seen it—and not a living soul in Binger that would walk out over that plain toward it. It's a bad business, young man, and if you're wise you'll let it rest where it is. Better call your search off, son, and tackle some of the other Injun legends around here. We've plenty to keep you busy, heaven knows!"

II.

But I was in no mood for advice; and though Compton gave me a pleasant room, I could not sleep a wink through eagerness for the next morning with its chances to see the daytime ghost and to question the Indians at the reservation. I meant to go about the whole thing slowly and thoroughly, equipping myself with all available data both white and red before I commenced any actual archaeological investigations. I rose and dressed at dawn, and when I heard others stirring I went downstairs. Compton was building the kitchen fire while his mother was busy in the pantry. When he saw me he nodded, and after a moment invited me out into the glamorous young sunlight. I knew where we were going, and as we walked along the lane I strained my eyes westward over the plains.

There was the mound—far away and very curious in its aspect of artificial regularity. It must have been from thirty to forty feet high, and all of a hundred yards from north to south as I looked at it. It was not as wide as that from east to west, Compton said, but had the contour of a rather thinnish ellipse. He, I knew, had been safely out to it and back several times. As I looked at the rim silhouetted against the deep blue of the west I tried to follow its minor irregularities, and became impressed with a sense of something moving upon it. My pulse mounted a bit feverishly, and I seized quickly on the high-powered binoculars which Compton had quietly offered me. Focussing them hastily, I saw at first only a tangle of underbrush on the distant mound's rim—and then something stalked into the field.

It was unmistakably a human shape, and I knew at once that I was seeing the daytime "Indian ghost". I did not wonder at the description, for surely the tall, lean, darkly robed being with the filleted black hair and seamed, coppery, expressionless, aquiline face looked more like an Indian than anything else in my previous experience. And yet my trained ethnologist's eye told me at once that this was no redskin of any sort hitherto known to history, but a creature of vast racial variation and of a wholly different culture-stream. Modern Indians are brachycephalic—round-headed—and you can't find any dolichocephalic or long-headed skulls except in ancient Pueblo deposits dating back 2500 years or more; yet this man's long-headedness was so pronounced that I recognised it at once, even at his vast distance and in the uncertain field of the binoculars. I saw, too, that the pattern of his robe represented a decorative tradition utterly remote from anything we recognise in southwestern native art. There were shining metal trappings, likewise, and a short sword or kindred weapon at his side, all wrought in a fashion wholly alien to anything I had ever heard of.

As he paced back and forth along the top of the mound I followed him for several minutes with the glass, noting the kinaesthetic quality of his stride and the poised way he carried his head; and there was borne in upon me the strong, persistent conviction that this man, whoever or whatever he might be, was certainly *not a savage*. He was the product of a *civilisation,* I felt instinctively, though of what civilisation I could not guess. At length he disappeared beyond the farther edge of the mound, as if descending the opposite and unseen slope; and I lowered the glass with a curious mixture of puzzled feelings. Compton was looking quizzically at me, and I nodded non-committally. "What do you make of that?" he ventured. "This is what we've seen here in Binger every day of our lives."

That noon found me at the Indian reservation talking with old Grey Eagle—who, through some miracle, was still alive; though he must have been close to a hundred and fifty years old. He was a strange, impressive figure—this stern, fearless leader of his kind who had talked with outlaws and traders in fringed buckskin and French officials in knee-breeches and three-cornered hats—and I was glad to see that, because of my air of deference toward him, he appeared to like me. His liking, however, took an unfortunately obstructive form as soon as he learned what I wanted; for all he would do was to warn me against the search I was about to make.

"You good boy—you no bother that hill. Bad medicine. Plenty devil under there—catchum when you dig. No dig, no hurt. Go and dig, no come back. Just same when me boy, just same when my father and he father boy. All time buck he walk in day, squaw with no head she walk in night. All time since white man with tin coats they come from sunset and below big river—long way back—three, four times more back than Grey Eagle—two times more back than Frenchmen—all same after then. More back than that, nobody go near little hills nor deep valleys with stone caves. Still more back, those old ones no hide, come out and make villages. Bring plenty gold. Me them. You them. Then big waters come. All change. Nobody come out, let nobody in. Get in, no get out. They no die—no get old like Grey Eagle with valleys in face and snow on head. Just same like air—some man, some spirit. Bad medicine. Sometimes at night spirit come out on half-man–half-horse-with-horn and fight where men once fight. Keep 'way them place. No good. You good boy—go 'way and let them old ones 'lone."

That was all I could get out of the ancient chief, and the rest of the Indians would say nothing at all. But if I was troubled, Grey Eagle was clearly more so; for he obviously felt a real regret at the thought of my invading the region he feared so abjectly. As I turned to leave the reservation he stopped me for a final ceremonial farewell, and once more tried to get my promise to abandon my search. When he saw that he could not, he produced something half-timidly from a buckskin pouch he wore, and extended it toward me very solemnly. It was a worn but finely minted metal disc about two inches in diameter, oddly figured and perforated, and suspended from a leathern cord.

"You no promise, then Grey Eagle no can tell what get you. But if anything help um, this good medicine. Come from my father—he get from he father—he get from he father—all way back, close to Tiráwa, all men's father. My father say, 'You keep 'way from those old ones, keep 'way from little hills and valleys with stone caves. But if old ones they come out to get you, then you shew um this medicine. They know. They make him long way back. They look, then they no do such bad medicine maybe. But no can tell. You keep 'way, just same. Them no good. No tell what they do.'"

As he spoke, Grey Eagle was hanging the thing around my neck, and I saw it was a very curious object indeed. The more I looked at it, the more I marvelled; for not only was its heavy, darkish, lustrous, and richly mottled substance an absolutely strange metal to me, but what was left of its design seemed to be of a marvellously artistic and utterly unknown workmanship. One side, so far as I could see, had borne an exquisitely modelled serpent design; whilst the other side had depicted a kind of octopus or other tentacled monster. There were some half-effaced hieroglyphs, too, of a kind which no archaeologist could identify or even place conjecturally. With Grey Eagle's permission I later had expert historians, anthropologists, geologists, and chemists pass carefully upon the disc, but from them I obtained only a chorus of bafflement. It defied either classification or analysis. The chemists called it an amalgam of unknown metallic elements of heavy atomic weight, and one geologist suggested that the substance must be of meteoric origin, shot from unknown gulfs of interstellar space. Whether it really saved my life or sanity or existence as a human being I cannot attempt to say, but Grey Eagle is sure of it. He has it again, now, and I wonder if it has any connexion with his inordinate age. All his fathers who had it lived far beyond the century mark, perishing only in battle. Is it possible that Grey Eagle, if kept from accidents, will *never die?* But I am ahead of my story.

When I returned to the village I tried to secure more mound-lore, but found only excited gossip and opposition. It was really flattering to see how solicitous the people were about my safety, but I had to set their almost frantic remonstrances aside. I shewed them Grey Eagle's charm, but none of them had ever heard of it before, or seen anything even remotely like it. They agreed that it could not be an Indian relic, and imagined that the old chief's ancestors must have obtained it from some trader.

When they saw they could not deter me from my trip, the Binger citizens sadly did what they could to aid my outfitting. Having known before my arrival the sort of work to be done, I had most of my supplies already with me—machete and trench-knife for shrub-clearing and excavating, electric torches for any underground phase which might develop, rope, field-glasses, tape-measure, micro-scope, and incidentals for emergencies—as much, in fact, as might be comfortably stowed in a convenient handbag. To this equipment I added only the heavy revolver which the sheriff forced upon me, and the pick and shovel which I thought might expedite my work.

I decided to carry these latter things slung over my shoulder with a stout cord—for I soon saw that I could not hope for any helpers or fellow-explorers. The village would watch me, no doubt, with all its available telescopes and field-glasses; but it would not send any citizen so much as a yard over the flat plain toward the lone hillock. My start was timed for early the next morning, and all the rest of that day I was treated with the awed and uneasy respect which people give to a man about to set out for certain doom.

When morning came—a cloudy though not a threatening morn-ing—the whole village turned out to see me start across the dust-blown plain. Binoculars shewed the lone man at his usual pacing on the mound, and I resolved to keep him in sight as steadily as possi-ble during my approach. At the last moment a vague sense of dread oppressed me, and I was just weak and whimsical enough to let Grey Eagle's talisman swing on my chest in full view of any beings or ghosts who might be inclined to heed it. Bidding au revoir to Compton and his mother, I started off at a brisk stride despite the bag in my left hand and the clanking pick and shovel strapped to my back; holding my field-glass in my right hand and taking a glance at the silent pacer from time to time. As I neared the mound I saw the man very clearly, and fancied I could trace an expression of infinite evil and decadence on his seamed, hairless features. I was startled, too, to see that his goldenly gleaming weapon-case bore hieroglyphs very similar to those on the unknown talisman I wore. All the creature's costume and trappings bespoke exquisite work-manship and cultivation. Then, all too abruptly, I saw him start down the farther side of the mound and out of sight. When I reached the place, about ten minutes after I set out, there was no one there.

There is no need of relating how I spent the early part of my search in surveying and circumnavigating the mound, taking measurements, and stepping back to view the thing from different angles. It had impressed me tremendously as I approached it, and there seemed to be a kind of latent menace in its too regular outlines. It was the only elevation of any sort on the wide, level plain; and I could not doubt for a moment that it was an artificial tumulus. The steep sides seemed wholly unbroken, and without marks of human tenancy or passage. There were no signs of a path toward the top; and, burdened as I was, I managed to scramble up only with considerable difficulty. When I reached the summit I found a roughly level elliptical plateau about 300 by 50 feet in dimensions; uniformly covered with rank grass and dense underbrush, and utterly incompatible with the constant presence of a pacing sentinel. This condition gave me a real shock, for it shewed beyond question that the "Old Indian", vivid though he seemed, could not be other than a collective hallucination.

I looked about with considerable perplexity and alarm, glancing wistfully back at the village and the mass of black dots which I knew was the watching crowd. Training my glass upon them, I saw that they were studying me avidly with their glasses; so to reassure them I waved my cap in the air with a show of jauntiness which I was far from feeling. Then, settling to my work I flung down pick, shovel, and bag; taking my machete from the latter and commencing to clear away underbrush. It was a weary task, and now and then I felt a curious shiver as some perverse gust of wind arose to hamper my motion with a skill approaching deliberateness. At times it seemed as if a half-tangible force were pushing me back as I worked—almost as if the air thickened in front of me, or as if formless hands tugged at my wrists. My energy seemed used up without producing adequate results, yet for all that I made some progress.

By afternoon I had clearly perceived that, toward the northern end of the mound, there was a slight bowl-like depression in the root-tangled earth. While this might mean nothing, it would be a good place to begin when I reached the digging stage, and I made a mental note of it. At the same time I noticed another and very peculiar thing—namely, that the Indian talisman swinging from my neck seemed to behave oddly at a point about seventeen feet southeast of the suggested bowl. Its gyrations were altered whenever I happened to stoop around that point, and it tugged downward as if attracted by some magnetism in the soil. The more I noticed this, the more it struck me, till at length I decided to do a little preliminary digging there without further delay.

As I turned up the soil with my trench-knife I could not help wondering at the relative thinness of the reddish regional layer. The country as a whole was all red sandstone earth, but here I found a strange black loam less than a foot down. It was such soil as one finds in the strange, deep valleys farther west and south, and must surely have been brought from a considerable distance in the prehistoric age when the mound was reared. Kneeling and digging, I felt the leathern cord around my neck tugged harder and harder, as something in the soil seemed to draw the heavy metal talisman more and more. Then I felt my implements strike a hard surface, and wondered if a rock layer rested beneath. Prying about with the trench-knife, I found that such was not the case. Instead, to my intense surprise and feverish interest, I brought up a mould-clogged, heavy object of cylindrical shape—about a foot long and four inches in diameter—to which my hanging talisman clove with glue-like tenacity. As I cleared off the black loam my wonder and tension increased at the bas-reliefs revealed by that process. The whole cylinder, ends and all, was covered with figures and hieroglyphs; and I saw with growing excitement that these things were in the same unknown tradition as those on Grey Eagle's charm and on the yellow metal trappings of the ghost I had seen through my binoculars.

Sitting down, I further cleaned the magnetic cylinder against the rough corduroy of my knickerbockers, and observed that it was made of the same heavy, lustrous unknown metal as the charm—hence, no doubt, the singular attraction. The carvings and chasings were very strange and very horrible—nameless monsters and designs fraught with insidious evil—and all were of the highest finish and craftsmanship. I could not at first make head or tail of the thing, and handled it aimlessly until I spied a cleavage near one end. Then I sought eagerly for some mode of opening, discovering at last that the end simply unscrewed.

The cap yielded with difficulty, but at last it came off, liberating a curious aromatic odour. The sole contents was a bulky roll of a yellowish, paper-like substance inscribed in greenish characters, and for a second I had the supreme thrill of fancying that I held a written key to unknown elder worlds and abysses beyond time. Almost immediately, however, the unrolling of one end shewed that the manuscript was in Spanish—albeit the formal, pompous Spanish of a long-departed day. In the golden sunset light I looked at the heading and the opening paragraph, trying to decipher the wretched and ill-punctuated script of the vanished writer. What manner of relic was this? Upon what sort of a discovery had I stumbled? The first words set me in a new fury of excitement and curiosity, for instead of diverting me from my original quest they startlingly confirmed me in that very effort.

The yellow scroll with the green script began with a bold, identifying caption and a ceremoniously desperate appeal for belief in incredible revelations to follow:

RELACIÓN DE PÁNFILO DE ZAMACONA
Y NUÑEZ, HIDALGO DE LUARCA EN
ASTURIAS, TOCANTE AL MUNDO SOTERRÁNEO
DE XINAIÁN, A. D. MDXLV

En el nombre de la santísima Trinidad, Padre, Hijo, y Espíritu-Santo, tres personas distintas y un solo. Dios verdadero, y de la santísima Virgen muestra Señora, YO, PÁNFILO DE ZAMACONA, HIJO DE PEDRO GUZMAN Y ZAMACONA, HIDALGO, Y DE LA DOÑA YNÉS ALVARADO Y NUÑEZ, DE LUARCA EN ASTURIAS, juro para que todo que deco está verdadero como sacramento. . . .

I paused to reflect on the portentous significance of what I was reading. "The Narrative of Pánfilo de Zamacona y Nuñez, gentleman, of Luarca in Asturias, *Concerning the Subterranean World of Xinaián, A. D. 1545*". . . Here, surely, was too much for any mind to absorb all at once. A subterranean world—again that persistent idea which filtered through all the Indian tales and through all the utterances of those who had come back from the mound. And the date—1545—what could this mean? In 1540 Coronado and his men had gone north from Mexico into the wilderness, but had they not turned back in 1542? My eye ran questingly down the opened part of the scroll, and almost at once seized on the name *Francisco Vásquez de Coronado*. The writer of this thing, clearly, was one of Coronado's men—but what had he been doing in this remote realm three years after his party had gone back? I must read further, for another glance told me that what was now unrolled was merely a summary of Coronado's northward march, differing in no essential way from the account known to history.

It was only the waning light which checked me before I could unroll and read more, and in my impatient bafflement I almost forgot to be frightened at the onrush of night in this sinister place. Others, however, had not forgotten the lurking terror, for I heard a loud distant hallooing from a knot of men who had gathered at the edge of the town. Answering the anxious hail, I restored the manuscript to its strange cylinder—to which the disc around my neck still clung until I pried it off and packed it and my smaller implements for departure. Leaving the pick and shovel for the next day's work, I took up my handbag, scrambled down the steep side of the mound, and in another quarter-hour was back in the village explaining and exhibiting my curious find. As darkness drew on, I glanced back at the mound I had so lately left, and saw with a shudder that the faint bluish torch of the nocturnal squaw-ghost had begun to glimmer.

It was hard work waiting to get at the bygone Spaniard's narrative; but I knew I must have quiet and leisure for a good translation, so reluctantly saved the task for the later hours of night. Promising the townsfolk a clear account of my findings in the morning, and giving them an ample opportunity to examine the bizarre and provocative cylinder, I accompanied Clyde Compton home and ascended to my room for the translating process as soon as I possibly could. My host and his mother were intensely eager to hear the tale, but I thought they had better wait till I could thoroughly absorb the text myself and give them the gist concisely and unerringly.

Opening my handbag in the light of a single electric bulb, I again took out the cylinder and noted the instant magnetism which pulled the Indian talisman to its carven surface. The designs glimmered evilly on the richly lustrous and unknown metal, and I could not help shivering as I studied the abnormal and blasphemous forms that leered at me with such exquisite workmanship. I wish now that I had carefully photographed all these designs—though perhaps it is just as well that I did not. Of one thing I am really glad, and that is that I could not then identify the squatting octopus-headed thing which dominated most of the ornate cartouches, and which the manuscript called "Tulu". Recently I have associated it, and the legends in the manuscript connected with it, with some new-found folklore of monstrous and unmentioned Cthulhu, a horror which seeped down from the stars while the young earth was still half-formed; and had I known of the connexion then, I could not have stayed in the same room with the thing. The secondary motif, a semi-anthropomorphic serpent, I did quite readily place as a proto-type of the Yig, Quetzalcoatl, and Kukulcan conceptions. Before opening the cylinder I tested its magnetic powers on metals other than that of Grey Eagle's disc, but found that no attraction existed. It was no common magnetism which pervaded this morbid frag-ment of unknown worlds and linked it to its kind.

At last I took out the manuscript and began translating—jotting down a synoptic outline in English as I went, and now and then re-gretting the absence of a Spanish dictionary when I came upon some especially obscure or archaic word or construction. There was a sense of ineffable strangeness in thus being thrown back nearly four centuries in the midst of my continuous quest—thrown back to a year when my own forbears were settled, homekeeping gentlemen of Somerset and Devon under Henry the Eighth, with never a thought of the adventure that was to take their blood to Virginia and the New World; yet when that new world possessed, even as now, the same brooding mystery of the mound which formed my present sphere and horizon. The sense of a throwback was all the stronger because I felt instinctively that the common problem of the Spaniard and myself was one of such abysmal time-lessness—of such unholy and unearthly eternity—that the scant four hundred years between us bulked as nothing in comparison. It took no more than a single look at that monstrous and insidious cylinder to make me realise the dizzying gulfs that yawned between all men of the known earth and the primal mysteries it represented. Before that gulf Pánfilo de Zamacona and I stood side by side; just as Aristotle and I, or Cheops and I, might have stood.

III.

Of his youth in Luarca, a small, placid port on the Bay of Biscay, Zamacona told little. He had been wild, and a younger son, and had come to New Spain in 1532, when only twenty years old. Sen-sitively imaginative, he had listened spellbound to the floating rumours of rich cities and unknown worlds to the north—and especially to the tale of the Franciscan friar Marcos de Niza, who came back from a trip in 1539 with glowing accounts of fabulous

Cíbola and its great walled towns with terraced stone houses. Hearing of Coronado's contemplated expedition in search of these wonders—and of the greater wonders whispered to lie beyond them in the land of buffaloes—young Zamacona managed to join the picked party of 300, and started north with the rest in 1540.

History knows the story of that expedition—how Cíbola was found to be merely the squalid Pueblo village of Zuñi, and how de Niza was sent back to Mexico in disgrace for his florid exaggerations; how Coronado first saw the Grand Canyon, and how at Cicuyé, on the Pecos, he heard from the Indian called El Turco of the rich and mysterious land of Quivira, far to the northeast, where gold, silver, and buffaloes abounded, and where there flowed a river two leagues wide. Zamacona told briefly of the winter camp at Tiguex on the Pecos, and of the northward start in April, when the native guide proved false and led the party astray amidst a land of prairie-dogs, salt pools, and roving, bison-hunting tribes.

When Coronado dismissed his larger force and made his final forty-two-day march with a very small and select detachment, Zamacona managed to be included in the advancing party. He spoke of the fertile country and of the great ravines with trees visible only from the edge of their steep banks; and of how all the men lived solely on buffalo-meat. And then came mention of the expedition's farthest limit—of the presumable but disappointing land of Quivira with its villages of grass houses, its brooks and rivers, its good black soil, its plums, nuts, grapes, and mulberries, and its maize-growing and copper-using Indians. The execution of El Turco, the false native guide, was casually touched upon, and there was a mention of the cross which Coronado raised on the bank of a great river in the autumn of 1541—a cross bearing the inscription, "Thus far came the great general, Francisco Vásquez de Coronado".

This supposed Quivira lay at about the fortieth parallel of north latitude, and I see that quite lately the New York archaeologist Dr. Hodge has identified it with the course of the Arkansas River through Barton and Rice Counties, Kansas. It is the old home of the Wichitas, before the Sioux drove them south into what is now Oklahoma, and some of the grass-house village sites have been found and excavated for artifacts. Coronado did considerable exploring hereabouts, led hither and thither by the persistent rumours of rich cities and hidden worlds which floated fearfully around on the Indians' tongues. These northerly natives seemed more afraid and reluctant to talk about the rumoured cities and worlds than the

Mexican Indians had been; yet at the same time seemed as if they could reveal a good deal more than the Mexicans had they been willing or dared to do so. Their vagueness exasperated the Spanish leader, and after many disappointing searches he began to be very severe toward those who brought him stories. Zamacona, more patient than Coronado, found the tales especially interesting; and learned enough of the local speech to hold long conversations with a young buck named Charging Buffalo, whose curiosity had led him into much stranger places than any of his fellow-tribesmen had dared to penetrate.

It was Charging Buffalo who told Zamacona of the queer stone doorways, gates, or cave-mouths at the bottom of some of those deep, steep, wooded ravines which the party had noticed on the northward march. These openings, he said, were mostly concealed by shrubbery; and few had entered them for untold aeons. Those who went to where they led, never returned—or in a few cases returned mad or curiously maimed. But all this was legend, for nobody was known to have gone more than a limited distance inside any of them within the memory of the grandfathers of the oldest living men. Charging Buffalo himself had probably been farther than anyone else, and he had seen enough to curb both his curiosity and his greed for the rumoured gold below.

Beyond the aperture he had entered there was a long passage running crazily up and down and round about, and covered with frightful carvings of monsters and horrors that no man had ever seen. At last, after untold miles of windings and descents, there was a glow of terrible blue light; and the passage opened upon a shocking nether world. About this the Indian would say no more, for he had seen something that had sent him back in haste. But the golden cities must be somewhere down there, he added, and perhaps a white man with the magic of the thunder-stick might succeed in getting to them. He would not tell the big chief Coronado what he knew, for Coronado would not listen to Indian talk any more. Yes—he could shew Zamacona the way if the white man would leave the party and accept his guidance. But he would not go inside the opening with the white man. It was bad in there.

The place was about a five days' march to the south, near the region of great mounds. These mounds had something to do with the evil world down there—they were probably ancient closed-up passages to it, for once the Old Ones below had had colonies on the surface and had traded with men everywhere, even in the lands that had sunk under the big waters. It was when those lands had sunk that the Old Ones closed themselves up below and refused to deal with surface people. The refugees from the sinking places had told them that the gods of outer earth were against men, and that no men could survive on the outer earth unless they were daemons in league with the evil gods. That is why they shut out all surface folk, and did fearful things to any who ventured down where they dwelt. There had been sentries once at the various openings, but after ages they were no longer needed. Not many people cared to talk about the hidden Old Ones, and the legends about them would probably have died out but for certain ghostly reminders of their presence now and then. It seemed that the infinite ancientness of these creatures had brought them strangely near to the borderline of spirit, so that their ghostly emanations were more commonly frequent and vivid. Accordingly the region of the great mounds was often convulsed with spectral nocturnal battles reflecting those which had been fought in the days before the openings were closed.

The Old Ones themselves were half-ghost—indeed, it was said that they no longer grew old or reproduced their kind, but flickered eternally in a state between flesh and spirit. The change was not complete, though, for they had to breathe. It was because the underground world needed air that the openings in the deep valleys were not blocked up as the mound-openings on the plains had been. These openings, Charging Buffalo added, were probably based on natural fissures in the earth. It was whispered that the Old Ones had come down from the stars to the world when it was very young, and had gone inside to build their cities of solid gold because the surface was not then fit to live on. They were the ancestors of all men, yet none could guess from what star—or what place beyond the stars—they came. Their hidden cities were still full of gold and silver, but men had better let them alone unless protected by very strong magic.

They had frightful beasts with a faint strain of human blood, on which they rode, and which they employed for other purposes. The things, so people hinted, were carnivorous, and like their masters, preferred human flesh; so that although the Old Ones themselves did not breed, they had a sort of half-human slave-class which also served to nourish the human and animal population. This had been very oddly recruited, and was supplemented by a second slave-class of reanimated corpses. The Old Ones knew how to make a corpse into an automaton which would last almost indefinitely and perform any sort of work when directed by streams of thought. Charging Buffalo said that the people had all come to talk by means of thought only; speech having been found crude and needless, except for religious devotions and emotional expression, as aeons of discovery and study rolled by. They worshipped Yig, the great father of serpents, and Tulu, the octopus-headed entity that had brought them down from the stars; appeasing both of these hideous monstrosities by means of human sacrifices offered up in a very curious manner which Charging Buffalo did not care to describe.

Zamacona was held spellbound by the Indian's tale, and at once resolved to accept his guidance to the cryptic doorway in the ravine. He did not believe the accounts of strange ways attributed by legend to the hidden people, for the experiences of the party had been such as to disillusion one regarding native myths of unknown lands; but he did feel that some sufficiently marvellous field of riches and adventure must indeed lie beyond the weirdly carved passages in the earth. At first he thought of persuading Charging Buffalo to tell his story to Coronado—offering to shield him against any effects of the leader's testy scepticism—but later he decided that a lone adventure would be better. If he had no aid, he would not have to share anything he found; but might perhaps become a great discoverer and owner of fabulous riches. Success would make him a greater figure than Coronado himself—perhaps a greater figure than anyone else in New Spain, including even the mighty viceroy Don Antonio de Mendoza.

On October 7, 1541, at an hour close to midnight, Zamacona stole out of the Spanish camp near the grass-house village and met Charging Buffalo for the long southward journey. He travelled as lightly as possible, and did not wear his heavy helmet and breastplate. Of the details of the trip the manuscript told very little, but Zamacona records his arrival at the great ravine on October 13th. The descent of the thickly wooded slope took no great time; and though the Indian had trouble in locating the shrubbery-hidden stone door again amidst the twilight of that deep gorge, the place was finally found. It was a very small aperture as doorways go, formed of monolithic sandstone jambs and lintel, and bearing signs of nearly effaced and now undecipherable carvings. Its height was perhaps seven feet, and its width not more than four. There were drilled places in the jambs which argued the bygone presence of a hinged door or gate, but all other traces of such a thing had long since vanished.

At sight of this black gulf Charging Buffalo displayed considerable fear, and threw down his pack of supplies with signs of
haste. He had provided Zamacona with a good stock of resinous
torches and provisions, and had guided him honestly and well; but
refused to share in the venture that lay ahead. Zamacona gave him
the trinkets he had kept for such an occasion, and obtained his
promise to return to the region in a month; afterward shewing the
way southward to the Pecos Pueblo villages. A prominent rock on
the plain above them was chosen as a meeting-place; the one arriving first to pitch camp until the other should arrive.

In the manuscript Zamacona expressed a wistful wonder as to
the Indian's length of waiting at the rendezvous—for he himself
could never keep that tryst. At the last moment Charging Buffalo
tried to dissuade him from his plunge into the darkness, but soon
saw it was futile, and gestured a stoical farewell. Before lighting his
first torch and entering the opening with his ponderous pack, the
Spaniard watched the lean form of the Indian scrambling hastily
and rather relievedly upward among the trees. It was the cutting of
his last link with the world; though he did not know that he was
never to see a human being—in the accepted sense of that term—
again.

Zamacona felt no immediate premonition of evil upon entering
that ominous doorway, though from the first he was surrounded by
a bizarre and unwholesome atmosphere. The passage, slightly
taller and wider than the aperture, was for many yards a level tunnel of Cyclopean masonry, with heavily worn flagstones under
foot, and grotesquely carved granite and sandstone blocks in sides
and ceiling. The carvings must have been loathsome and terrible indeed, to judge from Zamacona's description; according to which
most of them revolved around the monstrous beings Yig and Tulu.
They were unlike anything the adventurer had ever seen before,
though he added that the native architecture of Mexico came clos-
est to them of all things in the outer world. After some distance the
tunnel began to dip abruptly, and irregular natural rock appeared
on all sides. The passage seemed only partly artificial, and decorations were limited to occasional cartouches with shocking bas-
reliefs.

Following an enormous descent, whose steepness at times produced an acute danger of slipping and tobogganing, the passage
became exceedingly uncertain in its direction and variable in its
contour. At times it narrowed almost to a slit or grew so low that

stooping and even crawling were necessary, while at other times it broadened out into sizeable caves or chains of caves. Very little human construction, it was plain, had gone into this part of the tunnel; though occasionally a sinister cartouche or hieroglyphic on the wall, or a blocked-up lateral passageway, would remind Zamacona that this was in truth the aeon-forgotten high-road to a primal and unbelievable world of living things.

For three days, as best he could reckon, Pánfilo de Zamacona scrambled down, up, along, and around, but always predominately downward, through this dark region of palaeogean night. Once in a while he heard some secret being of darkness patter or flap out of his way, and on just one occasion he half glimpsed a great, bleached thing that set him trembling. The quality of the air was mostly very tolerable; though foetid zones were now and then met with, while one great cavern of stalactites and stalagmites afforded a depressing dampness. This latter, when Charging Buffalo had come upon it, had quite seriously barred the way; since the limestone deposits of ages had built fresh pillars in the path of the primordial abyss-denizens. The Indian, however, had broken through these; so that Zamacona did not find his course impeded. It was an unconscious comfort to him to reflect that someone else from the outside world had been there before—and the Indian's careful descriptions had removed the element of surprise and unexpectedness. More—Charging Buffalo's knowledge of the tunnel had led him to provide so good a torch supply for the journey in and out, that there would be no danger of becoming stranded in darkness. Zamacona camped twice, building a fire whose smoke seemed well taken care of by the natural ventilation.

At what he considered the end of the third day—though his cocksure guesswork chronology is not at any time to be given the easy faith that he gave it—Zamacona encountered the prodigious descent and subsequent prodigious climb which Charging Buffalo had described as the tunnel's last phase. As at certain earlier points, marks of artificial improvement were here discernible; and several times the steep gradient was eased by a flight of rough-hewn steps. The torch shewed more and more of the monstrous carvings on the walls, and finally the resinous flare seemed mixed with a fainter and more diffusive light as Zamacona climbed up and up after the last downward stairway. At length the ascent ceased, and a level passage of artificial masonry with dark, basaltic blocks led straight ahead. There was no need for a torch now, for all the air was glowing with a bluish, quasi-electric radiance that flickered like an aurora. It was the strange light of the inner world that the Indian had described—and in another moment Zamacona emerged from the tunnel upon a bleak, rocky hillside which climbed above him to a seething, impenetrable sky of bluish coruscations, and descended dizzily below him to an apparently illimitable plain shrouded in bluish mist.

He had come to the unknown world at last, and from his manuscript it is clear that he viewed the formless landscape as proudly and exaltedly as ever his fellow-countryman Balboa viewed the new-found Pacific from that unforgettable peak in Darien. Charging Buffalo had turned back at this point, driven by fear of something which he would only describe vaguely and evasively as a herd of bad cattle, neither horse nor buffalo, but like the things the mound-spirits rode at night—but Zamacona could not be deterred by any such trifle. Instead of fear, a strange sense of glory filled him; for he had imagination enough to know what it meant to stand alone in an inexplicable nether world whose existence no other white man suspected.

The soil of the great hill that surged upward behind him and spread steeply downward below him was dark grey, rock-strown, without vegetation, and probably basaltic in origin; with an unearthly cast which made him feel like an intruder on an alien planet. The vast distant plain, thousands of feet below, had no features he could distinguish; especially since it appeared to be largely veiled in a curling, bluish vapour. But more than hill or plain or cloud, the bluely luminous, coruscating sky impressed the adventurer with a sense of supreme wonder and mystery. What created this sky within a world he could not tell; though he knew of the northern lights, and had even seen them once or twice. He concluded that this subterraneous light was something vaguely akin to the aurora; a view which moderns may well endorse, though it seems likely that certain phenomena of radio-activity may also enter in.

At Zamacona's back the mouth of the tunnel he had traversed yawned darkly; defined by a stone doorway very like the one he had entered in the world above, save that it was of greyish-black basalt instead of red sandstone. There were hideous sculptures, still in good preservation and perhaps corresponding to those on the outer portal which time had largely weathered away. The absence of weathering here argued a dry, temperate climate; indeed, the Spaniard already began to note the delightfully spring-like stability of temperature which marks the air of the north's interior. On the stone jambs were works proclaiming the bygone presence of hinges, but of any actual door or gate no trace remained. Seating himself for rest and thought, Zamacona lightened his pack by removing an amount of food and torches sufficient to take him back through the tunnel. These he proceeded to cache at the opening, under a cairn hastily formed of the rock fragments which everywhere lay around. Then, readjusting his lightened pack, he commenced his descent toward the distant plain; preparing to invade a region which no living thing of outer earth had penetrated in a century or more, which no white man had ever penetrated, and from which, if legend were to be believed, no organic creature had ever returned sane.

Zamacona strode briskly along down the steep, interminable slope; his progress checked at times by the bad walking that came from loose rock fragments, or by the excessive precipitousness of the grade. The distance of the mist-shrouded plain must have been enormous, for many hours' walking brought him apparently no closer to it than he had been before. Behind him was always the great hill stretching upward into a bright aërial sea of bluish coruscations. Silence was universal; so that his own footsteps, and the fall of stones that he dislodged, struck on his ears with startling distinctness. It was at what he regarded as about noon that he first saw the abnormal footprints which set him to thinking of Charging Buffalo's terrible hints, precipitate flight, and strangely abiding terror.

The rock-strown nature of the soil gave few opportunities for tracks of any kind, but at one point a rather level interval had caused the loose detritus to accumulate in a ridge, leaving a considerable area of dark-grey loam absolutely bare. Here, in a rambling confusion indicating a large herd aimlessly wandering, Zamacona found the abnormal prints. It is to be regretted that he could not describe them more exactly, but the manuscript displayed far more vague fear than accurate observation. Just what it was that so frightened the Spaniard can only be inferred from his later hints regarding the beasts. He referred to the prints as 'not hooves, nor hands, nor feet, nor precisely paws—nor so large as to cause alarm on that account'. Just why or how long ago the things had been there, was not easy to guess. There was no vegetation visible, hence grazing was out of the question; but of course if the beasts were carnivorous they might well have been hunting smaller animals, whose tracks their own would tend to obliterate.

Glancing backward from this plateau to the heights above, Zamacona thought he detected traces of a great winding road which had once led from the tunnel downward to the plain. One could get the impression of this former highway only from a broad panoramic view, since a trickle of loose rock fragments had long ago obscured it; but the adventurer felt none the less certain that it had existed. It had not, probably, been an elaborately paved trunk route; for the small tunnel it reached seemed scarcely like a main avenue to the outer world. In choosing a straight path of descent Zamacona had not followed its curving course, though he must have crossed it once or twice. With his attention now called to it, he looked ahead to see if he could trace it downward toward the plain; and this he finally thought he could do. He resolved to investigate its surface when next he crossed it, and perhaps to pursue its line for the rest of the way if he could distinguish it.

Having resumed his journey, Zamacona came some time later upon what he thought was a bend of the ancient road. There were signs of grading and of some primal attempt at rock-surfacing, but not enough was left to make the route worth following. While rummaging about in the soil with his sword, the Spaniard turned up something that glittered in the eternal blue daylight, and was thrilled at beholding a kind of coin or medal of a dark, unknown, lustrous metal, with hideous designs on each side. It was utterly and bafflingly alien to him, and from his description I have no doubt but that it was a duplicate of the talisman given me by Grey Eagle almost four centuries afterward. Pocketing it after a long and curious examination, he strode onward; finally pitching camp at an hour which he guessed to be the evening of the outer world.

The next day Zamacona rose early and resumed his descent through this blue-litten world of mist and desolation and preternatural silence. As he advanced, he at last became able to distinguish a few objects on the distant plain below—trees, bushes, rocks, and a small river that came into view from the right and curved forward at a point to the left of his contemplated course. This river seemed to be spanned by a bridge connected with the descending roadway, and with care the explorer could trace the route of the road beyond it in a straight line over the plain. Finally he even thought he could detect towns scattered along the rectilinear ribbon; towns whose left-hand edges reached the river and sometimes crossed it. Where such crossings occurred, he saw as he descended, there were always signs of bridges either ruined or surviving. He was now in the midst of a sparse grassy vegetation, and saw that below him the growth became thicker and thicker. The road was easier to define now, since its surface discouraged the grass which the looser soil supported. Rock fragments were less frequent, and the barren upward vista behind him looked bleak and forbidding in contrast to his present milieu.

It was on this day that he saw the blurred mass moving over the distant plain. Since his first sight of the sinister footprints he had met with no more of these, but something about that slowly and deliberately moving mass peculiarly sickened him. Nothing but a herd of grazing animals could move just like that, and after seeing the footprints he did not wish to meet the things which had made them. Still, the moving mass was not near the road—and his curiosity and greed for fabled gold were great. Besides, who could really judge things from vague, jumbled footprints or from the panic-twisted hints of an ignorant Indian?

In straining his eyes to view the moving mass Zamacona became aware of several other interesting things. One was that certain parts of the now unmistakable towns glittered oddly in the misty blue light. Another was that, besides the towns, several similarly glittering structures of a more isolated sort were scattered here and there along the road and over the plain. They seemed to be embowered in clumps of vegetation, and those off the road had small avenues leading to the highway. No smoke or other signs of life could be discerned about any of the towns or buildings. Finally Zamacona saw that the plain was not infinite in extent, though the half-concealing blue mists had hitherto made it seem so. It was bounded in the remote distance by a range of low hills, toward a gap in which the river and roadway seemed to lead. All this—especially the glittering of certain pinnacles in the towns—had become very vivid when Zamacona pitched his second camp amidst the endless blue day. He likewise noticed the flocks of high-soaring birds, whose nature he could not clearly make out.

The next afternoon—to use the language of the outer world as the manuscript did at all times—Zamacona reached the silent plain and crossed the soundless, slow-running river on a curiously carved and fairly well-preserved bridge of black basalt. The water was clear, and contained large fishes of a wholly strange aspect. The roadway was now paved and somewhat overgrown with weeds and creeping vines, and its course was occasionally outlined by small pillars bearing obscure symbols. On every side the grassy level extended, with here and there a clump of trees or shrubbery, and with unidentifiable bluish flowers growing irregularly over the whole area. Now and then some spasmodic motion of the grass indicated the presence of serpents. In the course of several hours the traveller reached a grove of old and alien-looking evergreen-trees which he knew, from distant viewing, protected one of the glittering-roofed isolated structures. Amidst the encroaching vegetation he saw the hideously sculptured pylons of a stone gateway leading off the road, and was presently forcing his way through briers above a moss-crusted tessellated walk lined with huge trees and low monolithic pillars.

At last, in this hushed green twilight, he saw the crumbling and ineffably ancient facade of the building—a temple, he had no doubt. It was a mass of nauseous bas-reliefs; depicting scenes and beings, objects and ceremonies, which could certainly have no place on this or any sane planet. In hinting of these things Zamacona displays for the first time that shocked and pious hesitancy which impairs the informative value of the rest of his manuscript. We cannot help regretting that the Catholic ardour of Renaissance Spain had so thoroughly permeated his thought and feeling. The door of the place stood wide open, and absolute darkness filled the windowless interior. Conquering the repulsion which the mural sculptures had excited, Zamacona took out flint and steel, lighted a resinous torch, pushed aside curtaining vines, and sallied boldly across the ominous threshold.

For a moment he was quite stupefied by what he saw. It was not the all-covering dust and cobwebs of immemorial aeons, the fluttering winged things, the shriekingly loathsome sculptures on the walls, the bizarre form of the many basins and braziers, the sinister pyramidal altar with the hollow top, or the monstrous, octopus-headed abnormality in some strange, dark metal leering and squatting broodingly on its hieroglyphed pedestal, which robbed him of even the power to give a startled cry. It was nothing so unearthly as this—but merely the fact that, with the exception of the dust, the cobwebs, the winged things, and the gigantic emerald-eyed idol, every particle of substance in sight was composed of pure and evidently solid gold.

Even the manuscript, written in retrospect after Zamacona knew that gold is the most common structural metal of a nether world containing limitless lodes and veins of it, reflects the frenzied excitement which the traveller felt upon suddenly finding the real source

of all the Indian legends of golden cities. For a time the power of
detailed observation left him, but in the end his faculties were
recalled by a peculiar tugging sensation in the pocket of his doublet.
Tracing the feeling, he realised that the disc of strange metal he had
found in the abandoned road was being attracted strongly by the
vast octopus-headed, emerald-eyed idol on the pedestal, which he
now saw to be composed of the same unknown exotic metal. He
was later to learn that this strange magnetic substance—as alien to
the inner world as to the outer world of men—is the one precious
metal of the blue-lighted abyss. None knows what it is or where it
occurs in Nature, and the amount of it on this planet came down
from the stars with the people when great Tulu, the octopus-
headed god, brought them for the first time to this earth. Certainly,
its only known source was a stock of pre-existing artifacts, including multitudes of Cyclopean idols. It could never be placed or
analysed, and even its magnetism was exerted only on its own kind.
It was the supreme ceremonial metal of the hidden people, its use
being regulated by custom in such a way that its magnetic properties might cause no inconvenience. A very weakly magnetic alloy of
it with such base metals as iron, gold, silver, copper, or zinc, had
formed the sole monetary standard of the hidden people at one
period of their history.

Zamacona's reflections on the strange idol and its magnetism
were disturbed by a tremendous wave of fear as, for the first time in
this silent world, he heard a rumble of very definite and obviously
approaching sound. There was no mistaking its nature. It was a
thunderously charging herd of large animals; and, remembering the
Indian's panic, the footprints, and the moving mass distantly seen,
the Spaniard shuddered in terrified anticipation. He did not analyse
his position, or the significance of this onrush of great lumbering
beings, but merely responded to an elemental urge toward self-
protection. Charging herds do not stop to find victims in obscure
places, and on the outer earth Zamacona would have felt little or
no alarm in such a massive, grove-girt edifice. Some instinct,
however, now bred a deep and peculiar terror in his soul; and he
looked about frantically for any means of safety.

There being no available refuge in the great, gold-patined interior, he felt that he must close the long-disused door; which still
hung on its ancient hinges, doubled back against the inner wall.
Soil, vines, and moss had entered the opening from outside, so that
he had to dig a path for the great gold portal with his sword; but he

managed to perform this work very swiftly under the frightful stimulus of the approaching noise. The hoofbeats had grown still louder and more menacing by the time he began tugging at the heavy door itself; and for a while his fears reached a frantic height, as hope of starting the age-clogged metal grew faint. Then, with a creak, the thing responded to his youthful strength, and a frenzied siege of pulling and pushing ensued. Amidst the roar of unseen stampeding feet success came at last, and the ponderous golden door clanged shut, leaving Zamacona in darkness but for the single lighted torch he had wedged between the pillars of a basin-tripod. There was a latch, and the frightened man blessed his patron saint that it was still effective.

Sound alone told the fugitive the sequel. When the roar grew very near it resolved itself into separate footfalls, as if the evergreen grove had made it necessary for the herd to slacken speed and disperse. But feet continued to approach, and it became evident that the beasts were advancing among the trees and circling the hideously carven temple walls. In the curious deliberation of their tread Zamacona found something very alarming and repulsive, nor did he like the scuffling sounds which were audible even through the thick stone walls and heavy golden door. Once the door rattled ominously on its archaic hinges, as if under a heavy impact, but fortunately it still held. Then, after a seemingly endless interval, he heard retreating steps and realised that his unknown visitors were leaving. Since the herds did not seem to be very numerous, it would have perhaps been safe to venture out within a half-hour or less; but Zamacona took no chances. Opening his pack, he prepared his camp on the golden tiles of the temple's floor, with the great door still securely latched against all comers; drifting eventually into a sounder sleep than he could have known in the blue-litten spaces outside. He did not even mind the hellish, octopus-headed bulk of great Tulu, fashioned of unknown metal and leering with fishy, sea-green eyes, which squatted in the blackness above him on its monstrously hieroglyphed pedestal.

Surrounded by darkness for the first time since leaving the tunnel, Zamacona slept profoundly and long. He must have more than made up the sleep he had lost at his two previous camps, when the ceaseless glare of the sky had kept him awake despite his fatigue, for much distance was covered by other living feet while he lay in his healthily dreamless rest. It is well that he rested deeply, for there were many strange things to be encountered in his next period of consciousness.

IV.

What finally roused Zamacona was a thunderous rapping at the door. It beat through his dreams and dissolved all the lingering mists of drowsiness as soon as he knew what it was. There could be no mistake about it—it was a definite, human, and peremptory rapping; performed apparently with some metallic object, and with all the measured quality of conscious thought or will behind it. As the awakening man rose clumsily to his feet, a sharp vocal note was added to the summons—someone calling out, in a not unmusical voice, a formula which the manuscript tries to represent as *"oxi, oxi, giathcán ycá relex"*. Feeling sure that his visitors were men and not daemons, and arguing that they could have no reason for considering him an enemy, Zamacona decided to face them openly and at once; and accordingly fumbled with the ancient latch till the golden door creaked open from the pressure of those outside.

As the great portal swung back, Zamacona stood facing a group of about twenty individuals of an aspect not calculated to give him alarm. They seemed to be Indians; though their tasteful robes and trappings and swords were not such as he had seen among any of the tribes of the outer world, while their faces had many subtle differences from the Indian type. That they did not mean to be irresponsibly hostile, was very clear; for instead of menacing him in any way they merely probed him attentively and significantly with their eyes, as if they expected their gaze to open up some sort of communication. The longer they gazed, the more he seemed to know about them and their mission; for although no one had spoken since the vocal summons before the opening of the door, he found himself slowly realising that they had come from the great city beyond the low hills, mounted on animals, and that they had been summoned by animals who had reported his presence; that they were not sure what kind of person he was or just where he had come from, but that they knew he must be associated with that dimly remembered outer world which they sometimes visited in curious dreams. How he read all this in the gaze of the two or three leaders he could not possibly explain; though he learned why a moment later.

As it was, he attempted to address his visitors in the Wichita dialect he had picked up from Charging Buffalo; and after this failed to draw a vocal reply he successively tried the Aztec, Spanish, French, and Latin tongues—adding as many scraps of lame Greek, Galician, and Portuguese, and of the Bable peasant patois of his native Asturias, as his memory could recall. But not even this polyglot array—his entire linguistic stock—could bring a reply in kind. When, however, he paused in perplexity, one of the visitors began speaking in an utterly strange and rather fascinating language whose sounds the Spaniard later had much difficulty in representing on paper. Upon his failure to understand this, the speaker pointed first to his own eyes, then to his forehead, and then to his eyes again, as if commanding the other to gaze at him in order to absorb what he wanted to transmit.

Zamacona, obeying, found himself rapidly in possession of certain information. The people, he learned, conversed nowadays by means of unvocal radiations of thought; although they had formerly used a spoken language which still survived as the written tongue, and into which they still dropped orally for tradition's sake, or when strong feeling demanded a spontaneous outlet. He could understand them merely by concentrating his attention upon their eyes; and could reply by summoning up a mental image of what he wished to say, and throwing the substance of this into his glance. When the thought-speaker paused, apparently inviting a response, Zamacona tried his best to follow the prescribed pattern, but did not appear to succeed very well. So he nodded, and tried to describe himself and his journey by signs. He pointed upward, as if to the outer world, then closed his eyes and made signs as of a mole burrowing. Then he opened his eyes again and pointed downward, in order to indicate his descent of the great slope. Experimentally he blended a spoken word or two with his gestures—for example, pointing successively to himself and to all of his visitors and saying *"un hombre"*, and then pointing to himself alone and very carefully pronouncing his individual name, *Pánfilo de Zamacona*.

Before the strange conversation was over, a good deal of data had passed in both directions. Zamacona had begun to learn how to throw his thoughts, and had likewise picked up several words of the region's archaic spoken language. His visitors, moreover, had absorbed many beginnings of an elementary Spanish vocabulary. Their own old language was utterly unlike anything the Spaniard had ever heard, though there were times later on when he was to fancy an infinitely remote linkage with the Aztec, as if the latter represented some far stage of corruption, or some very thin infiltration of loan-words. The underground world, Zamacona learned, bore an ancient name which the manuscript records as *"Xinaián"*, but which, from the writer's supplementary explanations and diacritical marks, could probably be best represented to Anglo-Saxon ears by the phonetic arrangement *K'n-yan*.

It is not surprising that this preliminary discourse did not go beyond the merest essentials, but those essentials were highly important. Zamacona learned that the people of K'n-yan were almost infinitely ancient, and that they had come from a distant part of space where physical conditions are much like those of the earth. All this, of course, was legend now; and one could not say how much truth was in it, or how much worship was really due to the octopus-headed being Tulu who had traditionally brought them hither and whom they still reverenced for aesthetic reasons. But they knew of the outer world, and were indeed the original stock who had peopled it as soon as its crust was fit to live on. Between glacial ages they had had some remarkable surface civilisations, especially one at the South Pole near the mountain Kadath.

At some time infinitely in the past most of the outer world had sunk beneath the ocean, so that only a few refugees remained to bear the news to K'n-yan. This was undoubtedly due to the wrath of space-devils hostile alike to men and to men's gods—for it bore out rumours of a primordially earlier sinking which had submerged the gods themselves, including great Tulu, who still lay prisoned and dreaming in the watery vaults of the half-cosmic city Relex. No man not a slave of the space-devils, it was argued, could live long on the outer earth; and it was decided that all beings who remained there must be evilly connected. Accordingly traffic with the lands of sun and starlight abruptly ceased. The subterraneous approaches to K'n-yan, or such as could be remembered, were either blocked up or carefully guarded; and all encroachers were treated as dangerous spies and enemies.

But this was long ago. With the passing of ages fewer and fewer visitors came to K'n-yan, and eventually sentries ceased to be maintained at the unblocked approaches. The mass of the people forgot, except through distorted memories and myths and some very singular dreams, that an outer world existed; though educated folk never ceased to recall the essential facts. The last visitors ever recorded—centuries in the past—had not even been treated as devil-spies; faith in the old legendry having long before died out. They had been questioned eagerly about the fabulous outer regions; for scientific curiosity in K'n-yan was keen, and the myths, memories, dreams, and historical fragments relating to the earth's surface had often tempted scholars to the brink of an external expedition which they had not quite dared to attempt. The only thing demanded of such visitors was that they refrain from going back and informing the outer world of K'n-yan's positive existence; for after all, one could not be sure about these outer lands. They coveted gold and silver, and might prove highly troublesome intruders. Those who had obeyed the injunction had lived happily, though regrettably briefly, and had told all they could about their world—little enough, however, since their accounts were all so fragmentary and conflicting that one could hardly tell what to believe and what to doubt. One wished that more of them would come. As for those who disobeyed and tried to escape—it was very unfortunate about them. Zamacona himself was very welcome, for he appeared to be a higher-grade man, and to know much more about the outer world, than anyone else who had come down within memory. He could tell them much—and they hoped he would be reconciled to his lifelong stay.

Many things which Zamacona learned about K'n-yan in that first colloquy left him quite breathless. He learned, for instance, that during the past few thousand years the phenomena of old age and death had been conquered; so that men no longer grew feeble or died except through violence or will. By regulating the system, one might be as physiologically young and immortal as he wished; and the only reason why any allowed themselves to age, was that they enjoyed the sensation in a world where stagnation and commonplaceness reigned. They could easily become young again when they felt like it. Births had ceased, except for experimental purposes, since a large population had been found needless by a master-race which controlled Nature and organic rivals alike. Many, however, chose to die after a while; since despite the cleverest efforts to invent new pleasures, the ordeal of consciousness became too dull for sensitive souls—especially those in whom time and satiation had blinded the primal instincts and emotions of self-preservation. All the members of the group before Zamacona were from 500 to 1500 years old; and several had seen surface visitors before, though time had blurred the recollection. These visitors, by the way, had often tried to duplicate the longevity of the underground race; but had been able to do so only fractionally, owing to evolutionary differences developing during the million or two years of cleavage.

These evolutionary differences were even more strikingly shewn in another particular—one far stranger than the wonder of immortality itself. This was the ability of the people of K'n-yan to regulate the balance between matter and abstract energy, even where the bodies of living organic beings were concerned, by the sheer force of the technically trained will. In other words, with suitable effort a learned man of K'n-yan could dematerialise and rematerialise himself—or, with somewhat greater effort and subtler technique, any other object he chose; reducing solid matter to free external particles and recombining the particles again without damage. Had not Zamacona answered his visitors' knock when he did, he would have discovered this accomplishment in a highly puzzling way; for only the strain and bother of the process prevented the twenty men from passing bodily through the golden door without pausing for a summons. This art was much older than the art of perpetual life; and it could be taught to some extent, though never perfectly, to any intelligent person. Rumours of it had reached the outer world in past aeons; surviving in secret traditions and ghostly legendry. The men of K'n-yan had been amused by the primitive and imperfect spirit tales brought down by outer-world stragglers. In practical life this principle had certain industrial applications, but was generally suffered to remain neglected through lack of any particular incentive to its use. Its chief surviving form was in connexion with sleep, when for excitement's sake many dream-connoisseurs resorted to it to enhance the vividness of their visionary wanderings. By the aid of this method certain dreamers even paid half-material visits to a strange, nebulous realm of mounds and valleys and varying light which some believed to be the forgotten outer world. They would go thither on their beasts, and in an age of peace live over the old, glorious battles of their forefathers. Some philosophers thought that in such cases they actually coalesced with immaterial forces left behind by these warlike ancestors themselves.

The people of K'n-yan all dwelt in the great, tall city of Tsath beyond the mountains. Formerly several races of them had inhabited the entire underground world, which stretched down to unfathomable abysses and which included besides the blue-litten region a red-litten region called Yoth, where relics of a still older and non-human race were found by archaeologists. In the course of time, however, the men of Tsath had conquered and enslaved the rest; interbreeding them with certain horned and four-footed animals of the red-litten region, whose semi-human leanings were very peculiar, and which, though containing a certain artificially created element, may have been in part the degenerate descendants of those peculiar entities who had left the relics. As aeons passed, and mechanical discoveries made the business of life extremely easy, a concentration of the people of Tsath took place; so that all the rest of K'n-yan became relatively deserted.

It was easier to live in one place, and there was no object in maintaining a population of overflowing proportions. Many of the old mechanical devices were still in use, though others had been abandoned when it was seen that they failed to give pleasure, or that they were not necessary for a race of reduced numbers whose mental force could govern an extensive array of inferior and semi-human industrial organisms. This extensive slave-class was highly composite, being bred from ancient conquered enemies, from outer-world stragglers, from dead bodies curiously galvanised into effectiveness, and from the naturally inferior members of the ruling race of Tsath. The ruling type itself had become highly superior through selective breeding and social evolution—the nation having passed through a period of idealistic industrial democracy which gave equal opportunities to all, and thus, by raising the naturally intelligent to power, drained the masses of all their brains and stamina. Industry, being found fundamentally futile except for the supplying of basic needs and the gratification of inescapable yearnings, had become very simple. Physical comfort was ensured by an urban mechanisation of standardised and easily maintained pattern, and other elemental needs were supplied by scientific agriculture and stock-raising. Long travel was abandoned, and people went back to using the horned, half-human beasts instead of maintaining the profusion of gold, silver, and steel transportation machines which had once threaded land, water, and air. Zamacona could scarcely believe that such things had ever existed outside dreams, but was told he could see specimens of them in museums. He could also see the ruins of other vast magical devices by travelling a day's journey to the valley of Do-Hna, to which the race had spread during its period of greatest numbers. The cities and temples of this present plain were of a far more archaic period, and had never been other than religious and antiquarian shrines during the supremacy of the men of Tsath.

In government, Tsath was a kind of communistic or semi-anarchical state; habit rather than law determining the daily order of things. This was made possible by the age-old experience and paralysing ennui of the race, whose wants and needs were limited to physical fundamentals and to new sensations. An aeon-long tolerance not yet undermined by growing reaction had abolished all illusions of values and principles, and nothing but an approximation to custom was ever sought or expected. To see that the mutual encroachments of pleasure-seeking never crippled the mass life of the community—this was all that was desired. Family organisation had long ago perished, and the civil and social distinction of the sexes had disappeared. Daily life was organised in ceremonial patterns; with games, intoxication, torture of slaves, day-dreaming, gastronomic and emotional orgies, religious exercises, exotic experiments, artistic and philosophical discussions, and the like, as the principal occupations. Property—chiefly land, slaves, animals, shares in the common city enterprise of Tsath, and ingots of magnetic Tulu-metal, the former universal money standard—was allocated on a very complex basis which included a certain amount equally divided among all the freemen. Poverty was unknown, and labour consisted only of certain administrative duties imposed by an intricate system of testing and selection. Zamacona found difficulty in describing conditions so unlike anything he had previously known; and the text of his manuscript proved unusually puzzling at this point.

Art and intellect, it appeared, had reached very high levels in Tsath; but had become listless and decadent. The dominance of machinery had at one time broken up the growth of normal aesthetics, introducing a lifelessly geometrical tradition fatal to sound expression. This had soon been outgrown, but had left its mark upon all pictorial and decorative attempts; so that except for conventionalised religious designs, there was little depth or feeling in any later work. Archaistic reproductions of earlier work had been found much preferable for general enjoyment. Literature was all highly individual and analytical, so much so as to be wholly incomprehensible to Zamacona. Science had been profound and accurate, and all-embracing save in the one direction of astronomy. Of late, however, it was falling into decay, as people found it in-

creasingly useless to tax their minds by recalling its maddening in-
finitude of details and ramifications. It was thought more sensible
to abandon the deepest speculations and to confine philosophy to
conventional forms. Technology, of course, could be carried on by
rule of thumb. History was more and more neglected, but exact
and copious chronicles of the past existed in the libraries. It was
still an interesting subject, and there would be a vast number to re-
joice at the fresh outer-world knowledge brought in by Zamacona.
In general, though, the modern tendency was to feel rather than to
think; so that men were now more highly esteemed for inventing
new diversions than for preserving old facts or pushing back the
frontier of cosmic mystery.

Religion was a leading interest in Tsath, though very few actually
believed in the supernatural. What was desired was the aesthetic
and emotional exaltation bred by the mystical moods and sensuous
rites which attended the colourful ancestral faith. Temples to Great
Tulu, a spirit of universal harmony anciently symbolised as the
octopus-headed god who had brought all men down from the stars,
were the most richly constructed objects in all K'n-yan; while the
cryptic shrines of Yig, the principle of life symbolised as the Father
of all Serpents, were almost as lavish and remarkable. In time
Zamacona learned much of the orgies and sacrifices connected with
this religion, but seemed piously reluctant to describe them in his
manuscript. He himself never participated in any of the rites save
those which he mistook for perversions of his own faith; nor did he
ever lose an opportunity to try to convert the people to that faith of
the Cross which the Spaniards hoped to make universal.

Prominent in the contemporary religion of Tsath was a revived
and almost genuine veneration for the rare, sacred metal of Tulu—
that dark, lustrous, magnetic stuff which was nowhere found in
Nature, but which had always been with men in the form of idols
and hieratic implements. From the earliest times any sight of it in its
unalloyed form had impelled respect, while all the sacred archives
and litanies were kept in cylinders wrought of its purest substance.
Now, as the neglect of science and intellect was dulling the critically
analytical spirit, people were beginning to weave around the metal
once more that same fabric of awestruck superstition which had existed in primitive times.

Another function of religion was the regulation of the calendar,
born of a period when time and speed were regarded as prime
fetiches in man's emotional life. Periods of alternate waking and

sleeping, prolonged, abridged, and inverted as mood and conveni-
ence dictated, and timed by the tail-beats of Great Yig, the Serpent,
corresponded very roughly to terrestrial days and nights; though
Zamacona's sensations told him they must actually be almost twice
as long. The year-unit, measured by Yig's annual shedding of his
skin, was equal to about a year and a half of the outer world.
Zamacona thought he had mastered this calendar very well when
he wrote his manuscript, whence the confidently given date of
1545; but the document failed to suggest that his assurance in this
matter was fully justified.

As the spokesman of the Tsath party proceeded with his information, Zamacona felt a growing repulsion and alarm. It was not only
what was told, but the strange, telepathic manner of telling, and
the plain inference that return to the outer world would be impossible, that made the Spaniard wish he had never descended to this
region of magic, abnormality, and decadence. But he knew that
nothing but friendly acquiescence would do as a policy, hence
decided to coöperate in all his visitors' plans and furnish all the information they might desire. They, on their part, were fascinated
by the outer-world data which he managed haltingly to convey.

It was really the first draught of reliable surface information they
had had since the refugees straggled back from Atlantis and
Lemuria aeons before, for all their subsequent emissaries from outside had been members of narrow and local groups without any
knowledge of the world at large—Mayas, Toltecs, and Aztecs at
best, and mostly ignorant tribes of the plains. Zamacona was the
first European they had ever seen, and the fact that he was a youth
of education and brilliancy made him of still more emphatic value
as a source of knowledge. The visiting party shewed their breathless interest in all he contrived to convey, and it was plain that his
coming would do much to relieve the flagging interest of weary
Tsath in matters of geography and history.

The only thing which seemed to displease the men of Tsath was
the fact that curious and adventurous strangers were beginning to
pour into those parts of the upper world where the passages to
K'n-yan lay. Zamacona told them of the founding of Florida and
New Spain, and made it clear that a great part of the world was
stirring with the zest of adventure—Spanish, Portuguese, French,
and English. Sooner or later Mexico and Florida must meet in one
great colonial empire—and then it would be hard to keep outsiders
from the rumoured gold and silver of the abyss. Charging Buffalo

knew of Zamacona's journey into the earth. Would he tell Coronado, or somehow let a report get to the great viceroy, when he failed to find the traveller at the promised meeting-place? Alarm for the continued secrecy and safety of K'n-yan shewed in the faces of the visitors, and Zamacona absorbed from their minds the fact that from now on sentries would undoubtedly be posted once more at all the unblocked passages to the outside world which the men of Tsath could remember.

V.

The long conversation of Zamacona and his visitors took place in the green-blue twilight of the grove just outside the temple door. Some of the men reclined on the weeds and moss beside the half-vanished walk, while others, including the Spaniard and the chief spokesman of the Tsath party, sat on the occasional low monolithic pillars that lined the temple approach. Almost a whole terrestrial day must have been consumed in the colloquy, for Zamacona felt the need of food several times, and ate from his well-stocked pack while some of the Tsath party went back for provisions to the roadway, where they had left the animals on which they had ridden. At length the prime leader of the party brought the discourse to a close, and indicated that the time had come to proceed to the city.

There were, he affirmed, several extra beasts in the cavalcade, upon one of which Zamacona could ride. The prospect of mounting one of those ominous hybrid entities whose fabled nourishment was so alarming, and a single sight of which had set Charging Buffalo into such a frenzy of flight, was by no means reassuring to the traveller. There was, moreover, another point about the things which disturbed him greatly—the apparently preternatural intelligence with which some members of the previous day's roving pack had reported his presence to the men of Tsath and brought out the present expedition. But Zamacona was not a coward, hence followed the men boldly down the weed-grown walk toward the road where the things were stationed.

And yet he could not refrain from crying out in terror at what he saw when he passed through the great vine-draped pylons and emerged upon the ancient road. He did not wonder that the curious Wichita had fled in panic, and had to close his eyes a moment to retain his sanity. It is unfortunate that some sense of pious reticence prevented him from describing fully in his manuscript the nameless sight he saw. As it is, he merely hinted at the shocking morbidity of these great floundering white things, with black fur on their backs, a rudimentary horn in the centre of their foreheads, and an unmistakable trace of human or anthropoid blood in their flat-nosed, bulging-lipped faces. They were, he declared later in his manuscript, the most terrible objective entities he ever saw in his life, either in K'n-yan or in the outer world. And the specific quality of their supreme terror was something apart from any easily recognisable or describable feature. The main trouble was that they were not wholly products of Nature.

The party observed Zamacona's fright, and hastened to reassure him as much as possible. The beasts or *gyaa-yothn,* they explained, surely were curious things; but were really very harmless. The flesh they ate was not that of intelligent people of the master-race, but merely that of a special slave-class which had for the most part ceased to be thoroughly human, and which indeed was the principal meat stock of K'n-yan. They—or their principal ancestral element—had first been found in a wild state amidst the Cyclopean ruins of the deserted red-litten world of Yoth which lay below the blue-litten world of K'n-yan. That part of them was human, seemed quite clear; but men of science could never decide whether they were actually the descendants of the bygone entities who had lived and reigned in the strange ruins. The chief ground for such a supposition was the well-known fact that the vanished inhabitants of Yoth had been quadrupedal. This much was known from the very few manuscripts and carvings found in the vaults of Zin, beneath the largest ruined city of Yoth. But it was also known from these manuscripts that the beings of Yoth had possessed the art of synthetically creating life, and had made and destroyed several efficiently designed races of industrial and transportational animals in the course of their history—to say nothing of concocting all manner of fantastic living shapes for the sake of amusement and new sensations during the long period of decadence. The beings of Yoth had undoubtedly been reptilian in affiliations, and most physiologists of Tsath agreed that the present beasts had been very much inclined toward reptilianism before they had been crossed with the mammal slave-class of K'n-yan.

It argues well for the intrepid fire of those Renaissance Spaniards who conquered half the unknown world, that Pánfilo de Zamacona y Nuñez actually mounted one of the morbid beasts of Tsath and fell into place beside the leader of the cavalcade—the man named

Gll'-Hthaa-Ynn, who had been most active in the previous exchange of information. It was a repulsive business; but after all, the seat was very easy, and the gait of the clumsy *gyaa-yoth* surprisingly even and regular. No saddle was necessary, and the animal appeared to require no guidance whatever. The procession moved forward at a brisk gait, stopping only at certain abandoned cities and temples about which Zamacona was curious, and which Gll'-Hthaa-Ynn was obligingly ready to display and explain. The largest of these towns, B'graa, was a marvel of finely wrought gold, and Zamacona studied the curiously ornate architecture with avid interest. Buildings tended toward height and slenderness, with roofs bursting into a multitude of pinnacles. The streets were narrow, curving, and occasionally picturesquely hilly, but Gll'-Hthaa-Ynn said that the later cities of K'n-yan were far more spacious and regular in design. All these old cities of the plain shewed traces of levelled walls—reminders of the archaic days when they had been successively conquered by the now dispersed armies of Tsath.

There was one object along the route which Gll'-Hthaa-Ynn exhibited on his own initiative, even though it involved a detour of about a mile along a vine-tangled side path. This was a squat, plain temple of black basalt blocks without a single carving, and containing only a vacant onyx pedestal. The remarkable thing about it was its story, for it was a link with a fabled elder world compared to which even cryptic Yoth was a thing of yesterday. It had been built in imitation of certain temples depicted in the vaults of Zin, to house a very terrible black toad-idol found in the red-litten world and called Tsathoggua in the Yothic manuscripts. It had been a potent and widely worshipped god, and after its adoption by the people of K'n-yan had lent its name to the city which was later to become dominant in that region. Yothic legend said that it had come from a mysterious inner realm beneath the red-litten world—a black realm of peculiar-sensed beings which had no light at all, but which had had great civilisations and mighty gods before ever the reptilian quadrupeds of Yoth had come into being. Many images of Tsathoggua existed in Yoth, all of which were alleged to have come from the black inner realm, and which were supposed by Yothic archaeologists to represent the aeon-extinct race of that realm. The black realm called N'kai in the Yothic manuscripts had been explored as thoroughly as possible by these archaeologists, and singular stone troughs or burrows had excited infinite speculation.

When the men of K'n-yan discovered the red-litten world and de-
ciphered its strange manuscripts, they took over the Tsathoggua
cult and brought all the frightful toad images up to the land of blue
light—housing them in shrines of Yoth-quarried basalt like the one
Zamacona now saw. The cult flourished until it almost rivalled the
ancient cults of Yig and Tulu, and one branch of the race even took
it to the outer world, where the smallest of the images eventually
found a shrine at Olathoë, in the land of Lomar near the earth's
north pole. It was rumoured that this outer-world cult survived
even after the great ice-sheet and the hairy Gnophkehs destroyed
Lomar, but of such matters not much was definitely known in
K'n-yan.. In that world of blue light the cult came to an abrupt end,
even though the name of Tsath was suffered to remain.

What ended the cult was the partial exploration of the black
realm of N'kai beneath the red-litten world of Yoth. According to
the Yothic manuscripts, there was no surviving life in N'kai, but
something must have happened in the aeons between the days of
Yoth and the coming of men to the earth; something perhaps not
unconnected with the end of Yoth. Probably it had been an earth-
quake, opening up lower chambers of the lightless world which had
been closed against the Yothic archaeologists; or perhaps some
more frightful juxtaposition of energy and electrons, wholly inconceivable to any sort of vertebrate minds, had taken place. At
any rate, when the men of K'n-yan went down into N'kai's black
abyss with their great atom-power searchlights they found living
things—living things that oozed along stone channels and worshipped onyx and basalt images of Tsathoggua. But they were not
toads like Tsathoggua himself. Far worse—they were amorphous
lumps of viscous black slime that took temporary shapes for
various purposes. The explorers of K'n-yan did not pause for
detailed observations, and those who escaped alive sealed the
passage leading from red-litten Yoth down into the gulfs of nether
horror. Then all the images of Tsathoggua in the land of K'n-yan
were dissolved into the ether by disintegrating rays, and the cult
was abolished forever.

Aeons later, when naive fears were outgrown and supplanted by
scientific curiosity, the old legends of Tsathoggua and N'kai were
recalled, and a suitably armed and equipped exploring party went
down to Yoth to find the closed gate of the black abyss and see
what might still lie beneath. But they could not find the gate, nor
could any man ever do so in all the ages that followed. Nowadays

there were those who doubted that any abyss had ever existed, but the few scholars who could still decipher the Yothic manuscripts believed that the evidence for such a thing was adequate, even though the middle records of K'n-yan, with accounts of the one frightful expedition into N'kai, were more open to question. Some of the later religious cults tried to suppress remembrance of N'kai's existence, and attached severe penalties to its mention; but these had not begun to be taken seriously at the time of Zamacona's advent to K'n-yan.

As the cavalcade returned to the old highway and approached the low range of mountains, Zamacona saw that the river was very close on the left. Somewhat later, as the terrain rose, the stream entered a gorge and passed through the hills, while the road traversed the gap at a rather higher level close to the brink. It was about this time that light rainfall came. Zamacona noticed the occasional drops and drizzle, and looked up at the coruscating blue air, but there was no diminution of the strange radiance. Gll'-Hthaa-Ynn then told him that such condensations and precipitations of water-vapour were not uncommon, and that they never dimmed the glare of the vault above. A kind of mist, indeed, always hung about the lowlands of K'n-yan, and compensated for the complete absence of true clouds.

The slight rise of the mountain pass enabled Zamacona, by looking behind, to see the ancient and deserted plain in panorama as he had seen it from the other side. He seems to have appreciated its strange beauty, and to have vaguely regretted leaving it; for he speaks of being urged by Gll'-Hthaa-Ynn to drive his beast more rapidly. When he faced frontward again he saw that the crest of the road was very near; the weed-grown way leading starkly up and ending against a blank void of blue light. The scene was undoubtedly highly impressive—a steep green mountain wall on the right, a deep river-chasm on the left with another green mountain wall beyond it, and ahead, the churning sea of bluish coruscations into which the upward path dissolved. Then came the crest itself, and with it the world of Tsath outspread in a stupendous forward vista.

Zamacona caught his breath at the great sweep of peopled landscape, for it was a hive of settlement and activity beyond anything he had ever seen or dreamed of. The downward slope of the hill itself was relatively thinly strown with small farms and occasional temples; but beyond it lay an enormous plain covered like a chessboard with planted trees, irrigated by narrow canals cut from the river, and threaded by wide, geometrically precise roads of gold or basalt blocks. Great silver cables borne aloft on golden pillars linked the low, spreading buildings and clusters of buildings which rose here and there, and in some places one could see lines of partly ruinous pillars without cables. Moving objects shewed the fields to be under tillage, and in some cases Zamacona saw that men were ploughing with the aid of the repulsive, half-human quadrupeds.

But most impressive of all was the bewildering vision of clustered spires and pinnacles which rose afar off across the plain and shimmered flower-like and spectral in the coruscating blue light. At first Zamacona thought it was a mountain covered with houses and temples, like some of the picturesque hill cities of his own Spain, but a second glance shewed him that it was not indeed such. It was a city of the plain, but fashioned of such heaven-reaching towers that its outline was truly that of a mountain. Above it hung a curious greyish haze, through which the blue light glistened and took added overtones of radiance from the million golden minarets. Glancing at Gll'-Hthaa-Ynn, Zamacona knew that this was the monstrous, gigantic, and omnipotent city of Tsath.

As the road turned downward toward the plain, Zamacona felt a kind of uneasiness and sense of evil. He did not like the beast he rode, or the world that could provide such a beast, and he did not like the atmosphere that brooded over the distant city of Tsath. When the cavalcade began to pass occasional farms, the Spaniard noticed the forms that worked in the fields; and did not like their motions and proportions, or the mutilations he saw on most of them. Moreover, he did not like the way that some of these forms were herded in corrals, or the way they grazed on the heavy verdure. Gll'-Hthaa-Ynn indicated that these beings were members of the slave-class, and that their acts were controlled by the master of the farm, who gave them hypnotic impressions in the morning of all they were to do during the day. As semi-conscious machines, their industrial efficiency was nearly perfect. Those in the corrals were inferior specimens, classified merely as livestock.

Upon reaching the plain, Zamacona saw the larger farms and noted the almost human work performed by the repulsive horned *gyaa-yothn*. He likewise observed the more manlike shapes that toiled along the furrows, and felt a curious fright and disgust toward certain of them whose motions were more mechanical than those of the rest. These, Gll'-Hthaa-Ynn explained, were what men called the *y'm-bhi*—organisms which had died, but which had been mechanically reanimated for industrial purposes by means of atomic energy and thought-power. The slave-class did not share the immortality of the freemen of Tsath, so that with time the number of *y'm-bhi* had become very large. They were dog-like and faithful, but not so readily amenable to thought-commands as were living slaves. Those which most repelled Zamacona were those whose mutilations were greatest; for some were wholly headless, while others had suffered singular and seemingly capricious subtractions, distortions, transpositions, and graftings in various places. The Spaniard could not account for this condition, but Gll'-Hthaa-Ynn made it clear that these were slaves who had been used for the amusement of the people in some of the vast arenas; for the men of Tsath were connoisseurs of delicate sensation, and required a constant supply of fresh and novel stimuli for their jaded impulses. Zamacona, though by no means squeamish, was not favourably impressed by what he saw and heard.

Approached more closely, the vast metropolis became dimly horrible in its monstrous extent and inhuman height. Gll'-Hthaa-Ynn explained that the upper parts of the great towers were no longer used, and that many had been taken down to avoid the bother of maintenance. The plain around the original urban area was covered with newer and smaller dwellings, which in many cases were preferred to the ancient towers. From the whole mass of gold and stone a monotonous roar of activity droned outward over the plain, while cavalcades and streams of wagons were constantly entering and leaving over the great gold- or stone-paved roads.

Several times Gll'-Hthaa-Ynn paused to shew Zamacona some particular object of interest, especially the temples of Yig, Tulu, Nug, Yeb, and the Not-to-Be-Named One which lined the road at infrequent intervals, each in its embowering grove according to the custom of K'n-yan. These temples, unlike those of the deserted plain beyond the mountains, were still in active use; large parties of mounted worshippers coming and going in constant streams. Gll'-Hthaa-Ynn took Zamacona into each of them, and the Spaniard watched the subtle orgiastic rites with fascination and repulsion. The ceremonies of Nug and Yeb sickened him especially—so much, indeed, that he refrained from describing them in his manuscript. One squat, black temple of Tsathoggua was encountered, but it had been turned into a shrine of Shub-Niggurath, the All-Mother and wife of the Not-to-Be-Named One. This deity was a kind of sophisticated Astarte, and her worship struck the pious Catholic as supremely obnoxious. What he liked least of all were the emotional sounds emitted by the celebrants—jarring sounds in a race that had ceased to use vocal speech for ordinary purposes.

Close to the compact outskirts of Tsath, and well within the shadow of its terrifying towers, Gll'-Hthaa-Ynn pointed out a monstrous circular building before which enormous crowds were lined up. This, he indicated, was one of the many amphitheatres where curious sports and sensations were provided for the weary people of K'n-yan. He was about to pause and usher Zamacona inside the vast curved facade, when the Spaniard, recalling the mutilated forms he had seen in the fields, violently demurred. This was the first of those friendly clashes of taste which were to convince the people of Tsath that their guest followed strange and narrow standards.

Tsath itself was a network of strange and ancient streets; and despite a growing sense of horror and alienage, Zamacona was enthralled by its intimations of mystery and cosmic wonder. The dizzy giganticism of its overawing towers, the monstrous surge of teeming life through its ornate avenues, the curious carvings on its doorways and windows, the odd vistas glimpsed from balustraded plazas and tiers of titan terraces, and the enveloping grey haze which seemed to press down on the gorge-like streets in low ceiling-fashion, all combined to produce such a sense of adventurous expectancy as he had never known before. He was taken at once to a council of executives which held forth in a gold-and-copper palace behind a gardened and fountained park, and was for some time subjected to close, friendly questioning in a vaulted hall frescoed with vertiginous arabesques. Much was expected of him, he could see, in the way of historical information about the outside earth; but in return all the mysteries of K'n-yan would be unveiled to him. The one great drawback was the inexorable ruling that he might never return to the world of sun and stars and Spain which was his.

A daily programme was laid down for the visitor, with time apportioned judiciously among several kinds of activities. There were to be conversations with persons of learning in various places, and lessons in many branches of Tsathic lore. Liberal periods of research were allowed for, and all the libraries of K'n-yan both secular and sacred were to be thrown open to him as soon as he might master the written languages. Rites and spectacles were to be attended—except when he might especially object—and much time would be left for the enlightened pleasure-seeking and emotional titillation which formed the goal and nucleus of daily life. A house in the suburbs or an apartment in the city would be assigned him, and he would be initiated into one of the large affection-groups, including many noblewomen of the most extreme and art-enhanced beauty, which in latter-day K'n-yan took the place of family units. Several horned *gyaa-yothn* would be provided for his transportation and errand-running, and ten living slaves of intact body would serve to conduct his establishment and protect him from thieves and sadists and religious orgiasts on the public highways. There were many mechanical devices which he must learn to use, but Gll'-Hthaa-Ynn would instruct him immediately regarding the principal ones.

Upon his choosing an apartment in preference to a suburban villa, Zamacona was dismissed by the executives with great courtesy and ceremony, and was led through several gorgeous streets to a cliff-like carven structure of some seventy or eighty floors. Preparations for his arrival had already been instituted, and in a spacious ground-floor suite of vaulted rooms slaves were busy adjusting hangings and furniture. There were lacquered and inlaid tabourets, velvet and silk reclining-corners and squatting-cushions, and infinite rows of teakwood and ebony pigeon-holes with metal cylinders containing some of the manuscripts he was soon to read—standard classics which all urban apartments possessed. Desks with great stacks of membrane-paper and pots of the prevailing green pigment were in every room—each with graded sets of pigment brushes and other odd bits of stationery. Mechanical writing devices stood on ornate golden tripods, while over all was shed a brilliant blue light from energy-globes set in the ceiling. There were windows, but at this shadowy ground-level they were of scant illuminating value. In some of the rooms were elaborate baths, while the kitchen was a maze of technical contrivances. Supplies were brought, Zamacona was told, through the network of underground passages which lay beneath Tsath, and which had once accommodated curious mechanical transports. There was a stable on that underground level for the beasts, and Zamacona would presently be shewn how to find the nearest runway to the street. Before his inspection was finished, the permanent staff of slaves arrived and were introduced; and shortly afterward there came some half-dozen freemen and noblewomen of his future affection-group, who were to be his companions for several days, contributing what they could to his instruction and amusement. Upon their departure, another party would take their place, and so onward in rotation through a group of about fifty members.

VI.

Thus was Pánfilo de Zamacona y Nuñez absorbed for four years into the life of the sinister city of Tsath in the blue-litten nether world of K'n-yan. All that he learned and saw and did is clearly not told in his manuscript; for a pious reticence overcame him when he began to write in his native Spanish tongue, and he dared not set down everything. Much he consistently viewed with repulsion, and many things he steadfastly refrained from seeing or doing or eating. For other things he atoned by frequent countings of the beads of his rosary. He explored the entire world of K'n-yan, including the deserted machine-cities of the middle period on the gorse-grown plain of Nith, and made one descent into the red-litten world of Yoth to see the Cyclopean ruins. He witnessed prodigies of craft and machinery which left him breathless, and beheld human meta-morphoses, dematerialisations, rematerialisations, and reanima-tions which made him cross himself again and again. His very capacity for astonishment was blunted by the plethora of new marvels which every day brought him.

But the longer he stayed, the more he wished to leave, for the in-ner life of K'n-yan was based on impulses very plainly outside his radius. As he progressed in historical knowledge, he understood more; but understanding only heightened his distaste. He felt that the people of Tsath were a lost and dangerous race—more danger-ous to themselves than they knew—and that their growing frenzy of monotony-warfare and novelty-quest was leading them rapidly toward a precipice of disintegration and utter horror. His own visit, he could see, had accelerated their unrest; not only by intro-ducing fears of outside invasion, but by exciting in many a wish to sally forth and taste the diverse external world he described. As time progressed, he noticed an increasing tendency of the people to resort to dematerialisation as an amusement; so that the apartments and amphitheatres of Tsath became a veritable Witches' Sabbath of transmutations, age-adjustments, death-experiments, and projec-tions. With the growth of boredom and restlessness, he saw, cruelty and subtlety and revolt were growing apace. There was more and more cosmic abnormality, more and more curious sadism, more and more ignorance and superstition, and more and more desire to escape out of physical life into a half-spectral state of electronic dispersal.

All his efforts to leave, however, came to nothing. Persuasion was useless, as repeated trials proved; though the mature disillusion of the upper classes at first prevented them from resenting their guest's open wish for departure. In a year which he reckoned as 1543 Zamacona made an actual attempt to escape through the tunnel by which he had entered K'n-yan, but after a weary journey across the deserted plain he encountered forces in the dark passage which discouraged him from future attempts in that direction. As a means of sustaining hope and keeping the image of home in mind, he began about this time to make rough draughts of the manuscript relating his adventures; delighting in the loved, old Spanish words and the familiar letters of the Roman alphabet. Somehow he fancied he might get the manuscript to the outer world; and to make it convincing to his fellows he resolved to enclose it in one of the Tulu-metal cylinders used for sacred archives. That alien, magnetic substance could not but support the incredible story he had to tell.

But even as he planned, he had little real hope of ever establishing contact with the earth's surface. Every known gate, he knew, was guarded by persons or forces that it were better not to oppose. His attempt at escape had not helped matters, for he could now see a growing hostility to the outer world he represented. He hoped that no other European would find his way in; for it was possible that later comers might not fare as well as he. He himself had been a cherished fountain of data, and as such had enjoyed a privileged status. Others, deemed less necessary, might receive rather different treatment. He even wondered what would happen to him when the sages of Tsath considered him drained dry of fresh facts; and in self-defence began to be more gradual in his talks on earth-lore, conveying whenever he could the impression of vast knowledge held in reserve.

One other thing which endangered Zamacona's status in Tsath was his persistent curiosity regarding the ultimate abyss of N'kai, beneath red-litten Yoth, whose existence the dominant religious cults of K'n-yan were more and more inclined to deny. When exploring Yoth he had vainly tried to find the blocked-up entrance; and later on he experimented in the arts of dematerialisation and projection, hoping that he might thereby be able to throw his consciousness downward into the gulfs which his physical eyes could not discover. Though never becoming truly proficient in these processes, he did manage to achieve a series of monstrous and portentous dreams which he believed included some elements of actual projection into N'kai; dreams which greatly shocked and perturbed the leaders of Yig and Tulu-worship when he related them, and which he was advised by friends to conceal rather than exploit. In time those dreams became very frequent and maddening; containing things which he dared not record in his main manuscript, but of which he prepared a special record for the benefit of certain learned men in Tsath.

It may have been unfortunate—or it may have been mercifully fortunate—that Zamacona practiced so many reticences and reserved so many themes and descriptions for subsidiary manuscripts. The main document leaves one to guess much about the detailed manners, customs, thoughts, language, and history of K'n-yan, as well as to form any adequate picture of the visual aspect and daily life of Tsath. One is left puzzled, too, about the real motivations of the people; their strange passivity and craven unwarlikeness, and their almost cringing fear of the outer world despite their possession of atomic and dematerialising powers which would have made them unconquerable had they taken the trouble to organise armies as in the old days. It is evident that K'n-yan was far along in its decadence—reacting with mixed apathy and hysteria against the standardised and time-tabled life of stultifying regularity which machinery had brought it during its middle period. Even the grotesque and repulsive customs and modes of thought and feeling can be traced to this source; for in his historical research Zamacona found evidence of bygone eras in which K'n-yan had held ideas much like those of the classic and renaissance outer world, and had possessed a national character and art full of what Europeans regard as dignity, kindness, and nobility.

The more Zamacona studied these things, the more apprehensive about the future he became; because he saw that the omnipresent moral and intellectual disintegration was a tremendously deepseated and ominously accelerating movement. Even during his stay the signs of decay multiplied. Rationalism degenerated more and more into fanatical and orgiastic superstition, centring in a lavish adoration of the magnetic Tulu-metal, and tolerance steadily dissolved into a series of frenzied hatreds, especially toward the outer world of which the scholars were learning so much from him.

At times he almost feared that the people might some day lose their age-long apathy and brokenness and turn like desperate rats against the unknown lands above them, sweeping all before them by virtue of their singular and still-remembered scientific powers. But for the present they fought their boredom and sense of emptiness in other ways; multiplying their hideous emotional outlets and increasing the mad grotesqueness and abnormality of their diversions. The arenas of Tsath must have been accursed and unthinkable places— Zamacona never went near them. And what they would be in another century, or even in another decade, he did not dare to think. The pious Spaniard crossed himself and counted his beads more often than usual in those days.

In the year 1545, as he reckoned it, Zamacona began what may well be accepted as his final series of attempts to leave K'n-yan. His fresh opportunity came from an unexpected source—a female of his affection-group who conceived for him a curious individual infatuation based on some hereditary memory of the days of monogamous wedlock in Tsath. Over this female—a noblewoman of moderate beauty and of at least average intelligence named T'la-yub—Zamacona acquired the most extraordinary influence; finally inducing her to help him in an escape, under the promise that he would let her accompany him. Chance proved a great factor in the course of events, for T'la-yub came of a primordial family of gate-lords who had retained oral traditions of at least one passage to the outer world which the mass of people had forgotten even at the time of the great closing; a passage to a mound on the level plains of earth which had, in consequence, never been sealed up or guarded. She explained that the primordial gate-lords were not guards or sentries, but merely ceremonial and economic proprietors, half-feudal and baronial in status, of an era preceding the severance of surface-relations. Her own family had been so reduced at the time of the closing that their gate had been wholly overlooked; and they had ever afterward preserved the secret of its existence as a sort of hereditary secret—a source of pride, and of a sense of reserve power, to offset the feeling of vanished wealth and influence which so constantly irritated them.

Zamacona, now working feverishly to get his manuscript into final form in case anything should happen to him, decided to take with him on his outward journey only five beast-loads of unalloyed gold in the form of the small ingots used for minor decorations— enough, he calculated, to make him a personage of unlimited power in his own world. He had become somewhat hardened to the sight of the monstrous *gyaa-yothn* during his four years of residence in Tsath, hence did not shrink from using the creatures; yet he resolved to kill and bury them, and cache the gold, as soon as he reached the outer world, since he knew that even a glimpse of one of the things would drive any ordinary Indian mad. Later he could arrange for a suitable expedition to transport the treasure to Mexico. T'la-yub he would perhaps allow to share his fortunes, for she was by no means unattractive; though possibly he would arrange for her sojourn amongst the plains Indians, since he was not overanxious to preserve links with the manner of life in Tsath. For a wife, of course, he would choose a lady of Spain—or at worst, an Indian princess of normal outer-world descent and a regular and approved past. But for the present T'la-yub must be used as a guide. The manuscript he would carry on his own person, encased in a book-cylinder of the sacred and magnetic Tulu-metal.

The expedition itself is described in the addendum to Zamacona's manuscript, written later, and in a hand shewing signs of nervous strain. It set out amidst the most careful precautions, choosing a rest-period and proceeding as far as possible along the faintly lighted passages beneath the city. Zamacona and T'la-yub, disguised in slaves' garments, bearing provision-knapsacks, and leading the five laden beasts on foot, were readily taken for commonplace workers; and they clung as long as possible to the subterranean way—using a long and little-frequented branch which had formerly conducted the mechanical transports to the now ruined suburb of L'thaa. Amidst the ruins of L'thaa they came to the surface, thereafter passing as rapidly as possible over the deserted, blue-litten plain of Nith toward the Grh-yan range of low hills. There, amidst the tangled underbrush, T'la-yub found the long disused and half-fabulous entrance to the forgotten tunnel; a thing she had seen but once before—aeons in the past, when her father had taken her thither to shew her this monument to their family pride. It was hard work getting the laden *gyaa-yothn* to scrape through the obstructing vines and briers, and one of them displayed a rebelliousness destined to bear dire consequences—bolting away from the party and loping back toward Tsath on its detestable pads, golden burden and all.

It was nightmare work burrowing by the light of blue-ray torches upward, downward, forward, and upward again through a dank, choked tunnel that no foot had trodden since ages before the sinking of Atlantis; and at one point T'la-yub had to practice the fear-some art of dematerialisation on herself, Zamacona, and the laden beasts in order to pass a point wholly clogged by shifting earth-strata. It was a terrible experience for Zamacona; for although he had often witnessed dematerialisation in others, and even practiced it himself to the extent of dream-projection, he had never been fully subjected to it before. But T'la-yub was skilled in the arts of K'n-yan, and accomplished the double metamorphosis in perfect safety.

Thereafter they resumed the hideous burrowing through stalac-tited crypts of horror where monstrous carvings leered at every turn; alternately camping and advancing for a period which Zama-cona reckoned as about three days, but which was probably less. At last they came to a very narrow place where the natural or only slightly hewn cave-walls gave place to walls of wholly artificial masonry, carved into terrible bas-reliefs. These walls, after about a mile of steep ascent, ended with a pair of vast niches, one on each side, in which monstrous, nitre-encrusted images of Yig and Tulu squatted, glaring at each other across the passage as they had glared since the earliest youth of the human world. At this point the passage opened into a prodigious vaulted and circular chamber of human construction; wholly covered with horrible carvings, and revealing at the farther end an arched passageway with the foot of a flight of steps. T'la-yub knew from family tales that this must be very near the earth's surface, but she could not tell just how near. Here the party camped for what they meant to be their last rest-period in the subterraneous world.

It must have been hours later that the clank of metal and the pad-ding of beasts' feet awakened Zamacona and T'la-yub. A bluish glare was spreading from the narrow passage between the images of Yig and Tulu, and in an instant the truth was obvious. An alarm had been given at Tsath—as was later revealed, by the returning *gyaa-yoth* which had rebelled at the brier-choked tunnel-entrance —and a swift party of pursuers had come to arrest the fugitives. Resistance was clearly useless, and none was offered. The party of twelve beast-riders proved studiously polite, and the return com-menced almost without a word or thought-message on either side.

It was an ominous and depressing journey, and the ordeal of de-materialisation and rematerialisation at the choked place was all the more terrible because of the lack of that hope and expectancy which had palliated the process on the outward trip. Zamacona heard his captors discussing the imminent clearing of this choked place by intensive radiations, since henceforward sentries must be maintained at the hitherto unknown outer portal. It would not do to let outsiders get within the passage, for then any who might escape without due treatment would have a hint of the vastness of the inner world and would perhaps be curious enough to return in greater strength. As with the other passages since Zamacona's coming, sentries must be stationed all along, as far as the very outermost gate; sentries drawn from amongst all the slaves, the dead-alive *y'm-bhi,* or the class of discredited freemen. With the overrunning of the American plains by thousands of Europeans, as the Spaniard had predicted, every passage was a potential source of danger; and must be rigorously guarded until the technologists of Tsath could spare the energy to prepare an ultimate and entrance-hiding obliteration as they had done for many passages in earlier and more vigorous times.

Zamacona and T'la-yub were tried before three *gn'agn* of the supreme tribunal in the gold-and-copper palace behind the gardened and fountained park, and the Spaniard was given his liberty because of the vital outer-world information he still had to impart. He was told to return to his apartment and to his affection-group; taking up his life as before, and continuing to meet deputations of scholars according to the latest schedule he had been following. No restrictions would be imposed upon him so long as he might remain peacefully in K'n-yan—but it was intimated that such leniency would not be repeated after another attempt at escape. Zamacona had felt that there was an element of irony in the parting words of the chief *gn'ag*—an assurance that all of his *gyaa-yothn,* including the one which had rebelled, would be returned to him.

The fate of T'la-yub was less happy. There being no object in retaining her, and her ancient Tsathic lineage giving her act a greater aspect of treason than Zamacona's had possessed, she was ordered to be delivered to the curious diversions of the amphitheatre; and afterward, in a somewhat mutilated and half-dematerialised form, to be given the functions of a *y'm-bhi* or animated corpse-slave and stationed among the sentries guarding the passage whose existence she had betrayed. Zamacona soon heard, not without many pangs of regret he could scarcely have anticipated, that poor T'la-yub had emerged from the arena in a headless and otherwise incomplete state, and had been set as an outermost guard upon the mound in which the passage had been found to terminate. She was, he was told, a night-sentinel, whose automatic duty was to warn off all comers with a torch; sending down reports to a small garrison of twelve dead slave *y'm-bhi* and six living but partly dematerialised freemen in the vaulted, circular chamber if the approachers did not heed her warning. She worked, he was told, in conjunction with a day-sentinel—a living freeman who chose this post in preference to other forms of discipline for other offences against the state. Zamacona, of course, had long known that most of the chief gate-sentries were such discredited freemen.

It was now made plain to him, though indirectly, that his own penalty for another escape-attempt would be service as a gate-sentry—but in the form of a dead-alive *y'm-bhi* slave, and after amphitheatre-treatment even more picturesque than that which T'la-yub was reported to have undergone. It was intimated that he —or parts of him—would be reanimated to guard some inner section of the passage; within sight of others, where his abridged person might serve as a permanent symbol of the rewards of treason. But, his informants always added, it was of course inconceivable that he would ever court such a fate. So long as he remained peaceably in K'n-yan, he would continue to be a free, privileged, and respected personage.

Yet in the end Pánfilo de Zamacona did court the fate so direfully hinted to him. True, he did not really expect to encounter it; but the nervous latter part of his manuscript makes it clear that he was prepared to face its possibility. What gave him a final hope of scatheless escape from K'n-yan was his growing mastery of the art of dematerialisation. Having studied it for years, and having learned still more from the two instances in which he had been subjected to it, he now felt increasingly able to use it independently and effectively. The manuscript records several notable experiments in this art—minor successes accomplished in his apartment—and reflects Zamacona's hope that he might soon be able to assume the spectral form in full, attaining complete invisibility and preserving that condition as long as he wished.

Once he reached this stage, he argued, the outward way lay open to him. Of course he could not bear away any gold, but mere escape was enough. He would, though, dematerialise and carry away with him his manuscript in the Tulu-metal cylinder, even though it cost additional effort; for this record and proof must reach the outer world at all hazards. He now knew the passage to follow; and if he could thread it in an atom-scattered state, he did not see how any person or force could detect or stop him. The only trouble would be if he failed to maintain his spectral condition at all times. That was the one ever-present peril, as he had learned from his experiments. But must one not always risk death and worse in a life of adventure? Zamacona was a gentleman of Old Spain; of the blood that faced the unknown and carved out half the civilisation of the New World.

For many nights after his ultimate resolution Zamacona prayed to St. Pamphilus and other guardian saints, and counted the beads of his rosary. The last entry in the manuscript, which toward the end took the form of a diary more and more, was merely a single sentence—*"Es más tarde de lo que pensaba—tengo que marcharme"*. . . . "It is later than I thought; I must go." After that, only silence and conjecture—and such evidence as the presence of the manuscript itself, and what that manuscript could lead to, might provide.

VII.

When I looked up from my half-stupefied reading and note-taking the morning sun was high in the heavens. The electric bulb was still burning, but such things of the real world—the modern outer world—were far from my whirling brain. I knew I was in my room at Clyde Compton's at Binger—but upon what monstrous vista had I stumbled? Was this thing a hoax or a chronicle of madness? If a hoax, was it a jest of the sixteenth century or of to-day? The manuscript's age looked appallingly genuine to my not wholly unpracticed eyes, and the problem presented by the strange metal cylinder I dared not even think about.

Moreover, what a monstrously exact explanation it gave of all the baffling phenomena of the mound—of the seemingly meaningless and paradoxical actions of diurnal and nocturnal ghosts, and of the queer cases of madness and disappearance! It was even an accursedly *plausible* explanation—evilly *consistent*—if one could adopt the incredible. It must be a shocking hoax devised by someone who knew all the lore of the mound. There was even a hint of social satire in the account of that unbelievable nether world of horror and decay. Surely this was the clever forgery of some learned cynic—something like the leaden crosses in New Mexico, which a jester once planted and pretended to discover as a relique of some forgotten Dark Age colony from Europe.

Upon going down to breakfast I hardly knew what to tell Compton and his mother, as well as the curious callers who had already begun to arrive. Still in a daze, I cut the Gordian Knot by giving a few points from the notes I had made, and mumbling my belief that the thing was a subtle and ingenious fraud left there by some previous explorer of the mound—a belief in which everybody seemed to concur when told of the substance of the manuscript. It is curious how all that breakfast group—and all the others in Binger to whom the discussion was repeated—seemed to find a great clearing of the atmosphere in the notion that somebody was playing a joke on somebody. For the time we all forgot that the known, recent history of the mound presented mysteries as strange as any in the manuscript, and as far from acceptable solution as ever.

The fears and doubts began to return when I asked for volunteers to visit the mound with me. I wanted a larger excavating party—but the idea of going to that uncomfortable place seemed no more attractive to the people of Binger than it had seemed on the previous day. I myself felt a mounting horror upon looking toward the mound and glimpsing the moving speck which I knew was the daylight sentinel; for in spite of all my scepticism the morbidities of that manuscript stuck by me and gave everything connected with the place a new and monstrous significance. I absolutely lacked the resolution to look at the moving speck with my binoculars. Instead, I set out with the kind of bravado we display in nightmares—when, knowing we are dreaming, we plunge desperately into still thicker horrors, for the sake of having the whole thing over the sooner. My pick and shovel were already out there, so I had only my handbag of smaller paraphernalia to take. Into this I put the strange cylinder and its contents, feeling vaguely that I might possibly find something worth checking up with some part of the green-lettered Spanish text. Even a clever hoax might be founded on some actual attribute of the mound which a former explorer had discovered— and that magnetic metal was damnably odd! Grey Eagle's cryptic talisman still hung from its leathern cord around my neck.

I did not look very sharply at the mound as I walked toward it, but when I reached it there was nobody in sight. Repeating my upward scramble of the previous day, I was troubled by thoughts of what *might* lie close at hand *if*, by any miracle, any part of the manuscript *were* actually half-true. In such a case, I could not help reflecting, the hypothetical Spaniard Zamacona must have barely reached the outer world when overtaken by some disaster—per-

haps an involuntary rematerialisation. He would naturally, in that
event, have been seized by whichever sentry happened to be on duty
at the time—either the discredited freeman, or, as a matter of
supreme irony, the very T'la-yub who had planned and aided his
first attempt at escape—and in the ensuing struggle the cylinder
with the manuscript might well have been dropped on the mound's
summit, to be neglected and gradually buried for nearly four centuries. But, I added, as I climbed over the crest, one must not think
of extravagant things like that. Still, if there *were* anything in the
tale, it must have been a monstrous fate to which Zamacona had
been dragged back . . . the amphitheatre . . . mutilation . . . duty
somewhere in the dank, nitrous tunnel as a dead-alive slave . . . a
maimed corpse-fragment as an automatic interior sentry. . . .

It was a very real shock which chased this morbid speculation
from my head, for upon glancing around the elliptical summit I saw
at once that my pick and shovel had been stolen. This was a highly
provoking and disconcerting development; baffling, too, in view of
the seeming reluctance of all the Binger folk to visit the mound.
Was this reluctance a pretended thing, and had the jokers of the
village been chuckling over my coming discomfiture as they
solemnly saw me off ten minutes before? I took out my binoculars
and scanned the gaping crowd at the edge of the village. No—they
did not seem to be looking for any comic climax; yet was not the
whole affair at bottom a colossal joke in which all the villagers and
reservation people were concerned—legends, manuscript, cylinder,
and all? I thought of how I had seen the sentry from a distance, and
then found him unaccountably vanished; thought also of the conduct of old Grey Eagle, of the speech and expressions of Compton
and his mother, and of the unmistakable fright of most of the
Binger people. On the whole, it could not very well be a village-
wide joke. The fear and the problem were surely real, though obviously there were one or two jesting daredevils in Binger who had
stolen out to the mound and made off with the tools I had left.

Everything else on the mound was as I had left it—brush cut by
my machete, slight, bowl-like depression toward the north end,
and the hole I had made with my trench-knife in digging up the
magnetism-revealed cylinder. Deeming it too great a concession to
the unknown jokers to return to Binger for another pick and
shovel, I resolved to carry out my programme as best I could with
the machete and trench-knife in my handbag; so extracting these, I
set to work excavating the bowl-like depression which my eye had

picked as the possible site of a former entrance to the mound. As I proceeded, I felt again the suggestion of a sudden wind blowing against me which I had noticed the day before—a suggestion which seemed stronger, and still more reminiscent of unseen, formless, opposing hands laid on my wrists, as I cut deeper and deeper through the root-tangled red soil and reached the exotic black loam beneath. The talisman around my neck appeared to twitch oddly in the breeze—not in any one direction, as when attracted by the buried cylinder, but vaguely and diffusely, in a manner wholly unaccountable.

Then, quite without warning, the black, root-woven earth beneath my feet began to sink cracklingly, while I heard a faint sound of sifting, falling matter far below me. The obstructing wind, or forces, or hands now seemed to be operating from the very seat of the sinking, and I felt that they aided me by pushing as I leaped back out of the hole to avoid being involved in any cave-in. Bending down over the brink and hacking at the mould-caked root-tangle with my machete, I felt that they were against me again—but at no time were they strong enough to stop my work. The more roots I severed, the more falling matter I heard below. Finally the hole began to deepen of itself toward the centre, and I saw that the earth was sifting down into some large cavity beneath, so as to leave a good-sized aperture when the roots that had bound it were gone. A few more hacks of the machete did the trick, and with a parting cave-in and uprush of curiously chill and alien air the last barrier gave way. Under the morning sun yawned a huge opening at least three feet square, and shewing the top of a flight of stone steps down which the loose earth of the collapse was still sliding. My quest had come to something at last! With an elation of accomplishment almost overbalancing fear for the nonce, I replaced the trench-knife and machete in my handbag, took out my powerful electric torch, and prepared for a triumphant, lone, and utterly rash invasion of the fabulous nether world I had uncovered.

It was rather hard getting down the first few steps, both because of the fallen earth which had choked them and because of a sinister up-pushing of a cold wind from below. The talisman around my neck swayed curiously, and I began to regret the disappearing square of daylight above me. The electric torch shewed dank, water-stained, and salt-encrusted walls fashioned of huge basalt blocks, and now and then I thought I descried some trace of carving beneath the nitrous deposits. I gripped my handbag more tightly, and was glad of the comforting weight of the sheriff's heavy revolver in my right-hand coat pocket. After a time the passage began to wind this way and that, and the staircase became free from obstructions. Carvings on the walls were now definitely traceable, and I shuddered when I saw how clearly the grotesque figures resembled the monstrous bas-reliefs on the cylinder I had found. Winds and forces continued to blow malevolently against me, and at one or two bends I half fancied the torch gave glimpses of thin, transparent shapes not unlike the sentinel on the mound as my binoculars had shewed him. When I reached this stage of visual chaos I stopped for a moment to get a grip on myself. It would not do to let my nerves get the better of me at the very outset of what would surely be a trying experience, and the most important archaeological feat of my career.

But I wished I had not stopped at just that place, for the act fixed my attention on something profoundly disturbing. It was only a small object lying close to the wall on one of the steps below me, but that object was such as to put my reason to a severe test, and bring up a line of the most alarming speculations. That the opening above me had been closed against all material forms for generations was utterly obvious from the growth of shrub-roots and accumulation of drifting soil; yet the object before me was most distinctly *not* many generations old. For it was an electric torch much like the one I now carried—warped and encrusted in the tomb-like dampness, but none the less perfectly unmistakable. I descended a few steps and picked it up, wiping off the evil deposits on my rough coat. One of the nickel bands bore an engraved name and address, and I recognised it with a start the moment I made it out. It read "Jas. C. Williams, 17 Trowbridge St., Cambridge, Mass."—and I knew that it had belonged to one of the two daring college instructors who had disappeared on June 28, 1915. Only thirteen years ago, and yet I had just broken through the sod of centuries! How had the thing got there? Another entrance—or was there something after all in this mad idea of dematerialisation and rematerialisation?

Doubt and horror grew upon me as I wound still farther down the seemingly endless staircase. Would the thing never stop? The carvings grew more and more distinct, and assumed a narrative pictorial quality which brought me close to panic as I recognised many unmistakable correspondences with the history of K'n-yan as sketched in the manuscript now resting in my handbag. For the first time I began seriously to question the wisdom of my descent, and to wonder whether I had not better return to the upper air before I came upon something which would never let me return as a sane man. But I did not hesitate long, for as a Virginian I felt the blood of ancestral fighters and gentlemen-adventurers pounding a protest against retreat from any peril known or unknown.

My descent became swifter rather than slower, and I avoided studying the terrible bas-reliefs and intaglios that had unnerved me. All at once I saw an arched opening ahead, and realised that the prodigious staircase had ended at last. But with that realisation came horror in mounting magnitude, for before me there yawned a vast vaulted crypt of all-too-familiar outline—a great circular space answering in every least particular to the carving-lined chamber described in the Zamacona manuscript.

It was indeed the place. There could be no mistake. And if any room for doubt yet remained, that room was abolished by what I saw directly across the great vault. It was a second arched opening, commencing a long, narrow passage and having at its mouth two huge opposite niches bearing loathsome and titanic images of shockingly familiar pattern. There in the dark unclean Yig and hideous Tulu squatted eternally, glaring at each other across the passage as they had glared since the earliest youth of the human world.

From this point onward I ask no credence for what I tell—for what I *think* I saw. It is too utterly unnatural, too utterly monstrous and incredible, to be any part of sane human experience or objective reality. My torch, though casting a powerful beam ahead, naturally could not furnish any general illumination of the Cyclopean crypt; so I now began moving it about to explore the giant walls little by little. As I did so, I saw to my horror that the space was by no means vacant, but was instead littered with odd furniture and utensils and heaps of packages which bespoke a populous recent occupancy—no nitrous reliques of the past, but queerly shaped objects and supplies in modern, every-day use. As my torch rested on each article or group of articles, however, the distinctness of the outlines soon began to grow blurred; until in the end I could scarcely tell whether the things belonged to the realm of matter or to the realm of spirit.

All this while the adverse winds blew against me with increasing fury, and the unseen hands plucked malevolently at me and snatched at the strange magnetic talisman I wore. Wild conceits surged through my mind. I thought of the manuscript and what it said about the garrison stationed in this place—twelve dead slave *y'm-bhi* and six living but partly dematerialised freemen—that was in 1545—three hundred and eighty-three years ago. . . . What since then? Zamacona had predicted change . . . subtle disintegration . . . more dematerialisation . . . weaker and weaker . . . was it Grey Eagle's talisman that held them at bay—their sacred Tulu-metal— and were they feebly trying to pluck it off so that they might do to me what they had done to those who had come before? . . . It occurred to me with shuddering force that I was building my speculations out of a full belief in the Zamacona manuscript—this must not be—I must get a grip on myself—

But, curse it, every time I tried to get a grip I saw some fresh sight to shatter my poise still further. This time, just as my will power was driving the half-seen paraphernalia into obscurity, my glance and torch-beam had to light on two things of very different nature; two things of the eminently real and sane world; yet they did more to unseat my shaky reason than anything I had seen before—because I knew what they were, and knew how profoundly, in the course of Nature, they ought not to be there. *They were my own missing pick and shovel, side by side, and leaning neatly against the blasphemously carved wall of that hellish crypt.* God in heaven— and I had babbled to myself about daring jokers from Binger!

That was the last straw. After that the cursed hypnotism of the manuscript got at me, and I actually *saw* the half-transparent shapes of the things that were pushing and plucking; pushing and plucking—those leprous palaeogean things with something of humanity still clinging to them—the *complete* forms, and the forms that were morbidly and perversely *incomplete* . . . all these, and hideous *other entities*—the four-footed blasphemies with ape-like face and projecting horn . . . and not a sound so far in all that nitrous hell of inner earth. . . .

Then there *was* a sound—a flopping; a padding; a dull, advancing sound which heralded beyond question a being as structurally material as the pickaxe and the shovel—something wholly unlike the shadow-shapes that ringed me in, yet equally remote from any sort of life as life is understood on the earth's wholesome surface. My shattered brain tried to prepare me for what was coming, but could not frame any adequate image. I could only say over and over again to myself, "It is of the abyss, but it is *not* dematerialised." The padding grew more distinct, and from the mechanical cast of the tread I knew it was a dead thing that stalked in the darkness. Then

—oh, God, *I saw it in the full beam of my torch; saw it framed like a sentinel in the narrow passage between the nightmare idols of the serpent Yig and the octopus Tulu.* . . .

Let me collect myself enough to hint at what I saw; to explain why I dropped torch and handbag and fled empty-handed in the utter blackness, wrapped in a merciful unconsciousness which did not wear off until the sun and the distant yelling and the shouting from the village roused me as I lay gasping on the top of the accursed mound. I do not yet know what guided me again to the earth's surface. I only know that the watchers in Binger saw me stagger up into sight three hours after I had vanished; saw me lurch up and fall flat on the ground as if struck by a bullet. None of them dared to come out and help me; but they knew I must be in a bad state, so tried to rouse me as best they could by yelling in chorus and firing off revolvers.

It worked in the end, and when I came to I almost rolled down the side of the mound in my eagerness to get away from that black aperture which still yawned open. My torch and tools, and the handbag with the manuscript, were all down there; but it is easy to see why neither I nor anyone else ever went after them. When I staggered across the plain and into the village I dared not tell what I had seen. I only muttered vague things about carvings and statues and snakes and shaken nerves. And I did not faint again until somebody mentioned that the ghost-sentinel had reappeared about the time I had staggered half way back to town. I left Binger that evening, and have never been there since, though they tell me the ghosts still appear on the mound as usual.

But I have resolved to hint here at last what I dared not hint to the people of Binger on that terrible August afternoon. I don't know yet just how I can go about it—and if in the end you think my reticence strange, just remember that to imagine such a horror is one thing, *but to see it is another thing.* I saw it. I think you'll recall my citing early in this tale the case of a bright young man named Heaton who went out to that mound one day in 1891 and came back at night as the village idiot, babbling for eight years about horrors and then dying in an epileptic fit. What he used to keep moaning was *"That white man—oh, my God, what they did to him. . . ."*

Well, I saw the same thing that poor Heaton saw—and I saw it after reading the manuscript, so I know more of its history than he did. That makes it worse—for I know all that it *implies;* all that must be still brooding and festering and waiting down there. I told you it had padded mechanically toward me out of the narrow passage and had stood sentry-like at the entrance between the frightful eidola of Yig and Tulu. That was very natural and inevitable—because the thing *was* a sentry. It had been made a sentry for punishment, and it was quite dead—besides lacking head, arms, lower legs, and other customary parts of a human being. Yes—it had been a very human being once; and what is more, it had been *white*. Very obviously, if that manuscript was as true as I think it was, this being had been used for the *diversions of the amphitheatre* before its life had become wholly extinct and supplanted by automatic impulses controlled from outside.

On its white and only slightly hairy chest some letters had been gashed or branded—I had not stopped to investigate, but had merely noted that they were in an awkward and fumbling Spanish; an awkward Spanish implying a kind of ironic use of the language by an alien inscriber familiar neither with the idiom nor the Roman letters used to record it. The inscription had read *"Secuestrado a la voluntad de Xinaián en el cuerpo decapitado de Tlayúb"*—*"Seized by the will of K'n-yan in the headless body of T'la-yub."*

Hazel Heald

The Horror in the Museum

It was languid curiosity which first brought Stephen Jones to Rogers' Museum. Someone had told him about the queer underground place in Southwark Street across the river, where waxen things so much more horrible than the worst effigies at Madame Tussaud's were shewn, and he had strolled in one April day to see how disappointing he would find it. Oddly, he was not disappointed. There was something different and distinctive here, after all. Of course, the usual gory commonplaces were present—Landru, Dr. Crippen, Madame Demers, Rizzio, Lady Jane Grey, endless maimed victims of war and revolution, and monsters like Gilles de Rais and Marquis de Sade—but there were other things which had made him breathe faster and stay till the ringing of the closing bell. The man who had fashioned this collection could be no ordinary mountebank. There was imagination—even a kind of diseased genius—in some of this stuff.

Later he had learned about George Rogers. The man had been on the Tussaud staff, but some trouble had developed which led to his discharge. There were aspersions on his sanity and tales of his crazy forms of secret worship—though latterly his success with his own basement museum had dulled the edge of some criticisms while sharpening the insidious point of others. Teratology and the iconography of nightmare were his hobbies, and even he had had the prudence to screen off some of his worst effigies in a special alcove for adults only. It was this alcove which had fascinated Jones so much. There were lumpish hybrid things which only fantasy could spawn, moulded with devilish skill, and coloured in a horribly life-like fashion.

Some were the figures of well-known myth—gorgons, chimaeras, dragons, cyclops, and all their shuddersome congeners. Others were drawn from darker and more furtively whispered cycles of subterranean legend—black, formless Tsathoggua, many-tentacled Cthulhu, proboscidian Chaugnar Faugn, and other rumoured blasphemies from forbidden books like the *Necronomicon,* the *Book of Eibon,* or the *Unaussprechlichen Kulten* of von Junzt. But the worst were wholly original with Rogers, and represented shapes which no tale of antiquity had ever dared to suggest. Several were hideous parodies on forms of organic life we know, while others seemed taken from feverish dreams of other planets and other galaxies. The wilder paintings of Clark Ashton Smith might suggest a few—but nothing could suggest the effect of poignant, loathsome terror created by their great size and fiendishly cunning workmanship, and by the diabolically clever lighting conditions under which they were exhibited.

Stephen Jones, as a leisurely connoisseur of the bizarre in art, had sought out Rogers himself in the dingy office and workroom behind the vaulted museum chamber—an evil-looking crypt lighted dimly by dusty windows set slit-like and horizontal in the brick wall on a level with the ancient cobblestones of a hidden courtyard. It was here that the images were repaired—here, too, where some of them had been made. Waxen arms, legs, heads, and torsos lay in grotesque array on various benches, while on high tiers of shelves matted wigs, ravenous-looking teeth, and glassy, staring eyes were indiscriminately scattered. Costumes of all sorts hung from hooks, and in one alcove were great piles of flesh-coloured wax-cakes and shelves filled with paint-cans and brushes of every description. In the centre of the room was a large melting-furnace used to prepare the wax for moulding, its fire-box topped by a huge iron container on hinges, with a spout which permitted the pouring of melted wax with the merest touch of a finger.

Other things in the dismal crypt were less describable—isolated parts of problematical entities whose assembled forms were the phantoms of delirium. At one end was a door of heavy plank, fastened by an unusually large padlock and with a very peculiar symbol painted over it. Jones, who had once had access to the dreaded *Necronomicon*, shivered involuntarily as he recognised that symbol. This showman, he reflected, must indeed be a person of disconcertingly wide scholarship in dark and dubious fields.

Nor did the conversation of Rogers disappoint him. The man was tall, lean, and rather unkempt, with large black eyes which gazed combustively from a pallid and usually stubble-covered face. He did not resent Jones's intrusion, but seemed to welcome the chance of unburdening himself to an interested person. His voice was of singular depth and resonance, and harboured a sort of repressed intensity bordering on the feverish. Jones did not wonder that many had thought him mad.

With every successive call—and such calls became a habit as the weeks went by—Jones had found Rogers more communicative and confidential. From the first there had been hints of strange faiths and practices on the showman's part, and later on these hints expanded into tales—despite a few odd corroborative photographs—whose extravagance was almost comic. It was some time in June, on a night when Jones had brought a bottle of good whiskey and plied his host somewhat freely, that the really demented talk first appeared. Before that there had been wild enough stories—accounts of mysterious trips to Thibet, the African interior, the Arabian desert, the Amazon valley, Alaska, and certain little-known islands of the South Pacific, plus claims of having read such monstrous and half-fabulous books as the prehistoric Pnakotic fragments and the Dhol chants attributed to malign and non-human Leng—but nothing in all this had been so unmistakably insane as what had cropped out that June evening under the spell of the whiskey.

To be plain, Rogers began making vague boasts of having found certain things in Nature that no one had found before, and of having brought back tangible evidences of such discoveries. According to his bibulous harangue, he had gone farther than anyone else in interpreting the obscure and primal books he studied, and had been directed by them to certain remote places where strange survivals are hidden—survivals of aeons and life-cycles earlier than mankind, and in some cases connected with other dimensions and other worlds, communication with which was frequent in the forgotten pre-human days. Jones marvelled at the fancy which could conjure up such notions, and wondered just what Rogers' mental history had been. Had his work amidst the morbid grotesqueries of Madame Tussaud's been the start of his imaginative flights, or was the tendency innate, so that his choice of occupation was merely one of its manifestations? At any rate, the man's work was very closely linked with his notions. Even now there was no mistaking the trend of his blackest hints about the nightmare monstrosities in the screened-off "Adults only" alcove. Heedless of ridicule, he was trying to imply that not all of these daemoniac abnormalities were artificial.

It was Jones's frank scepticism and amusement at these irresponsible claims which broke up the growing cordiality. Rogers, it was clear, took himself very seriously; for he now became morose and resentful, continuing to tolerate Jones only through a dogged urge to break down his wall of urbane and complacent incredulity. Wild tales and suggestions of rites and sacrifices to nameless elder gods continued, and now and then Rogers would lead his guest to one of the hideous blasphemies in the screened-off alcove and point out features difficult to reconcile with even the finest human craftsmanship. Jones continued his visits through sheer fascination, though he knew he had forfeited his host's regard. At times he would try to humour Rogers with pretended assent to some mad hint or assertion, but the gaunt showman was seldom to be deceived by such tactics.

The tension came to a head later in September. Jones had casually dropped into the museum one afternoon, and was wandering through the dim corridors whose horrors were now so familiar, when he heard a very peculiar sound from the general direction of Rogers' workroom. Others heard it, too, and started nervously as the echoes reverberated through the great vaulted basement. The three attendants exchanged odd glances; and one of them, a dark, taciturn, foreign-looking fellow who always served Rogers as a repairer and assistant designer, smiled in a way which seemed to puzzle his colleagues and which grated very harshly on some facet of Jones's sensibilities. It was the yelp or scream of a dog, and was such a sound as could be made only under conditions of the utmost fright and agony combined. Its stark, anguished frenzy was appalling to hear, and in this setting of grotesque abnormality it held a double hideousness. Jones remembered that no dogs were allowed in the museum.

He was about to go to the door leading into the workroom, when the dark attendant stopped him with a word and a gesture. Mr. Rogers, the man said in a soft, somewhat accented voice at once apologetic and vaguely sardonic, was out, and there were standing orders to admit no one to the workroom during his absence. As for that yelp, it was undoubtedly something out in the courtyard behind the museum. This neighbourhood was full of stray mongrels, and their fights were sometimes shockingly noisy. There were no dogs in any part of the museum. But if Mr. Jones wished to see Mr. Rogers he might find him just before closing-time.

After this Jones climbed the old stone steps to the street outside and examined the squalid neighbourhood curiously. The leaning, decrepit buildings—once dwellings but now largely shops and warehouses—were very ancient indeed. Some of them were of a gabled type seeming to go back to Tudor times, and a faint miasmatic stench hung subtly about the whole region. Beside the dingy house whose basement held the museum was a low archway pierced by a dark cobbled alley, and this Jones entered in a vague wish to find the courtyard behind the workroom and settle the affair of the dog more comfortably in his mind. The courtyard was dim in the late afternoon light, hemmed in by rear walls even uglier and more intangibly menacing than the crumbling street facades of the evil old houses. Not a dog was in sight, and Jones wondered how the aftermath of such a frantic turmoil could have completely vanished so soon.

Despite the assistant's statement that no dog had been in the museum, Jones glanced nervously at the three small windows of the basement workroom—narrow, horizontal rectangles close to the grass-grown pavement, with grimy panes that stared repulsively and incuriously like the eyes of dead fish. To their left a worn flight of steps led to an opaque and heavily bolted door. Some impulse urged him to crouch low on the damp, broken cobblestones and peer in, on the chance that the thick green shades, worked by long cords that hung down to a reachable level, might not be drawn. The outer surfaces were thick with dirt, but as he rubbed them with his handkerchief he saw there was no obscuring curtain in the way of his vision.

So shadowed was the cellar from the inside that not much could be made out, but the grotesque working paraphernalia now and then loomed up spectrally as Jones tried each of the windows in turn. It seemed evident at first that no one was within; yet when he peered through the extreme right-hand window—the one nearest the entrance alley—he saw a glow of light at the farther end of the apartment which made him pause in bewilderment. There was no reason why any light should be there. It was an inner side of the room, and he could not recall any gas or electric fixture near that point. Another look defined the glow as a large vertical rectangle, and a thought occurred to him. It was in that direction that he had always noticed the heavy plank door with the abnormally large padlock—the door which was never opened, and above which was crudely smeared that hideous cryptic symbol from the fragmentary records of forbidden elder magic. It must be open now—and there was a light inside. All his former speculations as to where that door led, and as to what lay behind it, were now renewed with trebly disquieting force.

Jones wandered aimlessly around the dismal locality till close to six o'clock, when he returned to the museum to make the call on Rogers. He could hardly tell why he wished so especially to see the man just then, but there must have been some subconscious misgivings about that terribly unplaceable canine scream of the afternoon, and about the glow of light in that disturbing and usually unopened inner doorway with the heavy padlock. The attendants were leaving as he arrived, and he thought that Orabona—the dark foreign-looking assistant—eyed him with something like sly, repressed amusement. He did not relish that look—even though he had seen the fellow turn it on his employer many times.

The vaulted exhibition room was ghoulish in its desertion, but he strode quickly through it and rapped at the door of the office and workroom. Response was slow in coming, though there were footsteps inside. Finally, in response to a second knock, the lock rattled, and the ancient six-panelled portal creaked reluctantly open to reveal the slouching, feverish-eyed form of George Rogers. From the first it was clear that the showman was in an unusual mood. There was a curious mixture of reluctance and actual gloating in his welcome, and his talk at once veered to extravagances of the most hideous and incredible sort.

Surviving elder gods—nameless sacrifices—the other than artificial nature of some of the alcove horrors—all the usual boasts, but uttered in a tone of peculiarly increasing confidence. Obviously, Jones reflected, the poor fellow's madness was gaining on him. From time to time Rogers would send furtive glances toward the heavy, padlocked inner door at the end of the room, or toward a piece of coarse burlap on the floor not far from it, beneath which some small object appeared to be lying. Jones grew more nervous as the moments passed, and began to feel as hesitant about mentioning the afternoon's oddities as he had formerly been anxious to do so.

Rogers' sepulchrally resonant bass almost cracked under the excitement of his fevered rambling.

"Do you remember," he shouted, "what I told you about that ruined city in Indo-China where the Tcho-Tchos lived? You had to admit I'd been there when you saw the photographs, even if you did think I made that oblong swimmer in darkness out of wax. If you'd seen it writhing in the underground pools as I did. . . .

"Well, this is bigger still. I never told you about this, because I wanted to work out the later parts before making any claim. When you see the snapshots you'll know the geography couldn't have been faked, and I fancy I have another way of proving that It isn't any waxed concoction of mine. You've never seen it, for the experiments wouldn't let me keep It on exhibition."

The showman glanced queerly at the padlocked door.

"It all comes from that long ritual in the eighth Pnakotic fragment. When I got it figured out I saw it could have only one meaning. There were things in the north before the land of Lomar—before mankind existed—and this was one of them. It took us all the way to Alaska, and up the Noatak from Fort Morton, but the thing was there as we knew it would be. Great Cyclopean ruins, acres of them. There was less left than we had hoped for, but after three million years what could one expect? And weren't the Esquimau legends all in the right direction? We couldn't get one of the beggars to go with us, and had to sledge all the way back to Nome for Americans. Orabona was no good up in that climate—it made him sullen and hateful.

"I'll tell you later how we found It. When we got the ice blasted out of the pylons of the central ruin the stairway was just as we knew it would be. Some carvings still there, and it was no trouble keeping the Yankees from following us in. Orabona shivered like a leaf—you'd never think it from the damned insolent way he struts around here. He knew enough of the Elder Lore to be properly afraid. The eternal light was gone, but our torches shewed enough. We saw the bones of others who had been before us—aeons ago, when the climate was warm. Some of these bones were of things you couldn't even imagine. At the third level down we found the ivory throne the fragments said so much about—and I may as well tell you it wasn't empty.

"The thing on that throne didn't move—and we knew then that It needed the nourishment of sacrifice. But we didn't want to wake It then. Better to get It to London first. Orabona and I went to the surface for the big box, but when we had packed it we couldn't get

It up the three flights of steps. These steps weren't made for human beings, and their size bothered us. Anyway, it was devilish heavy. We had to have the Americans down to get It out. They weren't anxious to go into the place, but of course the worst thing was safely inside the box. We told them it was a batch of ivory carvings—archaeological stuff; and after seeing the carved throne they probably believed us. It's a wonder they didn't suspect hidden treasure and demand a share. They must have told queer tales around Nome later on; though I doubt if they ever went back to those ruins, even for the ivory throne."

Rogers paused, felt around in his desk, and produced an envelope of good-sized photographic prints. Extracting one and laying it face down before him, he handed the rest to Jones. The set was certainly an odd one: ice-clad hills, dog sledges, men in furs, and vast tumbled ruins against a background of snow—ruins whose bizarre outlines and enormous stone blocks could hardly be accounted for. One flashlight view shewed an incredible interior chamber with wild carvings and a curious throne whose proportion could not have been designed for a human occupant. The carvings on the gigantic masonry—high walls and peculiar vaulting overhead— were mainly symbolic, and involved both wholly unknown designs and certain hieroglyphs darkly cited in obscene legends. Over the throne loomed the same dreadful symbol which was now painted on the workroom wall above the padlocked plank door. Jones darted a nervous glance at the closed portal. Assuredly, Rogers had been to strange places and had seen strange things. Yet this mad interior picture might easily be a fraud—taken from a very clever stage setting. One must not be too credulous. But Rogers was continuing:

"Well, we shipped the box from Nome and got to London without any trouble. That was the first time we'd ever brought back anything that had a chance of coming alive. I didn't put It on display, because there were more important things to do for It. It needed the nourishment of sacrifice, for It was a god. Of course I couldn't get It the sort of sacrifices which It used to have in It's day, for such things don't exist now. But there were other things which might do. The blood is the life, you know. Even the lemurs and elementals that are older than the earth will come when the blood of men or beasts is offered under the right conditions."

The expression on the narrator's face was growing very alarming and repulsive, so that Jones fidgeted involuntarily in his chair.

Rogers seemed to notice his guest's nervousness, and continued with a distinctly evil smile.

"It was last year that I got It, and ever since then I've been trying rites and sacrifices. Orabona hasn't been much help, for he was always against the idea of waking It. He hates It—probably because he's afraid of what It will come to mean. He carries a pistol all the time to protect himself—fool, as if there were human protection against It! If I ever see him draw that pistol, I'll strangle him. He wanted me to kill It and make an effigy of It. But I've stuck by my plans, and I'm coming out on top in spite of all the cowards like Orabona and damned sniggering sceptics like you, Jones! I've chanted the rites and made certain sacrifices, *and last week the transition came.* The sacrifice was—received and enjoyed!"

Rogers actually licked his lips, while Jones held himself uneasily rigid. The showman paused and rose, crossing the room to the piece of burlap at which he had glanced so often. Bending down, he took hold of one corner as he spoke again.

"You've laughed enough at my work—now it's time for you to get some facts. Orabona tells me you heard a dog screaming around here this afternoon. *Do you know what that meant?*"

Jones started. For all his curiosity he would have been glad to get out without further light on the point which had so puzzled him. But Rogers was inexorable, and began to lift the square of burlap. Beneath it lay a crushed, almost shapeless mass which Jones was slow to classify. Was it a once-living thing which some agency had flattened, sucked dry of blood, punctured in a thousand places, and wrung into a limp, broken-boned heap of grotesqueness? After a moment Jones realised what it must be. It was what was left of a dog—a dog, perhaps of considerable size and whitish colour. Its breed was past recognition, for distortion had come in nameless and hideous ways. Most of the hair was burned off as by some pungent acid, and the exposed, bloodless skin was riddled by innumerable circular wounds or incisions. The form of torture necessary to cause such results was past imagining.

Electrified with a pure loathing which conquered his mounting disgust, Jones sprang up with a cry.

"You damned sadist—you madman—you do a thing like this and dare to speak to a decent man!"

Rogers dropped the burlap with a malignant sneer and faced his oncoming guest. His words held an unnatural calm.

"Why, you fool, do you think *I* did this? Let us admit that the results are unbeautiful from our limited human standpoint. What of it? It is not human and does not pretend to be. To sacrifice is merely to offer. I gave the dog to It. What happened is It's work, not mine. It needed the nourishment of the offering, and took it in It's own way. But let me shew you what It looks like."

As Jones stood hesitating, the speaker returned to his desk and took up the photograph he had laid face down without shewing. Now he extended it with a curious look. Jones took it and glanced at it in an almost mechanical way. After a moment the visitor's glance became sharper and more absorbed, for the utterly satanic force of the object depicted had an almost hypnotic effect. Certainly, Rogers had outdone himself in modelling the eldritch nightmare which the camera had caught. The thing was a work of sheer, infernal genius, and Jones wondered how the public would react when it was placed on exhibition. So hideous a thing had no right to exist—probably the mere contemplation of it, after it was done, had completed the unhinging of its maker's mind and led him to worship it with brutal sacrifices. Only a stout sanity could resist the insidious suggestion that the blasphemy was—or had once been— some morbid and exotic form of actual life.

The thing in the picture squatted or was balanced on what appeared to be a clever reproduction of the monstrously carved throne in the other curious photograph. To describe it with any ordinary vocabulary would be impossible, for nothing even roughly corresponding to it has ever come within the imagination of sane mankind. It represented something meant perhaps to be roughly connected with the vertebrates of this planet—though one could not be too sure of that. Its bulk was Cyclopean, for even squatted it towered to almost twice the height of Orabona, who was shewn beside it. Looking sharply, one might trace its approximations toward the bodily features of the higher vertebrates.

There was an almost globular torso, with six long, sinuous limbs terminating in crab-like claws. From the upper end a subsidiary globe bulged forward bubble-like; its triangle of three staring, fishy eyes, its foot-long and evidently flexible proboscis, and a distended lateral system analogous to gills, suggesting that it was a head. Most of the body was covered with what at first appeared to be fur, but which on closer examination proved to be a dense growth of dark, slender tentacles or sucking filaments, each tipped with a mouth suggesting the head of an asp. On the head and below the proboscis the tentacles tended to be longer and thicker, and marked with spiral stripes—suggesting the traditional serpent-locks of Medusa. To say that such a thing could have an *expression* seems paradoxical; yet Jones felt that that triangle of bulging fish-eyes and that obliquely poised proboscis all bespoke a blend of hate, greed, and sheer cruelty incomprehensible to mankind because mixed with other emotions not of the world or this solar system. Into this bestial abnormality, he reflected, Rogers must have poured at once all his malignant insanity and all his uncanny sculptural genius. The thing was incredible—and yet the photograph proved that it existed.

Rogers interrupted his reveries.

"Well—what do you think of It? Now do you wonder what crushed the dog and sucked it dry with a million mouths? It needed nourishment— and It will need more. It is a god, and I am the first priest of It's latter-day hierarchy. Iä! Shub-Niggurath! The Goat with a Thousand Young!"

Jones lowered the photograph in disgust and pity.

"See here, Rogers, this won't do. There are limits, you know. It's a great piece of work, and all that, but it isn't good for you. Better not see it any more—let Orabona break it up, and try to forget about it. And let me tear this beastly picture up, too."

With a snarl, Rogers snatched the photograph and returned it to the desk.

"Idiot—you—and you still think It's all a fraud! You still think I made It, and you still think my figures are nothing but lifeless wax! Why, damn you, you're a worse clod than a wax image yourself! But I've got proof this time, and you're going to know! Not just now, for It is resting after the sacrifice—but later. Oh, yes—you will not doubt the power of It then."

As Rogers glanced toward the padlocked inner door Jones retrieved his hat and stick from a nearby bench.

"Very well, Rogers, let it be later. I must be going now, but I'll call around tomorrow afternoon. Think my advice over and see if it doesn't sound sensible. Ask Orabona what he thinks, too."

Rogers actually bared his teeth in wild-beast fashion.

"Must be going now, eh? Afraid, after all! Afraid, for all your bold talk! You say the effigies are only wax, and yet you run away when I begin to prove that they aren't. You're like the fellows who take my standing bet that they daren't spend the night in the museum—they come boldly enough, but after an hour they shriek and hammer to get out! Want me to ask Orabona, eh? You two—

always against me! You want to break down the coming earthly reign of It!"

Jones preserved his calm.

"No, Rogers—there's nobody against you. And I'm not afraid of your figures, either, much as I admire your skill. But we're both a bit nervous tonight, and I fancy some rest will do us good."

Again Rogers checked his guest's departure.

"Not afraid, eh?—then why are you so anxious to go? Look here —do you or don't you dare to stay alone here in the dark? What's your hurry if you don't believe in It?"

Some new idea seemed to have struck Rogers, and Jones eyed him closely.

"Why, I've no special hurry—but what would be gained by my staying here alone? What would it prove? My only objection is that it isn't very comfortable for sleeping. What good would it do either of us?"

This time it was Jones who was struck with an idea. He continued in a tone of conciliation.

"See here, Rogers—I've just asked you what it would prove if I stayed, when we both know. It would prove that your effigies are just effigies, and that you oughtn't to let your imagination go the way it's been going lately. Suppose I *do* stay. If I stick it out till morning, will you agree to take a new view of things—go on a vacation for three months or so and let Orabona destroy that new thing of yours? Come, now—isn't that fair?"

The expression on the showman's face was hard to read. It was obvious that he was thinking quickly, and that of sundry conflicting emotions, malign triumph was getting the upper hand. His voice held a choking quality as he replied.

"Fair enough! *If you do stick it out,* I'll take your advice. But stick you must. We'll go out for dinner and come back. I'll lock you in the display room and go home. In the morning I'll come down ahead of Orabona—he comes half an hour before the rest—and see how you are. But don't try it unless you are *very* sure of your scepticism. Others have backed out—you have that chance. And I suppose a pounding on the outer door would always bring a constable. You may not like it so well after a while—you'll be in the same building, though not in the same room with It."

As they left the rear door into the dingy courtyard, Rogers took with him the piece of burlap—weighted with a gruesome burden. Near the centre of the court was a manhole, whose cover the showman lifted quietly, and with a shuddersome suggestion of familiarity. Burlap and all, the burden went down to the oblivion of a cloacal labyrinth. Jones shuddered, and almost shrank from the gaunt figure at his side as they emerged into the street.

By unspoken mutual consent, they did not dine together, but agreed to meet in front of the museum at eleven.

Jones hailed a cab, and breathed more freely when he had crossed Waterloo Bridge and was approaching the brilliantly lighted Strand. He dined at a quiet café, and subsequently went to his home in Portland Place to bathe and get a few things. Idly he wondered what Rogers was doing. He had heard that the man had a vast, dismal house in the Walworth Road, full of obscure and forbidden books, occult paraphernalia, and wax images which he did not choose to place on exhibition. Orabona, he understood, lived in separate quarters in the same house.

At eleven Jones found Rogers waiting by the basement door in Southwark Street. Their words were few, but each seemed taut with a menacing tension. They agreed that the vaulted exhibition room alone should form the scene of the vigil, and Rogers did not insist that the watcher sit in the special adult alcove of supreme horrors. The showman, having extinguished all the lights with switches in the workroom, locked the door of that crypt with one of the keys on his crowded ring. Without shaking hands he passed out the street door, locked it after him, and stamped up the worn steps to the sidewalk outside. As his tread receded, Jones realised that the long, tedious vigil had commenced.

II.

Later, in the utter blackness of the great arched cellar, Jones cursed the childish naiveté which had brought him there. For the first half-hour he had kept flashing on his pocket-light at intervals, but now just sitting in the dark on one of the visitors' benches had become a more nerve-racking thing. Every time the beam shot out it lighted up some morbid, grotesque object—a guillotine, a nameless hybrid monster, a pasty-bearded face crafty with evil, a body with red torrents streaming from a severed throat. Jones knew that no sinister reality was attached to these things, but after that first half-hour he preferred not to see them.

Why he had bothered to humour that madman he could scarcely imagine. It would have been much simpler merely to have let him alone, or to have called in a mental specialist. Probably, he reflected, it was the fellow-feeling of one artist for another. There was so much genius in Rogers that he deserved every possible chance to be helped quietly out of his growing mania. Any man who could imagine and construct the incredibly life-like things that he had produced was surely not far from actual greatness. He had the fancy of a Sime or a Doré joined to the minute, scientific craftsmanship of a Blatschka. Indeed, he had done for the world of nightmare what the Blatschkas with their marvellously accurate plant models of finely wrought and coloured glass had done for the world of botany.

At midnight the strokes of a distant clock filtered through the darkness, and Jones felt cheered by the message from a still-surviving outside world. The vaulted museum chamber was like a tomb—ghastly in its utter solitude. Even a mouse would be cheering company; yet Rogers had once boasted that—for "certain reasons", as he said—no mice or even insects ever came near the place. That was very curious, yet it seemed to be true. The deadness and silence were virtually complete. If only something would make a sound! He shuffled his feet, and the echoes came spectrally out of the absolute stillness. He coughed, but there was something mocking in the staccato reverberations. He could not, he vowed, begin talking to himself. That meant nervous disintegration. Time seemed to pass with abnormal and disconcerting slowness. He could have sworn that hours had elapsed since he last flashed the light on his watch, yet here was only the stroke of midnight.

He wished that his senses were not so preternaturally keen. Something in the darkness and stillness seemed to have sharpened them, so that they responded to faint intimations hardly strong enough to be called true impressions. His ears seemed at times to catch a faint, elusive susurrus which could not *quite* be identified with the nocturnal hum of the squalid streets outside, and he thought of vague, irrelevant things like the music of the spheres and the unknown, inaccessible life of alien dimensions pressing on our own. Rogers often speculated about such things.

The floating specks of light in his blackness-drowned eyes seemed inclined to take on curious symmetries of pattern and motion. He had often wondered about those strange rays from the unplumbed abyss which scintillate before us in the absence of all earthly illumination, but he had never known any that behaved just as these were behaving. They lacked the restful aimlessness of ordinary light-

specks—suggesting some will and purpose remote from any terrestrial conception.

Then there was that suggestion of odd stirrings. Nothing was
open, yet in spite of the general draughtlessness Jones felt that the
air was not uniformly quiet. There were intangible variations in
pressure—not quite decided enough to suggest the loathsome paw-
ings of unseen elementals. It was abnormally chilly, too. He did not
like any of this. The air tasted salty, as if it were mixed with the
brine of dark subterrene waters, and there was a bare hint of some
odour of ineffable mustiness. In the daytime he had never noticed
that the waxen figures had an odour. Even now that half-received
hint was not the way wax figures ought to smell. It was more like
the faint smell of specimens in a natural-history museum. Curious,
in view of Rogers' claims that his figures were not all artificial—
indeed, it was probably that claim which made one's imagination
conjure up the olfactory suspicion. One must guard against excesses
of the imagination—had not such things driven poor Rogers mad?

But the utter loneliness of this place was frightful. Even the distant chimes seemed to come from across cosmic gulfs. It made
Jones think of that insane picture which Rogers had shewed him—
the wildly carved chamber with the cryptic throne which the fellow
had claimed was part of a three-million-year-old ruin in the shunned
and inaccessible solitudes of the Arctic. Perhaps Rogers had been to
Alaska, but that picture was certainly nothing but stage scenery. It
couldn't normally be otherwise, with all that carving and those terrible symbols. And that monstrous shape supposed to have been
found on that throne—what a flight of diseased fancy! Jones wondered just how far he actually was from the insane masterpiece in
wax—probably it was kept behind that heavy, padlocked plank
door leading somewhere out of the workroom. But it would never
do to brood about a waxen image. Was not the present room full of
such things, some of them scarcely less horrible than the dreadful
"IT"? And beyond a thin canvas screen on the left was the "Adults
only" alcove with its nameless phantoms of delirium.

The proximity of the numberless waxen shapes began to get on
Jones's nerves more and more as the quarter-hours wore on. He
knew the museum so well that he could not get rid of their usual
images even in the total darkness. Indeed, the darkness had the effect of adding to the remembered images certain very disturbing
imaginative overtones. The guillotine seemed to creak, and the
bearded face of Landru—slayer of his fifty wives—twisted itself

into expressions of monstrous menace. From the severed throat of Madame Demers a hideous bubbling sound seemed to emanate, while the headless, legless victim of a trunk murder tried to edge closer and closer on its gory stumps. Jones began shutting his eyes to see if that would dim the images, but found it was useless. Besides, when he shut his eyes the strange, purposeful patterns of light-specks became more disturbingly pronounced.

Then suddenly he began trying to keep the hideous images he had formerly been trying to banish. He tried to keep them because they were giving place to still more hideous ones. In spite of himself his memory began reconstructing the utterly non-human blasphemies that lurked in the obscurer corners, and these lumpish hybrid growths oozed and wriggled toward him as though hunting him down in a circle. Black Tsathoggua moulded itself from a toad-like gargoyle to a long, sinuous line with hundreds of rudimentary feet, and a lean, rubbery night-gaunt spread its wings as if to advance and smother the watcher. Jones braced himself to keep from screaming. He knew he was reverting to the traditional terrors of his childhood, and resolved to use his adult reason to keep the phantoms at bay. It helped a bit, he found, to flash the light again. Frightful as were the images it shewed, these were not as bad as what his fancy called out of the utter blackness.

But there were drawbacks. Even in the light of his torch he could not help suspecting a slight, furtive trembling on the part of the canvas partition screening off the terrible "Adults only" alcove. He knew what lay beyond, and shivered. Imagination called up the shocking form of fabulous Yog-Sothoth—only a congeries of iridescent globes, yet stupendous in its malign suggestiveness. What was this accursed mass slowly floating toward him and bumping on the partition that stood in the way? A small bulge in the canvas far to the right suggested the sharp horn of Gnoph-keh, the hairy myth-thing of the Greenland ice, that walked sometimes on two legs, sometimes on four, and sometimes on six. To get this stuff out of his head Jones walked boldly toward the hellish alcove with torch burning steadily. Of course, none of his fears was true. Yet were not the long, facial tentacles of great Cthulhu actually swaying, slowly and insidiously? He knew they were flexible, but he had not realised that the draught caused by his advance was enough to set them in motion.

Returning to his former seat outside the alcove, he shut his eyes and let the symmetrical light-specks do their worst. The distant clock boomed a single stroke. Could it be only one? He flashed the light on his watch and saw that it was precisely that hour. It would be hard indeed waiting for morning. Rogers would be down at about eight o'clock, ahead of even Orabona. It would be light outside in the main basement long before that, but none of it could penetrate here. All the windows in this basement had been bricked up but the three small ones facing the court. A pretty bad wait, all told.

His ears were getting most of the hallucinations now—for he could swear he heard stealthy, plodding footsteps in the workroom beyond the closed and locked door. He had no business thinking of that unexhibited horror which Rogers called "It". The thing was a contamination—it had driven its maker mad, and now even its picture was calling up imaginative terrors. It could not be in the workroom—it was very obviously beyond that padlocked door of heavy planking. Those steps were certainly pure imagination.

Then he thought he heard the key turn in the workroom door. Flashing on his torch, he saw nothing but the ancient six-panelled portal in its proper position. Again he tried darkness and closed eyes, but there followed a harrowing illusion of creaking—not the guillotine this time, but the slow, furtive opening of the workroom door. He would not scream. Once he screamed, he would be lost. There was a sort of padding or shuffling audible now, and it was slowly advancing toward him. He must retain command of himself. Had he not done so when the nameless brain-shapes tried to close in on him? The shuffling crept nearer, and his resolution failed. He did not scream but merely gulped out a challenge.

"Who goes there? Who are you? What do you want?"

There was no answer, but the shuffling kept on. Jones did not know which he feared most to do—turn on his flashlight or stay in the dark while the thing crept upon him. This thing was different, he felt profoundly, from the other terrors of the evening. His fingers and throat worked spasmodically. Silence was impossible, and the suspense of utter blackness was beginning to be the most intolerable of all conditions. Again he cried out hysterically—"Halt! Who goes there?"—as he switched on the revealing beams of his torch. Then, paralysed by what he saw, he dropped the flashlight and screamed—not once but many times.

Shuffling toward him in the darkness was the gigantic, blasphemous form of a black thing not wholly ape and not wholly insect. Its hide hung loosely upon its frame, and its rugose, dead-eyed rudiment of a head swayed drunkenly from side to side. Its fore paws were extended, with talons spread wide, and its whole body was taut with murderous malignity despite its utter lack of facial expression. After the screams and the final coming of darkness it leaped, and in a moment had Jones pinned to the floor. There was no struggle, for the watcher had fainted.

Jones's fainting spell could not have lasted more than a moment, for the nameless thing was apishly dragging him through the darkness when he began recovering consciousness. What started him fully awake were the sounds which the thing was making—or rather, the voice with which it was making them. That voice was human, and it was familiar. Only one living being could be behind the hoarse, feverish accents which were chanting to an unknown horror.

"Iä! Iä!" it was howling. "I am coming, O Rhan-Tegoth, coming with the nourishment. You have waited long and fed ill, but now you shall have what was promised. That and more, for instead of Orabona it will be one of high degree who had doubted you. You shall crush and drain him, with all his doubts, and grow strong thereby. And ever after among men he shall be shewn as a monument to your glory. Rhan-Tegoth, infinite and invincible, I am your slave and high-priest. You are hungry, and I provide. I read the sign and have led you forth. I shall feed you with blood, and you shall feed me with power. Iä! Shub-Niggurath! The Goat with a Thousand Young!"

In an instant all the terrors of the night dropped from Jones like a discarded cloak. He was again master of his mind, for he knew the very earthly and material peril he had to deal with. This was no monster of fable, but a dangerous madman. It was Rogers, dressed in some nightmare covering of his own insane designing, and about to make a frightful sacrifice to the devil-god he had fashioned out of wax. Clearly, he must have entered the workroom from the rear courtyard, donned his disguise, and then advanced to seize his neatly trapped and fear-broken victim. His strength was prodigious, and if he was to be thwarted, one must act quickly. Counting on the madman's confidence in his unconsciousness he determined to take him by surprise, while his grasp was relatively lax. The feel of a threshold told him he was crossing into the pitch-black workroom.

With the strength of mortal fear Jones made a sudden spring from the half-recumbent posture in which he was being dragged. For an instant he was free of the astonished maniac's hands, and in another instant a lucky lunge in the dark had put his own hands at his captor's weirdly concealed throat. Simultaneously Rogers gripped him again, and without further preliminaries the two were locked in a desperate struggle of life and death. Jones's athletic training, without doubt, was his sole salvation; for his mad assailant, freed from every inhibition of fair play, decency, or even self-preservation, was an engine of savage destruction as formidable as a wolf or panther.

Guttural cries sometimes punctured the hideous tussle in the dark. Blood spurted, clothing ripped, and Jones at last felt the actual throat of the maniac, shorn of its spectral mask. He spoke not a word, but put every ounce of energy into the defence of his life. Rogers kicked, gouged, butted, bit, clawed, and spat—yet found strength to yelp out actual sentences at times. Most of his speech was in a ritualistic jargon full of references to "It" or "Rhan-Te-goth", and to Jones's overwrought nerves it seemed as if the cries echoed from an infinite distance of daemoniac snortings and bayings. Toward the last they were rolling on the floor, overturning benches or striking against the walls and the brick foundations of the central melting-furnace. Up to the very end Jones could not be certain of saving himself, but chance finally intervened in his favour. A jab of his knee against Rogers' chest produced a general relaxation, and a moment later he knew he had won.

Though hardly able to hold himself up, Jones rose and stumbled about the walls seeking the light-switch—for his flashlight was gone, together with most of his clothing. As he lurched along he dragged his limp opponent with him, fearing a sudden attack when the madman came to. Finding the switch-box, he fumbled till he had the right handle. Then, as the wildly disordered workroom burst into sudden radiance, he set about binding Rogers with such cords and belts as he could easily find. The fellow's disguise—or what was left of it—seemed to be made of a puzzlingly queer sort of leather. For some reason it made Jones's flesh crawl to touch it, and there seemed to be an alien, rusty odour about it. In the normal clothes beneath it was Rogers' key-ring, and this the exhausted victor seized as his final passport to freedom. The shades at the small, slit-like windows were all securely drawn, and he let them remain so.

Washing off the blood of battle at a convenient sink, Jones donned the most ordinary-looking and least ill-fitting clothes he

could find on the costume hooks. Testing the door to the courtyard, he found it fastened with a spring-lock which did not require
a key from the inside. He kept the key-ring, however, to admit him
on his return with aid—for plainly, the thing to do was to call in an
alienist. There was no telephone in the museum, but it would not
take long to find an all-night restaurant or chemist's shop where
one could be had. He had almost opened the door to go when a torrent of hideous abuse from across the room told him that Rogers—
whose visible injuries were confined to a long, deep scratch down
the left cheek—had regained consciousness.

"Fool! Spawn of Noth-Yidik and effluvium of K'thun! Son of the
dogs that howl in the maelstrom of Azathoth! You would have
been sacred and immortal, and now you are betraying It and It's
priest! Beware—for It is hungry! It would have been Orabona—
that damned treacherous dog ready to turn against me and It—but I
give you the first honour instead. Now you must both beware, for
It is not gentle without It's priest.

"Iä! Iä! Vengeance is at hand! Do you know you would have
been immortal? Look at the furnace! There is a fire ready to light,
and there is wax in the kettle. I would have done with you as I have
done with other once-living forms. Hei! You, who have vowed all
my effigies are waxen, would have become a waxen effigy yourself!
The furnace was all ready! When It had had It's fill, and you were
like that dog I shewed you, I would have made your flattened,
punctured fragments immortal! Wax would have done it. Haven't
you said I'm a great artist? Wax in every pore—wax over every
square inch of you—Iä! Iä! And ever after the world would have
looked at your mangled carcass and wondered how I ever imagined
and made such a thing! Hei! And Orabona would have come next,
and others after him—and thus would my waxen family have
grown!

"Dog—do you still think I *made* all my effigies? Why not say
preserved? You know by this time the strange places I've been to,
and the strange things I've brought back. Coward—you could
never face the dimensional shambler whose hide I put on to scare
you—the mere sight of it alive, or even the full-fledged thought of
it, would kill you instantly with fright! Iä! Iä! It waits hungry for
the blood that is the life!"

Rogers, propped against the wall, swayed to and fro in his
bonds.

"See here, Jones—if I let you go will you let me go? It must be taken care of by It's high-priest. Orabona will be enough to keep It alive—and when he is finished I will make his fragments immortal in wax for the world to see. It could have been you, but you have rejected the honour. I won't bother you again. Let me go, and I will share with you the power that It will bring me. Iä! Iä! Great is Rhan-Tegoth! Let me go! Let me go! It is starving down there beyond that door, and if It dies the Old Ones can never come back. Hei! Hei! Let me go!"

Jones merely shook his head, though the hideousness of the showman's imaginings revolted him. Rogers, now staring wildly at the padlocked plank door, thumped his head again and again against the brick wall and kicked with his tightly bound ankles. Jones was afraid he would injure himself, and advanced to bind him more firmly to some stationary object. Writhing, Rogers edged away from him and set up a series of frenetic ululations whose utter, monstrous unhumanness was appalling, and whose sheer volume was almost incredible. It seemed impossible that any human throat could produce noises so loud and piercing, and Jones felt that if this continued there would be no need to telephone for aid. It could not be long before a constable would investigate, even granting that there were no listening neighbours in this deserted warehouse district.

"Wza-y'ei! Wza-y'ei!" howled the madman. "Y'kaa haa bho—ii, Rhan-Tegoth—Cthulhu fhtagn—Ei! Ei! Ei! Ei!—Rhan-Tegoth, Rhan-Tegoth, Rhan-Tegoth!"

The tautly trussed creature, who had started squirming his way across the littered floor, now reached the padlocked plank door and commenced knocking his head thunderously against it. Jones dreaded the task of binding him further, and wished he were not so exhausted from the previous struggle. This violent aftermath was getting hideously on his nerves, and he began to feel a return of the nameless qualms he had felt in the dark. Everything about Rogers and his museum was so hellishly morbid and suggestive of black vistas beyond life! It was loathsome to think of the waxen masterpiece of abnormal genius which must at this very moment be lurking close at hand in the blackness beyond the heavy, padlocked door.

And now something happened which sent an additional chill down Jones's spine, and caused every hair—even the tiny growth on the backs of his hands—to bristle with a vague fright beyond classification. Rogers had suddenly stopped screaming and beating his head against the stout plank door, and was straining up to a sitting posture, head cocked on one side as if listening intently for something. All at once a smile of devilish triumph overspread his face, and he began speaking intelligibly again—this time in a hoarse whisper contrasting oddly with his former stentorian howling.

"Listen, fool! Listen hard! *It* has heard me, and is coming. Can't you hear It splashing out of It's tank down there at the end of the runway? I dug it deep, because there was nothing too good for It. It is amphibious, you know—you saw the gills in the picture. It came to the earth from lead-grey Yuggoth, where the cities are under the warm deep sea. It can't stand up in there—too tall—has to sit or crouch. Let me get my keys—we must let It out and kneel down before It. Then we will go out and find a dog or cat—or perhaps a drunken man—to give It the nourishment It needs."

It was not what the madman said, but the way he said it, that disorganised Jones so badly. The utter, insane confidence and sincerity in that crazed whisper were damnably contagious. Imagination, with such a stimulus, could find an active menace in the devilish wax figure that lurked unseen just beyond the heavy planking. Eyeing the door in unholy fascination, Jones noticed that it bore several distinct cracks, though no marks of violent treatment were visible on this side. He wondered how large a room or closet lay behind it, and how the waxen figure was arranged. The maniac's idea of a tank and runway was as clever as all his other imaginings.

Then, in one terrible instant, Jones completely lost the power to draw a breath. The leather belt he had seized for Rogers' further strapping fell from his limp hands, and a spasm of shivering convulsed him from head to foot. He might have known the place would drive him mad as it had driven Rogers—and now he *was* mad. He was mad, for he now harboured hallucinations more weird than any which had assailed him earlier that night. The madman was bidding him hear the splashing of a mythical monster in a tank beyond the door—and now, God help him, *he did hear it!*

Rogers saw the spasm of horror reach Jones's face and transform it to a staring mask of fear. He cackled.

"At last, fool, you believe! At last you know! You hear It and It comes! Get me my keys, fool—we must do homage and serve It!"

But Jones was past paying attention to any human words, mad or sane. Phobic paralysis held him immobile and half-conscious, with wild images racing phantasmagorically through his helpless imagination. There *was* a splashing. There *was* a padding or shuffling, as of great wet paws on a solid surface. Something *was* approaching. Into his nostrils, from the cracks in that nightmare plank door, poured a noisome animal stench like and yet unlike that of the mammal cages at the zoölogical gardens in Regent's Park.

He did not know now whether Rogers was talking or not. Everything real had faded away, and he was a statue obsessed with dreams and hallucinations so unnatural that they became almost objective and remote from him. He thought he heard a sniffing or snorting from the unknown gulf beyond the door, and when a sudden baying, trumpeting noise assailed his ears he could not feel sure that it came from the tightly bound maniac whose image swam uncertainly in his shaken vision. The photograph of that accursed, unseen wax thing persisted in floating through his consciousness. Such a thing had no right to exist. Had it not driven him mad?

Even as he reflected, a fresh evidence of madness beset him. Something, he thought, was fumbling with the latch of the heavy padlocked door. It was patting and pawing and pushing at the planks. There was a thudding on the stout wood, which grew louder and louder. The stench was horrible. And now the assault on that door from the inside was a malign, determined pounding like the strokes of a battering-ram. There was an ominous cracking—a splintering—a welling foetor—a falling plank—*a black paw ending in a crab-like claw.* . . .

"Help! Help! God help me! . . . Aaaaaaa! . . ."

With intense effort Jones is today able to recall a sudden bursting of his fear-paralysis into the liberation of frenzied automatic flight. What he evidently did must have paralleled curiously the wild, plunging flights of maddest nightmares; for he seems to have leaped across the disordered crypt at almost a single bound, yanked open the outside door, which closed and locked itself after him with a clatter, sprung up the worn stone steps three at a time, and raced frantically and aimlessly out of that dank cobblestoned court and through the squalid streets of Southwark.

Here the memory ends. Jones does not know how he got home, and there is no evidence of his having hired a cab. Probably he raced all the way by blind instinct—over Waterloo Bridge, along the Strand and Charing Cross, and up Haymarket and Regent Street to his own neighbourhood. He still had on the queer mélange of museum costumes when he grew conscious enough to call the doctor.

A week later the nerve specialists allowed him to leave his bed and walk in the open air.

But he had not told the specialists much. Over his whole experience hung a pall of madness and nightmare, and he felt that silence was the only course. When he was up, he scanned intently all the papers which had accumulated since that hideous night, but found no reference to anything queer at the museum. How much, after all, had been reality? Where did reality end and morbid dream begin? Had his mind gone wholly to pieces in that dark exhibition chamber, and had the whole fight with Rogers been a phantasm of fever? It would help to put him on his feet if he could settle some of these maddening points. He *must* have seen that damnable photograph of the wax image called "It", for no brain but Rogers' could ever have conceived such a blasphemy.

It was a fortnight before he dared to enter Southwark Street again. He went in the middle of the morning, when there was the greatest amount of sane, wholesome activity around the ancient, crumbling shops and warehouses. The museum's sign was still there, and as he approached he saw that the place was open. The gateman nodded in a pleasant recognition as he summoned up the courage to enter, and in the vaulted chamber below an attendant touched his cap cheerfully. Perhaps everything had been a dream. Would he dare to knock at the door of the workroom and look for Rogers?

Then Orabona advanced to greet him. His dark, sleek face was a trifle sardonic, but Jones felt that he was not unfriendly. He spoke with a trace of accent.

"Good morning, Mr. Jones. It is some time since we have seen you here. Did you wish Mr. Rogers? I'm sorry, but he is away. He had word of business in America, and had to go. Yes, it was very sudden. I am in charge now—here, and at the house. I try to maintain Mr. Rogers' high standard—till he is back."

The foreigner smiled—perhaps from affability alone. Jones scarcely knew how to reply, but managed to mumble out a few inquiries about the day after his last visit. Orabona seemed greatly amused by the questions, and took considerable care in framing his replies.

"Oh, yes, Mr. Jones—the twenty-eighth of last month. I remember it for many reasons. In the morning—before Mr. Rogers got here, you understand—I found the workroom in quite a mess. There was a great deal of—cleaning up—to do. There had been—

late work, you see. Important new specimen given its secondary baking process. I took complete charge when I came.

"It was a hard specimen to prepare—but of course Mr. Rogers has taught me a great deal. He is, as you know, a very great artist. When he came he helped me complete the specimen—helped very materially, I assure you—but he left soon without even greeting the men. As I tell you, he was called away suddenly. There were important chemical reactions involved. They made loud noises—in fact, some teamsters in the court outside fancy they heard several pistol shots—very amusing idea!

"As for the new specimen—that matter is very unfortunate. It is a great masterpiece—designed and made, you understand, by Mr. Rogers. He will see about it when he gets back."

Again Orabona smiled.

"The police, you know. We put it on display a week ago, and there were two or three faintings. One poor fellow had an epileptic fit in front of it. You see, it is a trifle—stronger—than the rest. Larger, for one thing. Of course, it was in the adult alcove. The next day a couple of men from Scotland Yard looked it over and said it was too morbid to be shewn. Said we'd have to remove it. It was a tremendous shame—such a masterpiece of art—but I didn't feel justified in appealing to the courts in Mr. Rogers' absence. He would not like so much publicity with the police now—but when he gets back—when he gets back—"

For some reason or other Jones felt a mounting tide of uneasiness and repulsion. But Orabona was continuing.

"You are a connoisseur, Mr. Jones. I am sure I violate no law in offering you a private view. It may be—subject, of course, to Mr. Rogers' wishes—that we shall destroy the specimen some day—but that would be a crime."

Jones had a powerful impulse to refuse the sight and flee precipitately, but Orabona was leading him forward by the arm with an artist's enthusiasm. The adult alcove, crowded with nameless horrors, held no visitors. In the farther corner a large niche had been curtained off, and to this the smiling assistant advanced.

"You must know, Mr. Jones, that the title of this specimen is 'The Sacrifice to Rhan-Tegoth'."

Jones started violently, but Orabona appeared not to notice.

"The shapeless, colossal god is a feature in certain obscure legends which Mr. Rogers has studied. All nonsense, of course, as you've so often assured Mr. Rogers. It is supposed to have come from outer space, and to have lived in the Arctic three million years ago. It treated its sacrifices rather peculiarly and horribly, as you shall see. Mr. Rogers had made it fiendishly life-like—even to the face of the victim."

Now trembling violently, Jones clung to the brass railing in front of the curtained niche. He almost reached out to stop Orabona when he saw the curtain beginning to swing aside, but some conflicting impulse held him back. The foreigner smiled triumphantly.

"Behold!"

Jones reeled in spite of his grip on the railing.

"God!—great God!"

Fully ten feet high despite a shambling, crouching attitude expressive of infinite cosmic malignancy, a monstrosity of unbelievable horror was shewn starting forward from a Cyclopean ivory throne covered with grotesque carvings. In the central pair of its six legs it bore a crushed, flattened, distorted, bloodless thing, riddled with a million punctures, and in places seared as with some pungent acid. Only the mangled head of the victim, lolling upside down at one side, revealed that it represented something once human.

The monster itself needed no title for one who had seen a certain hellish photograph. That damnable print had been all too faithful; yet it could not carry the full horror which lay in the gigantic actuality. The globular torso—the bubble-like suggestion of a head —the three fishy eyes—the foot-long proboscis—the bulging gills— the monstrous capillation of asp-like suckers—the six sinuous limbs with their black paws and crab-like claws—God! the familiarity of that black paw ending in a crab-like claw! . . .

Orabona's smile was utterly damnable. Jones choked, and stared at the hideous exhibit with a mounting fascination which perplexed and disturbed him. What half-revealed horror was holding and forcing him to look longer and search out details? This had driven Rogers mad . . . Rogers, supreme artist . . . said they weren't artificial. . . .

Then he localised the thing that held him. It was the crushed waxen victim's lolling head, and something that it implied. This head was not entirely devoid of a face, and that face was familiar. It was like the mad face of poor Rogers. Jones peered closer, hardly knowing why he was driven to do so. Wasn't it natural for a mad egotist to mould his own features into his masterpiece? Was there anything more that subconscious vision had seized on and suppressed in sheer terror?

The wax of the mangled face had been handled with boundless dexterity. Those punctures—how perfectly they reproduced the myriad wounds somehow inflicted on that poor dog! But there was something more. On the left cheek one could trace an irregularity which seemed outside the general scheme—as if the sculptor had sought to cover up a defect of his first modelling. The more Jones looked at it, the more mysteriously it horrified him—and then, suddenly, he remembered a circumstance which brought his horror to a head. That night of hideousness—the tussle—the bound madman —*and the long, deep scratch down the left cheek of the actual living Rogers*. . . .

Jones, releasing his desperate clutch on the railing, sank in a total faint.

Orabona continued to smile.

Hazel Heald

Winged Death

The Orange Hotel stands in High Street near the railway station in Bloemfontein, South Africa. On Sunday, January 24, 1932, four men sat shivering from terror in a room on its third floor. One was George C. Titteridge, proprietor of the hotel; another was police constable Ian De Witt of the Central Station; a third was Johannes Bogaert, the local coroner; the fourth, and apparently the least disorganised of the group, was Dr. Cornelius Van Keulen, the coroner's physician.

On the floor, uncomfortably evident amidst the stifling summer heat, was the body of a dead man—but this was not what the four were afraid of. Their glances wandered from the table, on which lay a curious assortment of things, to the ceiling overhead, across whose smooth whiteness a series of huge, faltering alphabetical characters had somehow been scrawled in ink; and every now and then Dr. Van Keulen would glance half-furtively at a worn leather blank-book which he held in his left hand. The horror of the four seemed about equally divided among the blank-book, the scrawled words on the ceiling, and a dead fly of peculiar aspect which floated in a bottle of ammonia on the table. Also on the table were an open inkwell, a pen and writing-pad, a physician's medical case, a bottle of hydrochloric acid, and a tumbler about a quarter full of black oxide of manganese.

The worn leather book was the journal of the dead man on the floor, and had at once made it clear that the name "Frederick N. Mason, Mining Properties, Toronto, Canada", signed in the hotel register, was a false one. There were other things—terrible things—which it likewise made clear; and still other things of far greater terror at which it hinted hideously without making them clear or even fully believable. It was the half-belief of the four men, fostered by lives spent close to the black, settled secrets of brooding Africa, which made them shiver so violently in spite of the searing January heat.

The blank-book was not a large one, and the entries were in a fine handwriting, which, however, grew careless and nervous-looking toward the last. It consisted of a series of jottings at first rather irregularly spaced, but finally becoming daily. To call it a diary would not be quite correct, for it chronicled only one set of its writer's activities. Dr. Van Keulen recognised the name of the dead man the moment he opened the cover, for it was that of an eminent member of his own profession who had been largely connected with African matters. In another moment he was horrified to find this name linked with a dastardly crime, officially unsolved, which had filled the newspapers some four months before. And the farther he read, the deeper grew his horror, awe, and sense of loathing and panic.

Here, in essence, is the text which the doctor read aloud in that sinister and increasingly noisome room while the three men around him breathed hard, fidgeted in their chairs, and darted frightened glances at the ceiling, the table, the thing on the floor, and one another:

JOURNAL OF
THOMAS SLAUENWITE, M.D.

Touching punishment of Henry Sargent Moore, Ph.D., of Brooklyn, New York, Professor of Invertebrate Biology in Columbia University, New York, N.Y. Prepared to be read after my death, for the satisfaction of making public the accomplishment of my revenge, which may otherwise never be imputed to me even if it succeeds.

January 5, 1929—I have now fully resolved to kill Dr. Henry Moore, and a recent incident has shewn me how I shall do it. From now on, I shall follow a consistent line of action; hence the beginning of this journal.

It is hardly necessary to repeat the circumstances which have driven me to this course, for the informed part of the public is familiar with all the salient facts. I was born in Trenton, New Jersey, on April 12, 1885, the son of Dr. Paul Slauenwite, formerly of Pretoria, Transvaal, South Africa. Studying medicine as part of my family tradition, I was led by my father (who died in 1916, while I was serving in France in a South African regiment) to specialise in African fevers; and after my graduation from Columbia spent much time in researches which took me from Durban, in Natal, up to the equator itself.

In Mombasa I worked out my new theory of the transmission and development of remittent fever, aided only slightly by the papers of the late government physician, Sir Norman Sloane, which I found in the house I occupied. When I published my results I became at a single stroke a famous authority. I was told of the probability of an almost supreme position in the South African health service, and even a probable knighthood, in the event of my becoming a naturalised citizen, and accordingly I took the necessary steps.

Then occurred the incident for which I am about to kill Henry Moore. This man, my classmate and friend of years in America and Africa, chose deliberately to undermine my claim to my own theory; alleging that Sir Norman Sloane had anticipated me in every essential detail, and implying that I had probably found more of his papers than I had stated in my account of the matter. To buttress this absurd accusation he produced certain personal letters from Sir Norman which indeed shewed that the older man had been over my ground, and that he would have published his results very soon but for his sudden death. This much I could only admit with regret. What I could not excuse was the jealous suspicion that I had stolen the theory from Sir Norman's papers. The British government, sensibly enough, ignored these aspersions, but withheld the half-promised appointment and knighthood on the ground that my theory, while original with me, was not in fact new.

I could soon see that my career in Africa was perceptibly checked; though I had placed all my hopes on such a career, even to the point of resigning American citizenship. A distinct coolness toward me had arisen among the Government set in Mombasa, especially among those who had known Sir Norman. It was then that I resolved to be even with Moore sooner or later, though I did not know how. He had been jealous of my early celebrity, and had taken advantage of his old correspondence with Sir Norman to ruin me. This from the friend whom I had myself led to take an interest in Africa—whom I had coached and inspired till he achieved his present moderate fame as an authority on African entomology. Even now, though, I will not deny that his attainments are profound. I made him, and in return he has ruined me. Now—some day—I shall destroy him.

When I saw myself losing ground in Mombasa, I applied for my present situation in the interior—at M'gonga, only fifty miles from the Uganda line. It is a cotton and ivory trading-post, with only eight white men besides myself. A beastly hole, almost on the equator, and full of every sort of fever known to mankind. Poisonous snakes and insects everywhere, and niggers with diseases nobody ever heard of outside medical college. But my work is not hard, and I have always had plenty of time to plan things to do to Henry Moore. It amuses me to give his *Diptera of Central and Southern Africa* a prominent place on my shelf. I suppose it actually is a standard manual—they use it at Columbia, Harvard, and the U. of Wis.—but my own suggestions are really responsible for half its strong points.

Last week I encountered the thing which decided me how to kill Moore. A party from Uganda brought in a black with a queer illness which I can't yet diagnose. He was lethargic, with a very low temperature, and shuffled in a peculiar way. Most of the others were afraid of him and said he was under some kind of witch-doctor spell; but Gobo, the interpreter, said he had been bitten by an insect. What it was, I can't imagine—for there is only a slight puncture on the arm. It is bright red, though, with a purple ring around it. Spectral-looking—I don't wonder the boys lay it to black magic. They seem to have seen cases like it before, and say there's really nothing to do about it.

Old N'Kuru, one of the Galla boys at the post, says it must be the bite of a devil-fly, which makes its victim waste away gradually and die, and then takes hold of his soul and personality if it is still alive itself—flying around with all his likes, dislikes, and consciousness. A queer legend—and I don't know of any local insect deadly enough to account for it. I gave this sick black—his name is Mevana—a good shot of quinine and took a sample of his blood for testing, but haven't made much progress. There is certainly a strange germ present, but I can't even remotely identify it. The nearest thing to it is the bacillus one finds in oxen, horses, and dogs that the tsetse-fly has bitten; but tsetse-flies don't infect human beings, and this is too far north for them anyway.

However—the important thing is that I've decided how to kill Moore. If this interior region has insects as poisonous as the natives say, I'll see that he gets a shipment of them from a source he won't suspect, and with plenty of assurances that they are harmless. Trust him to throw overboard all caution when it comes to studying an unknown species—and then we'll see how Nature takes its course! It ought not to be hard to find an insect that scares the blacks so much. First to see how poor Mevana turns out—and then to find my envoy of death.

Jan. 7—Mevana is no better, though I have injected all the antitoxins I know of. He has fits of trembling, in which he rants affrightedly about the way his soul will pass when he dies into the insect that bit him, but between them he remains in a kind of half-stupor. Heart action still strong, so I may pull him through. I shall try to, for he can probably guide me better than anyone else to the region where he was bitten.

Meanwhile I'll write to Dr. Lincoln, my predecessor here, for Allen, the head factor, says he had a profound knowledge of the local sicknesses. He ought to know about the death-fly if any white man does. He's at Nairobi now, and a black runner ought to get me a reply in a week—using the railway for half the trip.

Jan. 10—Patient unchanged, but I have found what I want! It was in an old volume of the local health records, which I've been going over diligently while waiting to hear from Lincoln. Thirty years ago there was an epidemic that killed off thousands of natives in Uganda, and it was definitely traced to a rare fly called *Glossina palpalis*—a sort of cousin of the *Glossina marsitans,* or tsetse. It lives in the bushes on the shores of lakes and rivers, and feeds on the blood of crocodiles, antelopes, and large mammals. When these food animals have the germ of trypanosomiasis, or sleeping-sickness, it picks it up and develops acute infectivity after an incubation period of thirty-one days. Then for seventy-five days it is sure death to anyone or anything it bites.

Without doubt, this must be the "devil-fly" the niggers talk about. Now I know what I'm heading for. Hope Mevana pulls through. Ought to hear from Lincoln in four or five days—he has a great reputation for success in things like this. My worst problem will be to get the flies to Moore without his recognising them. With his cursed plodding scholarship it would be just like him to know all about them since they're actually on record.

Jan. 15—Just heard from Lincoln, who confirms all that the records say about *Glossina palpalis*. He has a remedy for sleeping-sickness which has succeeded in a great number of cases when not given too late. Intermuscular injections of tryparsamide. Since Mevana was bitten about two months ago, I don't know how it will work—but Lincoln says that cases have been known to drag on eighteen months, so possibly I'm not too late. Lincoln sent over some of his stuff, so I've just given Mevana a stiff shot. In a stupor now. They've brought his principal wife from the village, but he doesn't even recognise her. If he recovers, he can certainly shew me where the flies are. He's a great crocodile hunter, according to report, and knows all Uganda like a book. I'll give him another shot tomorrow.

Jan. 16—Mevana seems a little brighter today, but his heart action is slowing up a bit. I'll keep up the injections, but not overdo them.

Jan. 17—Recovery really pronounced today. Mevana opened his eyes and shewed signs of actual consciousness, though dazed, after the injection. Hope Moore doesn't know about tryparsamide. There's a good chance he won't, since he never leaned much toward medicine. Mevana's tongue seemed paralysed, but I fancy that will pass off if I can only wake him up. Wouldn't mind a good sleep myself, but not of this kind!

Jan. 25—Mevana nearly cured! In another week I can let him take me into the jungle. He was frightened when he first came to— about having the fly take his personality after he died—but brightened up finally when I told him he was going to get well. His wife, Ugowe, takes good care of him now, and I can rest a bit. Then for the envoys of death!

Feb. 3—Mevana is well now, and I have talked with him about a hunt for flies. He dreads to go near the place where they got him, but I am playing on his gratitude. Besides, he has an idea that I can ward off disease as well as cure it. His pluck would shame a white man—there's no doubt that he'll go. I can get off by telling the head factor the trip is in the interest of local health work.

March 12—In Uganda at last! Have five boys besides Mevana, but they are all Gallas. The local blacks couldn't be hired to come near the region after the talk of what had happened to Mevana. This jungle is a pestilential place—steaming with miasmal vapours. All the lakes look stagnant. In one spot we came upon a trace of Cyclopean ruins which made even the Gallas run past in a wide circle. They say these megaliths are older than man, and that they used to be a haunt or outpost of "The Fishers from Outside"— whatever that means—and of the evil gods Tsadogwa and Clulu.

To this day they are said to have a malign influence, and to be connected somehow with the devil-flies.

March 15—Struck Lake Mlolo this morning—where Mevana was bitten. A hellish, green-scummed affair, full of crocodiles, Mevana has fixed up a fly-trap of fine wire netting baited with crocodile meat. It has a small entrance, and once the quarry get in, they don't know enough to get out. As stupid as they are deadly, and ravenous for fresh meat or a bowl of blood. Hope we can get a good supply. I've decided that I must experiment with them—finding a way to change their appearance so that Moore won't recognise them. Possibly I can cross them with some other species, producing a strange hybrid whose infection-carrying capacity will be undiminished. We'll see. I must wait, but am in no hurry now. When I get ready I'll have Mevana get me some infected meat to feed my envoys of death—and then for the post-office. Ought to be no trouble getting infection, for this country is a veritable pest-hole.

March 16—Good luck. Two cages full. Five vigorous specimens with wings glistening like diamonds. Mevana is emptying them into a large can with a tightly meshed top, and I think we caught them in the nick of time. We can get them to M'gonga without trouble. Taking plenty of crocodile meat for their food. Undoubtedly all or most of it is infected.

April 20—Back at M'gonga and busy in the laboratory. Have sent to Dr. Joost in Pretoria for some tsetse-flies for hybridisation experiments. Such a crossing, if it will work at all, ought to produce something pretty hard to recognise yet at the same time just as deadly as the *palpalis*. If this doesn't work, I shall try certain other diptera from the interior, and I have sent to Dr. Vandervelde at Nyangwe for some of the Congo types. I shan't have to send Mevana for more tainted meat after all; for I find I can keep cultures of the germ *Trypanosoma gambiense,* taken from the meat we got last month, almost indefinitely in tubes. When the time comes, I'll taint some fresh meat and feed my winged envoys a good dose—then *bon voyage* to them!

June 18—My tsetse-flies from Joost came today. Cages for breeding were all ready long ago, and I am now making selections. Intend to use ultra-violet rays to speed up the life-cycle. Fortunately I have the needed apparatus in my regular equipment. Naturally I tell no one what I'm doing. The ignorance of the few men here makes it easy for me to conceal my aims and pretend to be merely studying existing species for medical reasons.

June 29—The crossing is fertile! Good deposits of eggs last Wednesday, and now I have some excellent larvae. If the mature insects look as strange as these do, I need do nothing more. Am preparing separate numbered cages for the different specimens.

July 7—New hybrids are out! Disguise is excellent as to shape, but sheen of wings still suggests *palpalis*. Thorax has faint suggestions of the stripes of the tsetse. Slight variation in individuals. Am feeding them all on tainted crocodile meat, and after infectivity develops will try them on some of the blacks—apparently, of course, by accident. There are so many mildly venomous flies around here that it can easily be done without exciting suspicion. I shall loose an insect in my tightly screened dining-room when Batta, my house-boy, brings in breakfast—keeping well on guard myself. When it has done its work I'll capture or swat it—an easy thing because of its stupidity—or asphyxiate it by filling the room with chlorine gas. If it doesn't work the first time, I'll try again until it does. Of course, I'll have the tryparsamide handy in case I get bitten myself—but I shall be careful to avoid biting, for no antidote is really certain.

Aug. 10—Infectivity mature, and managed to get Batta stung in fine shape. Caught the fly on him, returning it to its cage. Eased up the pain with iodine, and the poor devil is quite grateful for the service. Shall try a variant specimen on Gamba, the factor's messenger, tomorrow. That will be all the tests I shall dare to make here, but if I need more I shall take some specimens to Ukala and get additional data.

Aug. 11—Failed to get Gamba, but recaptured the fly alive. Batta still seems as well as usual, and has no pain in the back where he was stung. Shall wait before trying to get Gamba again.

Aug. 14—Shipment of insects from Vandervelde at last. Fully seven distinct species, some more or less poisonous. Am keeping them well fed in case the tsetse crossing doesn't work. Some of these fellows look very unlike the *palpalis,* but the trouble is that they may not make a fertile cross with it.

Aug. 17—Got Gamba this afternoon, but had to kill the fly on him. It nipped him in the left shoulder. I dressed the bite, and Gamba is as grateful as Batta was. No change in Batta.

Aug. 20—Gamba unchanged so far—Batta too. Am experimenting with a new form of disguise to supplement the hybridisation—some sort of dye to change the telltale glitter of the *palpalis'* wings. A bluish tint would be best—something I could spray on a whole batch of insects. Shall begin by investigating things like Prussian and Turnbull's blue—iron and cyanogen salts.

Aug. 25—Batta complained of a pain in his back today—things may be developing.

Sept. 3—Have made fair progress in my experiments. Batta shews signs of lethargy, and says his back aches all the time. Gamba beginning to feel uneasy in his bitten shoulder.

Sept. 24—Batta worse and worse, and beginning to get frightened about his bite. Thinks it must be a devil-fly, and entreated me to kill it—for he saw me cage it—until I pretended to him that it had died long ago. Said he didn't want his soul to pass into it upon his death. I give him shots of plain water with a hypodermic to keep his morale up. Evidently the fly retains all the properties of the *palpalis*. Gamba down, too, and repeating all of Batta's symptoms. I may decide to give him a chance with tryparsamide, for the effect of the fly is proved well enough. I shall let Batta go on, however, for I want a rough idea of how long it takes to finish a case.

Dye experiments coming along finely. An isomeric form of ferrous ferrocyanide, with some admixture of potassium salts, can be dissolved in alcohol and sprayed on the insects with splendid effect. It stains the wings blue without affecting the dark thorax much, and doesn't wear off when I sprinkle the specimens with water. With this disguise, I think I can use the present tsetse hybrids and avoid bothering with any more experiments. Sharp as he is, Moore couldn't recognise a blue-winged fly with a half-tsetse thorax. Of course, I keep all this dye business strictly under cover. Nothing must ever connect me with the blue flies later on.

Oct. 9—Batta is lethargic and has taken to his bed. Have been giving Gamba tryparsamide for two weeks, and fancy he'll recover.

Oct. 25—Batta very low, but Gamba nearly well.

Nov. 18—Batta died yesterday, and a curious thing happened which gave me a real shiver in view of the native legends and Batta's own fears. When I returned to the laboratory after the death I heard the most singular buzzing and thrashing in cage 12, which contained the fly that bit Batta. The creature seemed frantic, but stopped still when I appeared—lighting on the wire netting and looking at me in the oddest way. It reached its legs through the wires as if it were bewildered. When I came back from dining with Allen, the thing was dead. Evidently it had gone wild and beaten its life out on the sides of the cage.

It certainly is peculiar that this should happen just as Batta died. If any black had seen it, he'd have laid it at once to the absorption of the poor devil's soul. I shall start my blue-stained hybrids on their way before long now. The hybrid's rate of killing seems a little ahead of the pure *palpalis'* rate, if anything. Batta died three months and eight days after infection—but of course there is always a wide margin of uncertainty. I almost wish I had let Gamba's case run on.

Dec. 5—Busy planning how to get my envoys to Moore. I must have them appear to come from some disinterested entomologist who has read his *Diptera of Central and Southern Africa* and believes he would like to study this "new and unidentifiable species". There must also be ample assurances that the blue-winged fly is harmless, as proved by the natives' long experience. Moore will be off his guard, and one of the flies will surely get him sooner or later—though one can't tell just when.

I'll have to rely on the letters of New York friends—they still speak of Moore from time to time—to keep me informed of early results, though I dare say the papers will announce his death. Above all, I must shew no interest in his case. I shall mail the flies while on a trip, but must not be recognised when I do it. The best plan will be to take a long vacation in the interior, grow a beard, mail the package at Ukala while passing as a visiting entomologist, and return here after shaving off the beard.

April 12, 1930—Back in M'gonga after my long trip. Everything has come off finely—with clockwork precision. Have sent the flies to Moore without leaving a trace. Got a Christmas vacation Dec. 15th, and set out at once with the proper stuff. Made a very good mailing container with room to include some germ-tainted crocodile meat as food for the envoys. By the end of February I had beard enough to shape into a close Vandyke.

Shewed up at Ukala March 9th and typed a letter to Moore on the trading-post machine. Signed it "Nevil Wayland-Hall"—supposed to be an entomologist from London. Think I took just the right tone—interest of a brother-scientist, and all that. Was artistically casual in emphasising the "complete harmlessness" of the specimens. Nobody suspected anything. Shaved the beard as soon as I hit the bush, so that there wouldn't be any uneven tanning by the time I got back here. Dispensed with native bearers except for one small stretch of swamp—I can do wonders with one knapsack, and my sense of direction is good. Lucky I'm used to such travelling. Explained my protracted absence by pleading a touch of fever and some mistakes in direction when going through the bush.

But now comes the hardest part psychologically—waiting for news of Moore without shewing the strain. Of course, he may possibly escape a bite until the venom is played out—but with his recklessness the chances are one hundred to one against him. I have no regrets; after what he did to me, he deserves this and more.

June 30, 1930—Hurrah! The first step worked! Just heard casually from Dyson of Columbia that Moore had received some new blue-winged flies from Africa, and that he is badly puzzled over them! No word of any bite—but if I know Moore's slipshod ways as I think I do, there'll be one before long!

August 27, 1930—Letter from Morton in Cambridge. He says Moore writes of feeling very run-down, and tells of an insect bite on the back of his neck—from a curious new specimen that he received about the middle of June. Have I succeeded? Apparently Moore doesn't connect the bite with his weakness. If this is the real stuff, then Moore was bitten well within the insect's period of infectivity.

Sept. 12, 1930—Victory! Another line from Dyson says that Moore is really in an alarming shape. He now traces his illness to the bite, which he received around noon on June 19, and is quite bewildered about the identity of the insect. Is trying to get in touch with the "Nevil Wayland-Hall" who sent him the shipment. Of the hundred-odd that I sent, about twenty-five seem to have reached him alive. Some escaped at the time of the bite, but several larvae have appeared from eggs laid since the time of mailing. He is, Dyson says, carefully incubating these larvae. When they mature I suppose he'll identify the tsetse-*palpalis* hybridisation—but that won't do him much good now. He'll wonder, though, why the blue wings aren't transmitted by heredity!

Nov. 8, 1930—Letters from half a dozen friends tell of Moore's serious illness. Dyson's came today. He says Moore is utterly at sea about the hybrids that came from the larvae and is beginning to think that the parents got their blue wings in some artificial way. Has to stay in bed most of the time now. No mention of using tryparsamide.

Feb. 13, 1931—Not so good! Moore is sinking, and seems to know no remedy, but I think he suspects me. Had a very chilly letter from Morton last month, which told nothing of Moore; and now Dyson writes—also rather constrainedly—that Moore is forming theories about the whole matter. He's been making a search for "Wayland-Hall" by telegraph—at London, Ukala, Nairobi, Mombasa, and other places—and of course finds nothing. I judge that he's told Dyson whom he suspects, but that Dyson doesn't believe it yet. Fear Morton does believe it.

I see that I'd better lay plans for getting out of here and effacing my identity for good. What an end to a career that started out so well! More of Moore's work—but this time he's paying for it in advance! Believe I'll go back to South Africa—and meanwhile will quietly deposit funds there to the credit of my new self—"Frederick Nasmyth Mason of Toronto, Canada, broker in mining properties". Will establish a new signature for identification. If I never have to take the step, I can easily re-transfer the funds to my present self.

Aug. 15, 1931—Half a year gone, and still suspense. Dyson and Morton—as well as several other friends—seem to have stopped writing me. Dr. James of San Francisco hears from Moore's friends now and then, and says Moore is in an almost continuous coma. He hasn't been able to walk since May. As long as he could talk he complained of being cold. Now he can't talk, though it is thought he still has glimmers of consciousness. His breathing is short and quick, and can be heard some distance away. No question but that *Trypanosoma gambiense* is feeding on him—but he holds out better than the niggers around here. Three months and eight days finished Batta, and here Moore is alive over a year after his biting. Heard rumours last month of an intensive search around Ukala for "Wayland-Hall". Don't think I need to worry yet, though, for there's absolutely nothing in existence to link me with this business.

Oct. 7, 1931—It's over at last! News in the *Mombasa Gazette*. Moore died September 20 after a series of trembling fits and with a temperature vastly below normal. So much for that! I said I'd get him, and I did! The paper had a three-column report of his long illness and death, and of the futile search for "Wayland-Hall". Obviously, Moore was a bigger character in Africa than I had realised. The insect that bit him has now been fully identified from the surviving specimens and developed larvae, and the wing-staining is also detected. It is universally realised that the flies were prepared and shipped with intent to kill. Moore, it appears, communicated certain suspicions to Dyson, but the latter—and the police—are maintaining secrecy because of absence of proof. All of Moore's enemies are being looked up, and the Associated Press hints that "an investigation, possibly involving an eminent physician now abroad, will follow".

One thing at the very end of the report—undoubtedly, the cheap romancing of a yellow journalist—gives me a curious shudder in view of the legends of the blacks and the way the fly happened to go wild when Batta died. It seems that an odd incident occurred on the night of Moore's death; Dyson having been aroused by the buzzing of a blue-winged fly—which immediately flew out the window—just before the nurse telephoned the death news from Moore's home, miles away in Brooklyn.

But what concerns me most is the African end of the matter. People at Ukala remember the bearded stranger who typed the letter and sent the package, and the constabulary are combing the country for any blacks who may have carried him. I didn't use many, but if officers question the Ubandes who took me through N'Kini jungle belt I'll have more to explain than I like. It looks as if the time has come for me to vanish; so tomorrow I believe I'll resign and prepare to start for parts unknown.

Nov. 9, 1931—Hard work getting my resignation acted on, but release came today. I didn't want to aggravate suspicion by decamping outright. Last week I heard from James about Moore's death—but nothing more than is in the papers. Those around him in New York seem rather reticent about details, though they all talk about a searching investigation. No word from any of my friends in the East. Moore must have spread some dangerous suspicions around before he lost consciousness—but there isn't an iota of proof he could have adduced.

Still, I am taking no chances. On Thursday I shall start for Mombasa, and when there will take a steamer down the coast to Durban. After that I shall drop from sight—but soon afterward the mining properties' broker Frederick Nasmyth Mason, from Toronto, will turn up in Johannesburg.

Let this be the end of my journal. If in the end I am not suspected, it will serve its original purpose after my death and reveal what would otherwise not be known. If, on the other hand, these suspicions do materialise and persist, it will confirm and clarify the vague charges, and fill in many important and puzzling gaps. Of course, if danger comes my way I shall have to destroy it.

Well, Moore is dead—as he amply deserves to be. Now Dr. Thomas Slauenwite is dead, too. And when the body formerly belonging to Thomas Slauenwite is dead, the public may have this record.

II.

Jan. 15, 1932—A new year—and a reluctant reopening of this journal. This time I am writing solely to relieve my mind, for it would be absurd to fancy that the case is not definitely closed. I am

settled in the Vaal Hotel, Johannesburg, under my new name, and
no one has so far challenged my identity. Have had some in-
conclusive business talks to keep up my part as a mine broker, and
believe I may actually work myself into that business. Later I shall
go to Toronto and plant a few evidences for my fictitious past.

But what is bothering me is an insect that invaded my room
around noon today. Of course I have had all sorts of nightmares
about blue flies of late, but those were only to be expected in view
of my prevailing nervous strain. This thing, however, was a waking
actuality, and I am utterly at a loss to account for it. It buzzed
around my bookshelf for fully a quarter of an hour, and eluded
every attempt to catch or kill it. The queerest thing was its colour
and aspect—for it had blue wings and was in every way a duplicate
of my hybrid envoys of death. How it could possibly be one of
these, in fact, I certainly don't know. I disposed of all the hybrids—
stained and unstained—that I didn't send to Moore, and can't recall
any instance of escape.

Can this be wholly an hallucination? Or could any of the specimens that escaped in Brooklyn when Moore was bitten have found
their way back to Africa? There was that absurd story of the blue
fly that waked Dyson when Moore died—but after all, the survival
and return of some of the things is not impossible. It is perfectly
plausible that the blue should stick to their wings, too, for the pigment I devised was almost as good as tattooing for permanence. By
elimination, that would seem to be the only rational explanation
for this thing; though it is very curious that the fellow has come as
far south as this. Possibly it's some hereditary homing instinct in-
herent in the tsetse strain. After all, that side of him belongs to
South Africa.

I must be on my guard against a bite. Of course the original
venom—if this is actually one of the flies that escaped from
Moore—was worn out ages ago; but the fellow must have fed as he
flew back from America, and he may well have come through Central Africa and picked up a fresh infectivity. Indeed, that's more
probable than not; for the *palpalis* half of his heredity would
naturally take him back to Uganda, and all the trypanosomiasis
germs. I still have some of the tryparsamide left—I couldn't bear to
destroy my medicine case, incriminating though it may be—but
since reading up on the subject I am not so sure about the drug's action as I was. It gives one a fighting chance—certainly it saved
Gamba—but there's always a large probability of failure.

It's devilish queer that this fly should have happened to come into my room—of all places in the wide expanse of Africa! Seems to strain coincidence to the breaking-point. I suppose that if it comes again, I shall certainly kill it. I'm surprised that it escaped me today, for ordinarily these fellows are extremely stupid and easy to catch. Can it be a pure illusion after all? Certainly the heat is getting me of late as it never did before—even up around Uganda.

Jan. 16—Am I going insane? The fly came again this noon, and acted so anomalously that I can't make head or tail of it. Only delusion on my part could account for what that buzzing pest seemed to do. It appeared from nowhere, and went straight to my bookshelf —circling again and again to front a copy of Moore's *Diptera of Central and Southern Africa*. Now and then it would light on top or back of the volume, and occasionally it would dart forward toward me and retreat before I could strike at it with a folded paper. Such cunning is unheard of among the notoriously stupid African diptera. For nearly half an hour I tried to get the cursed thing, but at last it darted out the window through a hole in the screen that I hadn't noticed. At times I fancied it deliberately mocked me by coming within reach of my weapon and then skilfully sidestepping as I struck out. I must keep a tight hold of my consciousness.

Jan. 17—Either I am mad or the world is in the grip of some sudden suspension of the laws of probability as we know them. That damnable fly came in from somewhere just before noon and commenced buzzing around the copy of Moore's *Diptera* on my shelf. Again I tried to catch it, and again yesterday's experience was repeated. Finally the pest made for the open inkwell on my table and dipped itself in—just the legs and thorax, keeping its wings clear. Then it sailed up to the ceiling and lit—beginning to crawl around in a curved patch and leaving a trail of ink. After a time it hopped a bit and made a single ink spot unconnected with the trail—then it dropped squarely in front of my face, and buzzed out of sight before I could get it.

Something about this whole business struck me as monstrously sinister and abnormal—more so than I could explain to myself. When I looked at the ink-trail on the ceiling from different angles, it seemed more and more familiar to me, and it dawned on me suddenly that it formed an absolutely perfect question-mark. What device could be more malignly appropriate? It is a wonder that I did not faint. So far the hotel attendants have not noticed it. Have not seen the fly this afternoon and evening, but am keeping my inkwell securely closed. I think my extermination of Moore must be preying on me, and giving me morbid hallucinations. Perhaps there is no fly at all.

Jan. 18—Into what strange hell of living nightmare am I plunged? What occurred today is something which could not normally happen—*and yet an hotel attendant has seen the marks on the ceiling and concedes their reality.* About eleven o'clock this morning, as I was writing on a manuscript, something darted down to the inkwell for a second and flashed aloft again before I could see what it was. Looking up, I saw that hellish fly on the ceiling as it had been before—crawling along and tracing another trail of curves and turns. There was nothing I could do, but I folded a newspaper in readiness to get the creature if it should fly near enough. When it had made several turns on the ceiling it flew into a dark corner and disappeared, and as I looked upward at the doubly defaced plastering I saw that the new ink-trail was that of a huge and unmistakable figure 5!

For a time I was almost unconscious from a wave of nameless menace for which I could not fully account. Then I summoned up my resolution and took an active step. Going out to a chemist's shop I purchased some gum and other things necessary for preparing a sticky trap—also a duplicate inkwell. Returning to my room, I filled the new inkwell with the sticky mixture and set it where the old one had been, leaving it open. Then I tried to concentrate my mind on some reading. About three o'clock I heard the accursed insect again, and saw it circling around the new inkwell. It descended to the sticky surface but did not touch it, and afterward sailed straight toward me—retreating before I could hit it. Then it went to the bookshelf and circled around Moore's treatise. There is something profound and diabolic about the way the intruder hovers near that book.

The worst part was the last. Leaving Moore's book, the insect flew over to the open window and began beating itself rhythmically against the wire screen. There would be a series of beats and then a series of equal length and another pause, and so on. Something about this performance held me motionless for a couple of moments, but after that I went over to the window and tried to kill the noxious thing. As usual, no use. It merely flew across the room to a lamp and began beating the same tattoo on the stiff cardboard shade. I felt a vague desperation, and proceeded to shut all the doors as well as the window whose screen had the imperceptible hole. It seemed very necessary to kill this persistent being, whose hounding was rapidly unseating my mind. Then, unconsciously counting, I began to notice that each of its series of beatings contained just *five* strokes.

Five—the same number that the thing had traced in ink on the ceiling in the morning! Could there be any conceivable connexion? The notion was maniacal, for that would argue a human intellect and a knowledge of written figures in the hybrid fly. A human intellect—did not that take one back to the most primitive legends of the Uganda blacks? And yet there was that infernal cleverness in eluding me as contrasted with the normal stupidity of the breed. As I laid aside my folded paper and sat down in growing horror, the insect buzzed aloft and disappeared through a hole in the ceiling where the radiator pipe went to the room above.

The departure did not soothe me, for my mind had started on a train of wild and terrible reflections. If this fly had a human intelligence, where did that intelligence come from? Was there any truth in the native notion that these creatures acquire the personality of their victims after the latter's death? If so, whose personality did this fly bear? I had reasoned out that it must be one of those which escaped from Moore at the time he was bitten. *Was this the envoy of death which had bitten Moore? If so, what did it want with me?* What did it want with me anyway? In a cold perspiration I remembered the actions of the fly that had bitten Batta when Batta died. Had its own personality been displaced by that of its dead victim? Then there was that sensational news account of the fly that waked Dyson when Moore died. As for that fly that was hounding me— could it be that a vindictive human personality drove it on? How it hovered around Moore's book!—I refused to think any farther than that. All at once I began to feel sure that the creature was indeed infected, and in the most virulent way. With a malign deliberation so evident in every act, it must surely have charged itself on purpose with the deadliest bacilli in all Africa. My mind, thoroughly shaken, was now taking the thing's human qualities for granted.

I now telephoned the clerk and asked for a man to stop up the radiator pipehole and other possible chinks in my room. I spoke of being tormented by flies, and he seemed to be quite sympathetic. When the man came, I shewed him the ink-marks on the ceiling, which he recognised without difficulty. So they are real! The resemblance to a question-mark and a figure 5 puzzled and fascinated him. In the end he stopped up all the holes he could find, and mended the window-screen, so that I can now keep both windows open. He evidently thought me a bit eccentric, especially since no insects were in sight while he was here. But I am past minding that.

So far the fly has not appeared this evening. God knows what it is, what it wants, or what will become of me!

Jan. 19—I am utterly engulfed in horror. *The thing has touched me.* Something monstrous and daemoniac is at work around me, and I am a helpless victim. In the morning, when I returned from breakfast, that winged fiend from hell brushed into the room over my head, and began beating itself against the window-screen as it did yesterday. This time, though, each series of beats contained only *four* strokes. I rushed to the window and tried to catch it, but it escaped as usual and flew over to Moore's treatise, where it buzzed around mockingly. Its vocal equipment is limited, but I noticed that its spells of buzzing came in groups of four.

By this time I was certainly mad, for I called out to it, *"Moore, Moore, for God's sake, what do you want?"* When I did so, the creature suddenly ceased its circling, flew toward me, and made a low, graceful dip in the air, somehow suggestive of a bow. Then it flew back to the book. At least, I seemed to see it do all this—though I am trusting my senses no longer.

And then the worst thing happened. I had left my door open, hoping the monster would leave if I could not catch it; but about 11:30 I shut the door, concluding it had gone. Then I settled down to read. Just at noon I felt a tickling on the back of my neck, but when I put my hand up nothing was there. In a moment I felt the tickling again—and before I could move, that nameless spawn of hell sailed into view from behind, did another of those mocking, graceful dips in the air, and flew out through the keyhole—which I had never dreamed was large enough to allow its passage.

That the thing had touched me, I could not doubt. It had touched me without injuring me—and then I remembered in a sudden cold fright that Moore had been bitten *on the back of the neck at noon.* No invasion since then—but I have stuffed all the keyholes with paper and shall have a folded paper ready for use whenever I open the door to leave or enter.

Jan. 20—I cannot yet believe fully in the supernatural, yet I fear none the less that I am lost. The business is too much for me. Just before noon today that devil appeared *outside* the window and repeated its beating operations; but this time in series of *three.* When I went to the window it flew off out of sight. I still have resolution enough to take one more defensive step. Removing both window-screens, I coated them with my sticky preparation—the one I used in the inkwell—outside and inside, and set them back in place. If that creature attempts another tattoo, it will be its last!

Rest of the day in peace. Can I weather this experience without becoming a maniac?

Jan. 21—On board train for Bloemfontein.

I am routed. The thing is winning. It has a diabolic intelligence against which all my devices are powerless. It appeared outside the window this morning, *but did not touch the sticky screen.* Instead, it sheered off without lighting and began buzzing around in circles —*two at a time,* followed by a pause in the air. After several of these performances it flew off out of sight over the roofs of the city. My nerves are just about at the breaking-point, for these *suggestions of numbers* are capable of a hideous interpretation. Monday the thing dwelt on the figure *five;* Tuesday it was *four;* Wednesday it was *three;* and now today it is *two. Five, four, three, two*—what can this be save some monstrous and unthinkable *counting-off of days?* For what purpose, only the evil powers of the universe can know. I spent all the afternoon packing and arranging about my trunks, and now I have taken the night express for Bloemfontein. Flight may be useless, but what else can one do?

Jan. 22—Settled at the Orange Hotel, Bloemfontein—a comfortable and excellent place—but the horror followed me. I had shut all the doors and windows, stopped all the keyholes, looked for any possible chinks, and pulled down all the shades—but just before noon I heard a dull tap on one of the window-screens. I waited— and after a long pause another tap came. A second pause, and still another single tap. Raising the shade, I saw that accursed fly, as I had expected. It described one large, slow circle in the air, and then flew out of sight. I was left as weak as a rag, and had to rest on the couch. *One!* This was clearly the burden of the monster's present message. *One* tap, *one* circle. Did this mean *one* more day for me before some unthinkable doom? Ought I to flee again, or entrench myself here by sealing up the room?

After an hour's rest I felt able to act, and ordered a large reserve supply of canned and packaged food—also linen and towels—sent in. Tomorrow I shall not under any circumstances open any crevice of door or window. When the food and linen came the black looked at me queerly, but I no longer care how eccentric—or insane —I may appear. I am hounded by powers worse than the ridicule of mankind. Having received my supplies, I went over every square millimeter of the walls, and stopped up every microscopic opening I could find. At last I feel able to get real sleep.

[*Handwriting here becomes irregular, nervous, and very difficult to decipher.*]

Jan. 23—It is just before noon, and I feel that something very terrible is about to happen. Didn't sleep as late as I expected, even though I got almost no sleep on the train the night before. Up early, and have had trouble getting concentrated on anything—reading or writing. That slow, deliberate counting-off of days is too much for me. I don't know which has gone wild—Nature or my head. Until about eleven I did very little except walk up and down the room.

Then I heard a rustle among the food packages brought in yesterday, and that daemoniac fly crawled out before my eyes. I grabbed something flat and made passes at the thing despite my panic fear, but with no more effect than usual. As I advanced, that blue-winged horror retreated as usual to the table where I had piled my books, and lit for a second on Moore's *Diptera of Central and Southern Africa*. Then as I followed, it flew over to the mantel clock and lit on the dial near the figure 12. Before I could think up another move it had begun to crawl around the dial very slowly and deliberately—in the direction of the hands. It passed under the minute hand, curved down and up, passed under the hour hand, and finally came to a stop exactly at the figure 12. As it hovered there it fluttered its wings with a buzzing noise.

Is this a portent of some sort? I am getting as superstitious as the blacks. The hour is now a little after eleven. Is twelve the end? I have just one last resort, brought to my mind through utter desperation. Wish I had thought of it before. Recalling that my medicine case contains both of the substances necessary to generate chlorine gas, I have resolved to fill the room with that lethal vapour—asphyxiating the fly while protecting myself with an ammonia-sealed handkerchief tied over my face. Fortunately I have a good supply of ammonia. This crude mask will probably neutralise the acrid chlorine fumes till the insect is dead—or at least helpless enough to crush. But I must be quick. How can I be sure that the thing will not suddenly dart for me before my preparations are complete? I ought not to be stopping to write in this journal.

Later—Both chemicals—hydrochloric acid and manganese dioxide—on the table all ready to mix. I've tied the handkerchief over my nose and mouth, and have a bottle of ammonia ready to keep it soaked until the chlorine is gone. Have battened down both windows. But I don't like the actions of that hybrid daemon. It stays on the clock, but is very slowly crawling around backward from the 12 mark to meet the gradually advancing minute-hand.

Is this to be my last entry in this journal? It would be useless to try to deny what I suspect. Too often a grain of incredible truth lurks behind the wildest and most fantastic of legends. Is the personality of Henry Moore trying to get at me through this bluewinged devil? Is this the fly that bit him, and that in consequence absorbed his consciousness when he died? If so, and if it bites me, will my own personality displace Moore's and enter that buzzing body when I die of the bite later on? Perhaps, though, I need not die even if it gets me. There is always a chance with tryparsamide. And I regret nothing. Moore had to die, be the outcome what it will.

Slightly later.

The fly has paused on the clock-dial near the 45-minute mark. It is now 11:30. I am saturating the handkerchief over my face with ammonia, and keeping the bottle handy for further applications. This will be the final entry before I mix the acid and manganese and liberate the chlorine. I ought not to be losing time, but it steadies me to get things down on paper. But for this record, I'd have lost all my reason long ago. The fly seems to be getting restless, and the minute-hand is approaching it. Now for the chlorine. . . .

[End of the journal]

On Sunday, Jan. 24, 1932, after repeated knocking had failed to gain any response from the eccentric man in Room 303 of the Orange Hotel, a black attendant entered with a pass key and at once fled shrieking downstairs to tell the clerk what he had found. The clerk, after notifying the police, summoned the manager; and the latter accompanied Constable De Witt, Coroner Bogaert, and Dr. Van Keulen to the fatal room.

The occupant lay dead on the floor—his face upward, and bound with a handkerchief which smelled strongly of ammonia. Under this covering the features shewed an expression of stark, utter fear which transmitted itself to the observers. On the back of the neck Dr. Van Keulen found a virulent insect bite—dark red, with a purple ring around it—which suggested a tsetse-fly or something less innocuous. An examination indicated that death must be due to heart-failure induced by sheer fright rather than to the bite—though a subsequent autopsy indicated that the germ of trypanosomiasis had been introduced into the system.

On the table were several objects—a worn leather blank-book containing the journal just described, a pen, writing-pad, and open inkwell, a doctor's medicine case with the initials "T. S." marked in gold, bottles of ammonia and hydrochloric acid, and a tumbler about a quarter full of black manganese dioxide. The ammonia bottle demanded a second look because something besides the fluid seemed to be in it. Looking closer, Coroner Bogaert saw that the alien occupant was a fly.

It seemed to be some sort of hybrid with vague tsetse affiliations, but its wings—shewing faintly blue despite the action of the strong ammonia—were a complete puzzle. Something about it waked a faint memory of newspaper reading in Dr. Van Keulen—a memory which the journal was soon to confirm. Its lower parts seemed to have been stained with ink, so thoroughly that even the ammonia had not bleached them. Possibly it had fallen at one time into the inkwell, though the wings were untouched. But how had it managed to fall into the narrow-necked ammonia bottle? It was as if the creature had deliberately crawled in and committed suicide!

But the strangest thing of all was what Constable De Witt noticed on the smooth white ceiling overhead as his eyes roved about curiously. At his cry the other three followed his gaze—even Dr. Van Keulen, who had for some time been thumbing through the worn leather book with an expression of mixed horror, fascination, and incredulity. The thing on the ceiling was a series of shaky, straggling ink-tracks, such as might have been made by the crawling of some ink-drenched insect. At once everyone thought of the stains on the fly so oddly found in the ammonia bottle.

But these were no ordinary ink-tracks. Even a first glance revealed something hauntingly familiar about them, and closer inspection brought gasps of startled wonder from all four observers. Coroner Bogaert instinctively looked around the room to see if there were any conceivable instrument or arrangement of piled-up furniture which could make it possible for those straggling marks to have been drawn by human agency. Finding nothing of the sort, he resumed his curious and almost awestruck upward glance.

For beyond a doubt these inky smudges formed definite letters of the alphabet—letters coherently arranged in English words. The doctor was the first to make them out clearly, and the others listened breathlessly as he recited the insane-sounding message so incredibly scrawled in a place no human hand could reach:

"SEE MY JOURNAL—*IT* GOT ME FIRST—I DIED—THEN I SAW I WAS IN *IT*—THE BLACKS ARE RIGHT—STRANGE POWERS IN NATURE—NOW I WILL DROWN WHAT IS LEFT—"

Presently, amidst the puzzled hush that followed, Dr. Van Keulen commenced reading aloud from the worn leather journal.

Hazel Heald

The Horror in the Burying-Ground

When the state highway to Rutland is closed, travellers are forced
to take the Stillwater road past Swamp Hollow. The scenery is
superb in places, yet somehow the route has been unpopular for
years. There is something depressing about it, especially near Stillwater itself. Motorists feel subtly uncomfortable about the tightly
shuttered farmhouse on the knoll just north of the village, and
about the white-bearded half-wit who haunts the old burying-
ground on the south, apparently talking to the occupants of some
of the graves.

Not much is left of Stillwater, now. The soil is played out, and
most of the people have drifted to the towns across the distant river
or to the city beyond the distant hills. The steeple of the old white
church has fallen down, and half of the twenty-odd straggling
houses are empty and in various stages of decay. Normal life is
found only around Peck's general store and filling-station, and it is
here that the curious stop now and then to ask about the shuttered
house and the idiot who mutters to the dead.

Most of the questioners come away with a touch of distaste and
disquiet. They find the shabby loungers oddly unpleasant and full
of unnamed hints in speaking of the long-past events brought up.
There is a menacing, portentous quality in the tones which they use

to describe very ordinary events—a seemingly unjustified tendency to assume a furtive, suggestive, confidential air, and to fall into awesome whispers at certain points—which insidiously disturbs the listener. Old Yankees often talk like that; but in this case the melancholy aspect of the half-mouldering village, and the dismal nature of the story unfolded, give these gloomy, secretive mannerisms an added significance. One feels profoundly the quintessential horror that lurks behind the isolated Puritan and his strange repressions— feels it, and longs to escape precipitately into clearer air.

The loungers whisper impressively that the shuttered house is that of old Miss Sprague—Sophie Sprague, whose brother Tom was buried on the seventeenth of June, back in '86. Sophie was never the same after that funeral—that and the other thing which happened the same day—and in the end she took to staying in all the time. Won't even be seen now, but leaves notes under the back-door mat and has her things brought from the store by Ned Peck's boy. Afraid of something—the old Swamp Hollow burying-ground most of all. Never could be dragged near there since her brother— and the other one—were laid away. Not much wonder, though, seeing the way crazy Johnny Dow rants. He hangs around the burying-ground all day and sometimes at night, and claims he talks with Tom—and the other. Then he marches by Sophie's house and shouts things at her—that's why she began to keep the shutters closed. He says things are coming from somewhere to get her some-time. Ought to be stopped, but one can't be too hard on poor Johnny. Besides, Steve Barbour always had his opinions.

Johnny does his talking to two of the graves. One of them is Tom Sprague's. The other, at the opposite end of the graveyard, is that of Henry Thorndike, who was buried on the same day. Henry was the village undertaker—the only one in miles—and never liked around Stillwater. A city fellow from Rutland—been to college and full of book learning. Read queer things nobody else ever heard of, and mixed chemicals for no good purpose. Always trying to invent something new—some new-fangled embalming-fluid or some foolish kind of medicine. Some folks said he had tried to be a doctor but failed in his studies and took to the next best profession. Of course, there wasn't much undertaking to do in a place like Stillwater, but Henry farmed on the side.

Mean, morbid disposition—and a secret drinker if you could judge by the empty bottles in his rubbish heap. No wonder Tom Sprague hated him and blackballed him from the Masonic lodge, and warned him off when he tried to make up to Sophie. The way he experimented on animals was against Nature and Scripture. Who could forget the state that collie dog was found in, or what happened to old Mrs. Akeley's cat? Then there was the matter of Deacon Leavitt's calf, when Tom had led a band of the village boys to demand an accounting. The curious thing was that the calf came alive after all in the end, though Tom had found it as stiff as a poker. Some said the joke was on Tom, but Thorndike probably thought otherwise, since he had gone down under his enemy's fist before the mistake was discovered.

Tom, of course, was half drunk at the time. He was a vicious brute at best, and kept his poor sister half cowed with threats. That's probably why she is such a fear-racked creature still. There were only the two of them, and Tom would never let her leave because that meant splitting the property. Most of the fellows were too afraid of him to shine up to Sophie—he stood six feet one in his stockings—but Henry Thorndike was a sly cuss who had ways of doing things behind folk's backs. He wasn't much to look at, but Sophie never discouraged him any. Mean and ugly as he was, she'd have been glad if anybody could have freed her from her brother. She may not have stopped to wonder how she could get clear of him after he got her clear of Tom.

Well, that was the way things stood in June of '86. Up to this point, the whispers of the loungers at Peck's store are not so unbearably portentous; but as they continue, the element of secretiveness and malign tension grows. Tom Sprague, it appears, used to go to Rutland on periodic sprees, his absences being Henry Thorndike's great opportunities. He was always in bad shape when he got back, and old Dr. Pratt, deaf and half blind though he was, used to warn him about his heart, and about the danger of delirium tremens. Folks could always tell by the shouting and cursing when he was home again.

It was on the ninth of June—on a Wednesday, the day after young Joshua Goodenough finished building his new-fangled silo—that Tom started out on his last and longest spree. He came back the next Tuesday morning and folks at the store saw him lashing his bay stallion the way he did when whiskey had a hold of him. Then there came shouts and shrieks and oaths from the Sprague house, and the first thing anybody knew Sophie was running over to old Dr. Pratt's at top speed.

The doctor found Thorndike at Sprague's when he got there, and

Tom was on the bed in his room, with eyes staring and foam around his mouth. Old Pratt fumbled around and gave the usual tests, then shook his head solemnly and told Sophie she had suffered a great bereavement—that her nearest and dearest had passed through the pearly gates to a better land, just as everybody knew he would if he didn't let up on his drinking.

Sophie kind of sniffled, the loungers whisper, but didn't seem to take on much. Thorndike didn't do anything but smile—perhaps at the ironic fact that he, always an enemy, was now the only person who could be of any use to Thomas Sprague. He shouted something in old Dr. Pratt's half-good ear about the need of having the funeral early on account of Tom's condition. Drunks like that were always doubtful subjects, and any extra delay—with merely rural facilities—would entail consequences, visual and otherwise, hardly acceptable to the deceased's loving mourners. The doctor had muttered that Tom's alcoholic career ought to have embalmed him pretty well in advance, but Thorndike assured him to the contrary, at the same time boasting of his own skill, and of the superior methods he had devised through his experiments.

It is here that the whispers of the loungers grow acutely disturbing. Up to this point the story is usually told by Ezra Davenport, or Luther Fry, if Ezra is laid up with chilblains, as he is apt to be in winter; but from there on old Calvin Wheeler takes up the thread, and his voice has a damnably insidious way of suggesting hidden horror. If Johnny Dow happens to be passing by there is always a pause, for Stillwater does not like to have Johnny talk too much with strangers.

Calvin edges close to the traveller and sometimes seizes a coat-lapel with his gnarled, mottled hand while he half shuts his watery blue eyes.

"Well, sir," he whispers, "Henry he went home an' got his undertaker's fixin's—crazy Johnny Dow lugged most of 'em, for he was always doin' chores for Henry—an' says as Doc Pratt an' crazy Johnny should help lay out the body. Doc always did say as how he thought Henry talked too much—a-boastin' what a fine workman he was, an' how lucky it was that Stillwater had a reg'lar undertaker instead of buryin' folks jest as they was, like they do over to Whitby.

"'Suppose,' says he, 'some fellow was to be took with some of them paralysin' cramps like you read about. How'd a body like it when they lowered him down and begun shovelin' the dirt back?

How'd he like it when he was chokin' down there under the new headstone, scratchin' an' tearin' if he chanced to get back the power, but all the time knowin' it wasn't no use? No, sir, I tell you it's a blessin' Stillwater's got a smart doctor as knows when a man's dead and when he ain't, and a trained undertaker who can fix a corpse so he'll stay put without no trouble.'

"That was the way Henry went on talkin', most like he was talkin' to poor Tom's remains; and old Doc Pratt he didn't like what he was able to catch of it, even though Henry did call him a smart doctor. Crazy Johnny kept watchin' of the corpse, and it didn't make it none too pleasant the way he'd slobber about things like, 'He ain't cold, Doc,' or 'I see his eyelids move,' or 'There's a hole in his arm jest like the ones I git when Henry gives me a syringe full of what makes me feel good.' Thorndike shut him up on that, though we all knowed he'd been givin' poor Johnny drugs. It's a wonder the poor fellow ever got clear of the habit.

"But the worst thing, accordin' to the doctor, was the way the body jerked up when Henry begun to shoot it full of embalmin'-fluid. He'd been boastin' about what a fine new formula he'd got practicin' on cats and dogs, when all of a sudden Tom's corpse began to double up like it was alive and fixin' to wrassle. Land of Goshen, but Doc says he was scared stiff, though he knowed the way corpses act when the muscles begin to stiffen. Well, sir, the long and short of it is, that the corpse sat up an' grabbed a holt of Thorndike's syringe so that it got stuck in Henry hisself, an' give him as neat a dose of his own embalmin'-fluid as you'd wish to see. That got Henry pretty scared, though he yanked the point out and managed to get the body down again and shot full of the fluid. He kept measurin' more of the stuff out as though he wanted to be sure there was enough, and kept reassurin' himself as not much had got into him, but crazy Johnny begun singin' out, 'That's what you give Lige Hopkins's dog when it got all dead an' stiff an' then waked up agin. Now you're a-going to get dead an' stiff like Tom Sprague be! Remember it don't set to work till after a long spell if you don't get much.'

"Sophie, she was downstairs with some of the neighbours—my wife Matildy, she that's dead an' gone this thirty year, was one of them. They were all tryin' to find out whether Thorndike was over when Tom came home, and whether findin' him there was what set poor Tom off. I may as well say as some folks thought it mighty funny that Sophie didn't carry on more, nor mind the way Thorndike had smiled. Not as anybody was hintin' that Henry helped Tom off with some of his queer cooked-up fluids and syringes, or that Sophie would keep still if she thought so—but you know how folks will guess behind a body's back. We all knowed the nigh crazy way Thorndike had hated Tom—not without reason, at that—and Emily Barbour says to my Matildy as how Henry was lucky to have ol' Doc Pratt right on the spot with a death certificate as didn't leave no doubt for nobody."

When old Calvin gets to this point he usually begins to mumble indistinguishably in his straggling, dirty white beard. Most listeners try to edge away from him, and he seldom appears to heed the gesture. It is generally Fred Peck, who was a very small boy at the time of the events, who continues the tale.

Thomas Sprague's funeral was held on Thursday, June 17th, only two days after his death. Such haste was thought almost indecent in remote and inaccessible Stillwater, where long distances had to be covered by those who came, but Thorndike had insisted that the peculiar condition of the deceased demanded it. The undertaker had seemed rather nervous since preparing the body, and could be seen frequently feeling his pulse. Old Dr. Pratt thought he must be worrying about the accidental dose of embalming-fluid. Naturally, the story of the "laying out" had spread, so that a double zest animated the mourners who assembled to glut their curiosity and morbid interest.

Thorndike, though he was obviously upset, seemed intent on doing his professional duty in magnificent style. Sophie and others who saw the body were most startled by its utter lifelikeness, and the mortuary virtuoso made doubly sure of his job by repeating certain injections at stated intervals. He almost wrung a sort of reluctant admiration from the townsfolk and visitors, though he tended to spoil that impression by his boastful and tasteless talk. Whenever he administered to his silent charge he would repeat that eternal rambling about the good luck of having a first-class undertaker. What—he would say as if directly addressing the body—if Tom had had one of those careless fellows who bury their subjects alive? The way he harped on the horrors of premature burial was truly barbarous and sickening.

Services were held in the stuffy best room—opened for the first time since Mrs. Sprague died. The tuneless little parlour organ groaned disconsolately, and the coffin, supported on trestles near the hall door, was covered with sickly-smelling flowers. It was obvious that a record-breaking crowd was assembling from far and near, and Sophie endeavoured to look properly grief-stricken for their benefit. At unguarded moments she seemed both puzzled and uneasy, dividing her scrutiny between the feverish-looking undertaker and the life-like body of her brother. A slow disgust at Thorndike seemed to be brewing within her, and neighbours whispered freely that she would soon send him about his business now that Tom was out of the way—that is, if she could, for such a slick customer was sometimes hard to deal with. But with her money and remaining looks she might be able to get another fellow, and he'd probably take care of Henry well enough.

As the organ wheezed into *Beautiful Isle of Somewhere* the Methodist church choir added their lugubrious voices to the gruesome cacophony, and everyone looked piously at Deacon Leavitt—everyone, that is, except crazy Johnny Dow, who kept his eyes glued to the still form beneath the glass of the coffin. He was muttering softly to himself.

Stephen Barbour—from the next farm—was the only one who noticed Johnny. He shivered as he saw that the idiot was talking directly to the corpse, and even making foolish signs with his fingers as if to taunt the sleeper beneath the plate glass. Tom, he reflected, had kicked poor Johnny around on more than one occasion, though probably not without provocation. Something about this whole event was getting on Stephen's nerves. There was a suppressed tension and brooding abnormality in the air for which he could not account. Johnny ought not to have been allowed in the house—and it was curious what an effort Thorndike seemed to be making not to look at the body. Every now and then the undertaker would feel his pulse with an odd air.

The Reverend Silas Atwood droned on in a plaintive monotone about the deceased—about the striking of Death's sword in the midst of this little family, breaking the earthly tie between this loving brother and sister. Several of the neighbours looked furtively at one another from beneath lowered eyelids, while Sophie actually began to sob nervously. Thorndike moved to her side and tried to reassure her, but she seemed to shrink curiously away from him. His motions were distinctly uneasy, and he seemed to feel acutely the abnormal tension permeating the air. Finally, conscious of his duty as master of ceremonies, he stepped forward and announced in a sepulchral voice that the body might be viewed for the last time.

Slowly the friends and neighbours filed past the bier, from which Thorndike roughly dragged crazy Johnny away. Tom seemed to be resting peacefully. That devil had been handsome in his day. A few genuine sobs—and many feigned ones—were heard, though most of the crowd were content to stare curiously and whisper afterward. Steve Barbour lingered long and attentively over the still face, and moved away shaking his head. His wife, Emily, following after him, whispered that Henry Thorndike had better not boast so much about his work, for Tom's eyes had come open. They had been shut when the services began, for she had been up and looked. But they certainly looked natural—not the way one would expect after two days.

When Fred Peck gets this far he usually pauses as if he did not like to continue. The listener, too, tends to feel that something unpleasant is ahead. But Peck reassures his audience with the statement that what happened isn't as bad as folks like to hint. Even Steve never put into words what he may have thought, and crazy Johnny, of course, can't be counted at all.

It was Luella Morse—the nervous old maid who sang in the choir —who seems to have touched things off. She was filing past the coffin like the rest, but stopped to peer a little closer than anyone else except the Barbours had peered. And then, without warning, she gave a shrill scream and fell in a dead faint.

Naturally, the room was at once a chaos of confusion. Old Dr. Pratt elbowed his way to Luella and called for some water to throw in her face, and others surged up to look at her and at the coffin. Johnny Dow began chanting to himself, "He knows, he knows, he kin hear all we're a-sayin' and see all we're a-doin', and they'll bury him that way"—but no one stopped to decipher his mumbling except Steve Barbour.

In a very few moments Luella began to come out of her faint, and could not tell exactly what had startled her. All she could whisper was, "The way he looked—the way he looked." But to other eyes the body seemed exactly the same. It was a gruesome sight, though, with those open eyes and that high colouring.

And then the bewildered crowd noticed something which put both Luella and the body out of their minds for a moment. It was Thorndike—on whom the sudden excitement and jostling crowd seemed to be having a curiously bad effect. He had evidently been knocked down in the general bustle, and was on the floor trying to drag himself to a sitting posture. The expression on his face was terrifying in the extreme, and his eyes were beginning to take on a glazed, fishy expression. He could scarcely speak aloud, but the husky rattle of his throat held an ineffable desperation which was obvious to all.

"Get me home, quick, and let me be. That fluid I got in my arm by mistake . . . heart action . . . this damned excitement . . . too much . . . wait . . . wait . . . don't think I'm dead if I seem to . . . only the fluid—just get me home and wait . . . I'll come to later, don't know how long . . . all the time I'll be conscious and know what's going on . . . don't be deceived. . . ."

As his words trailed off into nothingness old Dr. Pratt reached him and felt his pulse—watching a long time and finally shaking his head. "No use doing anything—he's gone. Heart no good—and that fluid he got in his arm must have been bad stuff. I don't know what it is."

A kind of numbness seemed to fall on all the company. New death in the chamber of death! Only Steve Barbour thought to bring up Thorndike's last choking words. Was he surely dead, when he himself had said he might falsely seem so? Wouldn't it be better to wait a while and see what would happen? And for that matter, what harm would it do if Doc Pratt were to give Tom Sprague another looking over before burial?

Crazy Johnny was moaning, and had flung himself on Thorndike's body like a faithful dog. "Don't ye bury him, don't ye bury him! He ain't dead no more nor Lige Hopkins's dog nor Deacon Leavitt's calf was when he shot 'em full. He's got some stuff he puts into ye to make ye seem like dead when ye ain't! Ye seem like dead but ye know everything what's a-goin' on, and the next day ye come to as good as ever. Don't ye bury him—he'll come to under the earth an' he can't scratch up! He's a good man, an' not like Tom Sprague. Hope to Gawd Tom scratches an' chokes for hours an' hours. . . ."

But no one save Barbour was paying any attention to poor Johnny. Indeed, what Steve himself had said had evidently fallen on deaf ears. Uncertainty was everywhere. Old Doc Pratt was applying final tests and mumbling about death certificate blanks, and unctuous Elder Atwood was suggesting that something be done about a double interment. With Thorndike dead there was no undertaker this side of Rutland, and it would mean a terrible expense if one were to be brought from there, and if Thorndike were not embalmed in this hot June weather—well, one couldn't tell.

And there were no relatives or friends to be critical unless Sophie chose to be—but Sophie was on the other side of the room, staring silently, fixedly, and almost morbidly into her brother's coffin.

Deacon Leavitt tried to restore a semblance of decorum, and had poor Thorndike carried across the hall to the sitting-room, meanwhile sending Zenas Wells and Walter Perkins over to the undertaker's house for a coffin of the right size. The key was in Henry's trousers pocket. Johnny continued to whine and paw at the body, and Elder Atwood busied himself with inquiring about Thorndike's denomination—for Henry had not attended local services. When it was decided that his folks in Rutland—all dead now—had been Baptists, the Reverend Silas decided that Deacon Leavitt had better offer the brief prayer.

It was a gala day for the funeral-fanciers of Stillwater and vicinity. Even Luella had recovered enough to stay. Gossip, murmured and whispered, buzzed busily while a few composing touches were given to Thorndike's cooling, stiffening form. Johnny had been cuffed out of the house, as most agreed he should have been in the first place, but his distant howls were now and then wafted gruesomely in.

When the body was encoffined and laid out beside that of Thomas Sprague, the silent, almost frightening-looking Sophie gazed intently at it as she had gazed at her brother's. She had not uttered a word for a dangerously long time, and the mixed expression on her face was past all describing or interpreting. As the others withdrew to leave her alone with the dead she managed to find a sort of mechanical speech, but no one could make out the words, and she seemed to be talking first to one body and then the other.

And now, with what would seem to an outsider the acme of gruesome unconscious comedy, the whole funeral mummery of the afternoon was listlessly repeated. Again the organ wheezed, again the choir screeched and scraped, again a droning incantation arose, and again the morbidly curious spectators filed past a macabre object—this time a dual array of mortuary repose. Some of the more sensitive people shivered at the whole proceeding, and again Stephen Barbour felt an underlying note of eldritch horror and daemoniac abnormality. God, how life-like both of those corpses were . . . and how in earnest poor Thorndike had been about not wanting to be judged dead . . . and how he hated Tom Sprague . . . but what could one do in the face of common sense—a dead man was a dead man, and there was old Doc Pratt with his years of experience . . . if nobody else bothered, why should one bother oneself? . . . Whatever Tom had got he had probably deserved . . . and if Henry had done anything to him, the score was even now . . . well, Sophie was free at last. . . .

As the peering procession moved at last toward the hall and the outer door, Sophie was alone with the dead once more. Elder Atwood was out in the road talking to the hearse-driver from Lee's livery stable, and Deacon Leavitt was arranging for a double quota of pall-bearers. Luckily the hearse would hold two coffins. No hurry—Ed Plummer and Ethan Stone were going ahead with shovels to dig the second grave. There would be three livery hacks and any number of private rigs in the cavalcade—no use trying to keep the crowd away from the graves.

Then came that frantic scream from the parlour where Sophie and the bodies were. Its suddenness almost paralysed the crowd and brought back the same sensation which had surged up when Luella had screamed and fainted. Steve Barbour and Deacon Leavitt started to go in, but before they could enter the house Sophie was bursting forth, sobbing and gasping about "That face at the window! . . . that face at the window! . . ."

At the same time a wild-eyed figure rounded the corner of the house, removing all mystery from Sophie's dramatic cry. It was, very obviously, the face's owner—poor crazy Johnny, who began to leap up and down, pointing at Sophie and shrieking, "She knows! She knows! I seen it in her face when she looked at 'em and talked to 'em! She knows, and she's a-lettin' 'em go down in the earth to scratch an' claw for air. . . . But they'll talk to her so's she kin hear 'em . . . they'll talk to her, an' appear to her . . . and some day they'll come back an' git her!"

Zenas Wells dragged the shrieking half-wit to a woodshed behind the house and bolted him in as best he could. His screams and poundings could be heard at a distance, but nobody paid him any further attention. The procession was made up, and with Sophie in the first hack it slowly covered the short distance past the village to the Swamp Hollow burying-ground.

Elder Atwood made appropriate remarks as Thomas Sprague was laid to rest, and by the time he was through, Ed and Ethan had finished Thorndike's grave on the other side of the cemetery—to which the crowd presently shifted. Deacon Leavitt then spoke ornamentally, and the lowering process was repeated. People had begun to drift off in knots, and the clatter of receding buggies and carryalls was quite universal, when the shovels began to fly again. As the earth thudded down on the coffin-lids, Thorndike's first, Steve Barbour noticed the queer expressions flitting over Sophie Sprague's face. He couldn't keep track of them all, but behind the rest there seemed to lurk a sort of wry, perverse, half-suppressed look of vague triumph. He shook his head.

Zenas had run back and let crazy Johnny out of the woodshed before Sophie got home, and the poor fellow at once made frantically for the graveyard. He arrived before the shovelmen were through, and while many of the curious mourners were still lingering about. What he shouted into Tom Sprague's partly filled grave, and how he clawed at the loose earth of Thorndike's freshly finished mound across the cemetery, surviving spectators still shudder to recall. Jotham Blake, the constable, had to take him back to the town farm by force, and his screams waked dreadful echoes.

This is where Fred Peck usually leaves off the story. What more, he asks, is there to tell? It was a gloomy tragedy, and one can scarcely wonder that Sophie grew queer after that. That is all one hears if the hour is so late that old Calvin Wheeler has tottered home, but when he is still around he breaks in again with that damnably suggestive and insidious whisper. Sometimes those who hear him dread to pass either the shuttered house or the graveyard afterward, especially after dark.

"Heh, heh . . . Fred was only a little shaver then, and don't remember no more than half of what was goin' on! You want to know why Sophie keeps her house shuttered, and why crazy Johnny still keeps a-talkin' to the dead and a-shoutin' at Sophie's windows? Well, sir, I don't know's I know all there is to know, but I hear what I hear."

Here the old man ejects his cud of tobacco and leans forward to buttonhole the listener.

"It was that same night, mind ye—toward mornin', and just eight hours after them burials—when we heard the first scream from Sophie's house. Woke us all up—Steve and Emily Barbour and me and Matildy goes over hot-footin', all in night gear, and finds Sophie all dressed and dead fainted on the settin'-room floor. Lucky she hadn't locked the door. When we got her to she was shakin' like a leaf, and wouldn't let on by so much as a word what was ailin' her. Matildy and Emily done what they could to quiet her down, but Steve whispered things to me as didn't make me none too easy. Come about an hour when we allowed we'd be goin' home soon, that Sophie she begun to tip her head on one side like she was a-listenin' to somethin'. Then on a sudden she screamed again, and keeled over in another faint.

"Well, sir, I'm tellin' what I'm tellin', and won't do no guessin' like Steve Barbour would a done if he dared. He always was the greatest hand for hintin' things . . . died ten years ago of pneumony. . . .

"What we heard so faint-like was just poor crazy Johnny, of course. 'Taint more than a mile to the buryin'-ground, and he must a got out of the window where they'd locked him up at the town farm—even if Constable Blake says he didn't get out that night. From that day to this he hangs around them graves a-talkin' to the both of them—cussin' and kickin' at Tom's mound, and puttin' posies and things on Henry's. And when he ain't a-doin' that he's hangin' around Sophie's shuttered windows howlin' about what's a-comin' soon to git her.

"She wouldn't never go near the buryin'-ground, and now she won't come out of the house at all nor see nobody. Got to sayin' there was a curse on Stillwater—and I'm dinged if she ain't half right, the way things is a-goin' to pieces these days. There certainly was somethin' queer about Sophie right along. Once when Sally Hopkins was a-callin' on her—in '97 or '98, I think it was—there was an awful rattlin' at her winders—and Johnny was safe locked up at the time—at least, so Constable Dodge swore up and down. But I ain't takin' no stock in their stories about noises every seventeenth of June, or about faint shinin' figures a-tryin' Sophie's door and winders every black mornin' about two o'clock.

"You see, it was about two o'clock in the mornin' that Sophie heard the sounds and keeled over twice that first night after the buryin'. Steve and me, and Matildy and Emily, heard the second lot, faint as it was, just like I told you. And I'm a-tellin' you again as how it must a been crazy Johnny over to the buryin'-ground, let Jotham Blake claim what he will. There ain't no tellin' the sound of a man's voice so far off, and with our heads full of nonsense it ain't no wonder we thought there was two voices—and voices that hadn't ought to be speakin' at all.

"Steve, he claimed to have heard more than I did. I verily believe he took some stock in ghosts. Matildy and Emily was so scared they didn't remember what they heard. And curious enough, nobody else in town—if anybody was awake at the ungodly hour—never said nothin' about hearin' no sounds at all.

"Whatever it was, was so faint it might have been the wind if there hadn't been words. I made out a few, but don't want to say as I'd back up all Steve claimed to have caught. . . .

"'She-devil' . . . 'all the time' . . . 'Henry' . . . and 'alive' was plain . . . and so was 'you know' . . . 'said you'd stand by' . . . 'get rid of him' and 'bury me' . . . in a kind of changed voice. . . . Then there was that awful 'comin' again some day'—in a death-like squawk . . . but you can't tell me Johnny couldn't have made those sounds. . . .

"Hey, you! What's takin' you off in such a hurry? Mebbe there's more I could tell you if I had a mind. . . ."

William Lumley

The Diary of Alonzo Typer

EDITOR'S NOTE: Alonzo Hasbrouck Typer of Kingston, N.Y., was last seen and recognised on April 17, 1908, around noon, at the Hotel Richmond in Batavia. He was the only survivor of an ancient Ulster County family, and was fifty-three years old at the time of his disappearance.

Mr. Typer was educated privately and at Columbia and Heidelberg Universities. All his life was spent as a student; the field of his researches including many obscure and generally feared borderlands of human knowledge. His papers on vampirism, ghouls, and poltergeist phenomena were privately printed after rejection by many publishers. He resigned from the Society for Psychical Research in 1902 after a series of peculiarly bitter controversies.

At various times Mr. Typer travelled extensively, sometimes dropping out of sight for long periods. He is known to have visited obscure spots in Nepal, India, Thibet, and Indo-China, and passed most of the year 1899 on mysterious Easter Island. The extensive search for Mr. Typer after his disappearance yielded no results, and his estate was divided among distant cousins in New York City.

The diary herewith presented was allegedly found in the ruins of a large country house near Attica, N.Y., which had borne a curiously sinister reputation for generations before its collapse. The edifice was very old, antedating the general white settlement of the region, and had formed the home of a strange and secretive family named van der Heyl, which had migrated from Albany in 1746 under a curious cloud of witchcraft suspicion. The structure probably dated from about 1760.

Of the history of the van der Heyls very little is known. They remained entirely aloof from their normal neighbours, employed negro servants brought directly from Africa and speaking little English, and educated their children privately and at European colleges. Those of them who went out into the world were soon lost to sight, though not before gaining evil repute for association with Black Mass groups and cults of even darker significance.

Around the dreaded house a straggling village arose, populated by Indians and later by renegades from the surrounding country, which bore the dubious name of Chorazin. Of the singular hereditary strains which afterward appeared in the mixed Chorazin villagers, several monographs have been written by ethnologists. Just behind the village, and in sight of the van der Heyl house, is a steep hill crowned with a peculiar ring of ancient standing stones which the Iroquois always regarded with fear and loathing. The origin and nature of the stones, whose date, according to archaeological and climatological evidence, must be fabulously early, is a problem still unsolved.

From about 1795 onward, the legends of the incoming pioneers and later population have much to say about strange cries and chants proceeding at certain seasons from Chorazin and from the great house and hill of standing stones; though there is reason to suppose that the noises ceased about 1872, when the entire van der Heyl household—servants and all—suddenly and simultaneously disappeared.

Thenceforward the house was deserted; for other disastrous events—including three unexplained deaths, five disappearances, and four cases of sudden insanity—occurred when later owners and interested visitors attempted to stay in it. The house, village, and extensive rural areas on all sides reverted to the state and were auctioned off in the absence of discoverable van der Heyl heirs. Since about 1890 the owners (successively the late Charles A. Shields and his son Oscar S. Shields, of Buffalo) have left the entire property in a state of absolute neglect, and have warned all inquirers not to visit the region.

Of those known to have approached the house during the last forty years, most were occult students, police officers, newspaper men, and odd characters from abroad. Among the latter was a mysterious Eurasian, probably from Cochin-China, whose later appearance with blank mind and bizarre mutilations excited wide press notice in 1903.

Mr. Typer's diary—a book about $6 \times 3\frac{1}{2}$ inches in size, with tough paper and an oddly durable binding of thin sheet metal—was discovered in the possession of one of the decadent Chorazin villagers on Nov. 16, 1935, by a state policeman sent to investigate the rumoured collapse of the deserted van der Heyl mansion. The house had indeed fallen, obviously from sheer age and decrepitude, in the severe gale of Nov. 12. Disintegration was peculiarly complete, and no thorough search of the ruins could be made for several weeks. John Eagle, the swarthy, simian-faced, Indian-like villager who had the diary, said that he found the book quite near the surface of the debris, in what must have been an upper front room.

Very little of the contents of the house could be identified, though an enormous and astonishingly solid brick vault in the cellar (whose ancient iron door had to be blasted open because of the strangely figured and perversely tenacious lock) remained intact and presented several puzzling features. For one thing, the walls were covered with still undeciphered hieroglyphs roughly incised in the brickwork. Another peculiarity was a huge circular aperture in the rear of the vault, blocked by a cave-in evidently caused by the collapse of the house.

But strangest of all was the apparently *recent* deposit of some foetid, slimy, pitch-black substance on the flagstoned floor, extending in a yard-broad, irregular line with one end at the blocked circular aperture. Those who first opened the vault declared that the place smelled like the snake-house at a zoo.

The diary, which was apparently designed solely to cover an investigation of the dreaded van der Heyl house by the vanished Mr. Typer, has been proved by handwriting experts to be genuine. The script shews signs of increasing nervous strain as it progresses toward the end, in places becoming almost illegible. Chorazin villagers—whose stupidity and taciturnity baffle all students of the region and its secrets—admit no recollection of Mr. Typer as distinguished from other rash visitors to the dreaded house.

The text of the diary is here given verbatim and without comment. How to interpret it, and what, other than the writer's madness, to infer from it, the reader must decide for himself. Only the future can tell what its value may be in solving a generation-old mystery. It may be remarked that genealogists confirm Mr. Typer's belated memory in the matter of *Adriaen Sleght*.

THE DIARY

April 17, 1908

Arrived here about 6 p.m. Had to walk all the way from Attica in the teeth of an oncoming storm, for no one would rent me a horse or rig, and I can't run an automobile. This place is even worse than I had expected, and I dread what is coming, even though I long at the same time to learn the secret. All too soon will come the night— the old Walpurgis Sabbat horror—and after that time in Wales I know what to look for. Whatever comes, I shall not flinch. Prodded by some unfathomable urge, I have given my whole life to the quest of unholy mysteries. I came here for nothing else, and will not quarrel with fate.

It was very dark when I got here, though the sun had by no means set. The storm-clouds were the densest I had ever seen, and I could not have found my way but for the lightning flashes. The village is a hateful little backwater, and its few inhabitants no better than idiots. One of them saluted me in a queer way, as if he knew me. I could see very little of the landscape—just a small, swampy valley of strange brown weed-stalks and dead fungi surrounded by scraggly, evilly twisted trees with bare boughs. But behind the village is a dismal-looking hill on whose summit is a circle of great stones with another stone at the centre. That, without question, is the vile primordial thing V—— told me about at the N——estbat.

The great house lies in the midst of a park all overgrown with curious-looking briers. I could scarcely break through, and when I did the vast age and decrepitude of the building almost stopped me from entering. The place looked filthy and diseased, and I wondered how so leprous a bulk could hang together. It is wooden; and though its original lines are hidden by a bewildering tangle of wings added at various dates, I think it was first built in the square colonial fashion of New England. Probably that was easier to build than a Dutch stone house—and then, too, I recall that Dirck van der Heyl's wife was from Salem, a daughter of the unmentionable Abaddon Corey. There was a small pillared porch, and I got under it just as the storm burst. It was a fiendish tempest—black as midnight, with rain in sheets, thunder and lightning like the day of general dissolution, and a wind that actually clawed at me. The door was unlocked, so I took out my electric torch and went inside. Dust was inches thick on floor and furniture, and the place smelled like a mould-caked tomb. There was a hall reaching all the way through, and a curving staircase on the right. I ploughed a way upstairs and selected this front room to camp out in. The whole place seems fully furnished, though most of the furniture is breaking down. This is written at eight o'clock, after a cold meal from my travelling-case. After this the village people will bring me supplies—though they won't agree to come any closer than the ruins of the park gate until (as they say) later. I wish I could get rid of an unpleasant feeling of familiarity with this place.

Later

I am conscious of several presences in this house. One in particular is decidedly hostile toward me—a malevolent will which is seeking to break down my own and overcome me. I must not countenance this for an instant, but must use all my forces to resist it. It is appallingly evil, and definitely non-human. I think it must be allied to powers outside earth—powers in the spaces behind time and beyond the universe. It towers like a colossus, bearing out what is said in the Aklo writings. There is such a feeling of vast size connected with it that I wonder these chambers can contain its bulk—and yet it has no visible bulk. Its age must be unutterably vast—shockingly, indescribably so.

April 18

Slept very little last night. At 3 a.m. a strange, creeping wind began to pervade the whole region—ever rising until the house rocked as if in a typhoon. As I went down the staircase to see to the rattling front door the darkness took half-visible forms in my imagination. Just below the landing I was pushed violently from behind —by the wind, I suppose, though I could have sworn I saw the dissolving outlines of a gigantic black paw as I turned quickly about. I did not lose my footing, but safely finished the descent and shot the heavy bolt of the dangerously shaking door.

I had not meant to explore the house till dawn; yet now, unable to sleep again and fired with mixed terror and curiosity, I felt reluctant to postpone my search. With my powerful torch I ploughed through the dust to the great south parlour, where I knew the portraits would be. There they were, just as V—— had said, and as I seemed to know from some obscurer source as well. Some were so blackened, mouldy, and dust-clouded that I could make little or nothing of them, but from those I could trace I recognised that they were indeed of the hateful line of the van der Heyls. Some of the paintings seemed to suggest faces I had known; but just *what* faces, I could not recall.

The outlines of that frightful hybrid Joris—spawned in 1773 by old Dirck's youngest daughter—were clearest of all, and I could trace the green eyes and the serpent look in his face. Every time I shut off the flashlight that face would seem to glow in the dark until I half fancied it shone with a faint, greenish light of its own. The more I looked, the more evil it seemed, and I turned away to avoid hallucinations of changing expression.

But that to which I turned was even worse. The long, dour face, small, closely set eyes, and swine-like features identified it at once, even though the artist had striven to make the snout look as human as possible. This was what V—— had whispered about. As I stared in horror, I thought the eyes took on a reddish glow—and for a moment the background seemed replaced by an alien and seemingly irrelevant scene—a lone, bleak moor beneath a dirty yellow sky, whereon grew a wretched-looking blackthorn bush. Fearing for my sanity, I rushed from that accursed gallery to the dust-cleared corner upstairs where I have my "camp".

Later

Decided to explore some of the labyrinthine wings of the house by daylight. I cannot get lost, for my footprints are distinct in the ankle-deep dust—and I can trace other identifying marks when necessary. It is curious how easily I learn the intricate windings of the corridors. Followed a long, outflung northerly "ell" to its extremity, and came to a locked door, which I forced. Beyond was a very small room quite crowded with furniture, and with the panelling badly worm-eaten. On the outer wall I spied a black space behind the rotting woodwork, and discovered a narrow secret passage leading downward to unknown black depths. It was a steeply inclined chute or tunnel without steps or hand-holds, and I wondered what its use could have been.

Above the fireplace was a mouldy painting, which I found on close inspection to be that of a young woman in the dress of the late eighteenth century. The face is of classic beauty, yet with the most fiendishly evil expression which I have ever known the human countenance to bear. Not merely callousness, greed, and cruelty, but some quality hideous beyond human comprehension seems to sit upon those finely carved features. And as I looked it seemed to me that the artist—or the slow processes of mould and decay—had imparted to that pallid complexion a sickly greenish cast, and the least suggestion of an almost imperceptibly scaly texture. Later I ascended to the attic, where I found several chests of strange books—many of utterly alien aspect in letters and in physical form alike. One contained variants of the Aklo formulae which I had never known to exist. I have not yet examined the books on the dusty shelves downstairs.

April 19

There are certainly unseen presences here, even though the dust as yet bears no footprints but my own. Cut a path through the briers yesterday to the park gate where my supplies are left, but this morning I found it closed. Very odd, since the bushes are hardly stirring with spring sap. Again I had that feeling of something at hand so colossal that the chambers can scarcely contain it. This time I feel more than one of the presences is of such a size, and I know now that the third Aklo ritual—which I found in that book in the attic yesterday—would make such beings solid and visible. Whether I shall dare to try this materialisation remains to be seen. The perils are great.

Last night I began to glimpse evanescent shadow-faces and forms in the dim corners of the halls and chambers—faces and forms so hideous and loathsome that I dare not describe them. They seem allied in substance to that titanic paw which tried to push me down the stairs night before last—and must of course be phantoms of my disturbed imagination. What I am seeking would not be quite like these things. I have seen the paw again—sometimes alone and sometimes with its mate—but I have resolved to ignore all such phenomena.

Early this afternoon I explored the cellar for the first time—descending by a ladder found in a storeroom, since the wooden steps had rotted away. The whole place is a mass of nitrous encrustations, with amorphous mounds marking the spots where various objects have disintegrated. At the farther end is a narrow passage which seems to extend under the northerly "ell" where I found the little locked room, and at the end of this is a heavy brick wall with a locked iron door. Apparently belonging to a vault of some sort, this wall and door bear evidences of eighteenth-century workmanship and must be contemporary with the oldest additions to the house— clearly pre-Revolutionary. On the lock—which is obviously older than the rest of the ironwork—are engraved certain symbols which I cannot decipher.

V—— had not told me about this vault. It fills me with a greater disquiet than anything else I have seen, for every time I approach it I have an almost irresistible impulse to *listen* for something. Hitherto no untoward *sounds* have marked my stay in this malign place. As I left the cellar I wished devoutly that the steps were still there—for my progress up the ladder seemed maddeningly slow. I do not want to go down there again—and yet some evil genius urges me to try it *at night* if I would learn what is to be learned.

April 20

I have sounded the depths of horror—only to be made aware of still lower depths. Last night the temptation was too strong, and in the black small hours I descended once more into that nitrous, hellish cellar with my flashlight—tiptoeing among the amorphous heaps to that terrible brick wall and locked door. I made no sound, and refrained from whispering any of the incantations I knew, but I listened—listened with mad intentness.

At last I heard the sounds from beyond those barred plates of sheet iron—the menacing padding and muttering, as of gigantic night-things within. Then, too, there was a damnable slithering, as of a vast serpent or sea-beast dragging its monstrous folds over a paved floor. Nearly paralysed with fright, I glanced at the huge rusty lock, and at the alien, cryptic hieroglyphs graven upon it. They were signs I could not recognise, and something in their vaguely Mongoloid technique hinted at a blasphemous and indescribable antiquity. At times I fancied I could see them glowing with a greenish light.

I turned to flee, but found that vision of the titan paws before me—the great talons seeming to swell and become more tangible as I gazed. Out of the cellar's evil blackness they stretched, with shadowy hints of scaly wrists beyond them, and with a waxing, malignant will guiding their horrible gropings. Then I heard from behind me—within that abominable vault—a fresh burst of muffled reverberations which seemed to echo from far horizons like distant thunder. Impelled by this greater fear, I advanced toward the shadowy paws with my flashlight and saw them vanish before the full force of the electric beam. Then up the ladder I raced, torch between my teeth, nor did I rest till I had regained my upstairs "camp".

What is to be my ultimate end, I dare not imagine. I came as a seeker, but now I know that something is seeking me. I could not leave if I wished. This morning I tried to go to the gate for my supplies, but found the briers twisted tightly in my path. It was the same in every direction—behind and on all sides of the house. In places the brown, barbed vines had uncurled to astonishing heights —forming a steel-like hedge against my egress. The villagers are connected with all this. When I went indoors I found my supplies in the great front hall, though without any clue to how they came there. I am sorry now that I swept the dust away. I shall scatter some more and see what prints are left.

This afternoon I read some of the books in the great shadowy library at the rear of the ground floor, and formed certain suspicions which I cannot bear to mention. I had never seen the text of Pnakotic Manuscripts or of the Eltdown Shards before, and would not have come here had I known what they contain. I believe it is too late now—for the awful Sabbat is only ten days away. It is for that night of horror that *they* are saving me.

April 21

I have been studying the portraits again. Some have names attached, and I noticed one—of an evil-faced woman, painted some two centuries ago—which puzzled me. It bore the name of Trintje van der Heyl Sleght, and I have a distinct impression that I once met the name of Sleght before, in some significant connexion. It was not horrible then, though it becomes so now. I must rack my brain for the clue.

The *eyes* of these pictures haunt me. Is it possible that some of them are emerging more distinctly from their shrouds of dust and decay and mould? The serpent-faced and swine-faced warlocks stare horribly at me from their blackened frames, and a score of other hybrid faces are beginning to peer out of shadowy backgrounds. There is a hideous look of family resemblance in them all —and that which is human is more horrible than that which is non-human. I wish they reminded me less of other faces—faces I have known in the past. They were an accursed line, and Cornelis of Leyden was the worst of them. It was *he* who broke down the barrier after his father had found that other key. I am sure that V——knows only a fragment of the horrible truth, so that I am indeed unprepared and defenceless. What of the line before old Claes? What he did in 1591 could never have been done without generations of evil heritage, or some link with the outside. And what of the branches this monstrous line has sent forth? Are they scattered over the world, all awaiting their common heritage of horror? I must recall the place where I once so particularly noticed the name of Sleght.

I wish I could be sure that these pictures stay always in their frames. For several hours now I have been seeing momentary presences like the earlier paws and shadow-faces and forms, but closely duplicating some of the ancient portraits. Somehow I can never glimpse a presence and the portrait it resembles at the same time—the light is always wrong for one or the other, or else the presence and the portrait are in different rooms.

Perhaps, as I have hoped, the presences are mere figments of imagination; but I cannot be sure now. Some are female, and of the same hellish beauty as the picture in the little locked room. Some are like no portrait I have seen, yet make me feel that their painted features lurk unrecognised beneath the mould and soot of canvases I cannot decipher. A few, I desperately fear, have approached materialisation in solid or semi-solid form—and some have a dreadful and unexplained familiarity.

There is one woman who in fell loveliness excels all the rest. Her poisonous charms are like a honeyed flower growing on the brink of hell. When I look at her closely she vanishes, only to reappear later. Her face has a greenish cast, and now and then I fancy I can spy a suspicion of the squamose in its smooth texture. Who is she? Is she that being who must have dwelt in the little locked room a century and more ago?

My supplies were again left in the front hall—that, clearly, is to be the custom. I had sprinkled dust about to catch footprints, but this morning the whole hall was swept clean by some unknown agency.

April 22

This has been a day of horrible discovery. I explored the cobwebbed attic again, and found a carved, crumbling chest—plainly from Holland—full of blasphemous books and papers far older than any hitherto encountered here. There was a Greek *Necronom-*

icon, a Norman-French *Livre d'Eibon,* and a first edition of old
Ludvig Prinn's *De Vermis Mysteriis.* But the old bound manuscript
was the worst. It was in low Latin, and full of the strange, crabbed
handwriting of Claes van der Heyl—being evidently the diary or
notebook kept by him between 1560 and 1580. When I unfastened
the blackened silver clasp and opened the yellowed leaves a coloured drawing fluttered out—the likeness of a monstrous creature
resembling nothing so much as a squid, beaked and tentacled, with
great yellow eyes, and with certain abominable approximations to
the human form in its contours.

I had never before seen so utterly loathsome and nightmarish a
form. On the paws, feet, and head-tentacles were curious claws—
reminding me of the colossal shadow-shapes which have groped so
horribly in my path—while the entity as a whole sat upon a great
throne-like pedestal inscribed with unknown hieroglyphs of vaguely
Chinese cast. About both writing and image there hung an air of
sinister evil so profound and pervasive that I could not think it the
product of any one world or age. Rather must that monstrous
shape be a focus for all the evil in unbounded space, throughout the
aeons past and to come—and those eldritch symbols be vile sentient eikons endowed with a morbid life of their own and ready to
wrest themselves from the parchment for the reader's destruction.
To the meaning of that monster and of those hieroglyphs I had no
clue, but I knew that both had been traced with a hellish precision
and for no namable purpose. As I studied the leering characters,
their kinship to the symbols on that ominous lock in the cellar became more and more manifest. I left the picture in the attic, for
never could sleep come to me with such a thing nearby.

All the afternoon and evening I read in the manuscript book of
old Claes van der Heyl, and what I read will cloud and make horrible whatever period of life lies ahead of me. The genesis of the
world, and of previous worlds, unfolded itself before my eyes. I
learned of the city Shamballah, built by the Lemurians fifty million
years ago, yet inviolate still behind its walls of psychic force in the
eastern desert. I learned of the Book of Dzyan, whose first six chapters antedate the earth, and which was old when the lords of Venus
came through space in their ships to civilise our planet. And I saw
recorded in writing for the first time that name which others had
spoken to me in whispers, and which I had known in a closer and
more horrible way—the shunned and dreaded name of *Yian-Ho.*

In several places I was held up by passages requiring a key. Eventually, from various allusions, I gathered that old Claes had not dared to embody all his knowledge in one book, but had left certain points for another. Neither volume can be wholly intelligible without its fellow; hence I have resolved to find the second one if it lies anywhere within this accursed house. Though plainly a prisoner, I have not lost my lifelong zeal for the unknown; and am determined to probe the cosmos as deeply as possible before doom comes.

April 23

Searched all the morning for the second diary, and found it about noon in a desk in the little locked room. Like the first, it is in Claes van der Heyl's barbarous Latin; and it seems to consist of disjointed notes referring to various sections of the other. Glancing through the leaves, I spied at once the abhorred name of Yian-Ho—of Yian-Ho, that lost and hidden city wherein brood aeon-old secrets, and of which dim memories older than the body lurk behind the minds of all men. It was repeated many times, and the text around it was strown with crudely drawn hieroglyphs plainly akin to those on the pedestal in that hellish drawing I had seen. Here, clearly, lay the key to that monstrous tentacled shape and its forbidden message. With this knowledge I ascended the creaking stairs to the attic of cobwebs and horror.

When I tried to open the attic door it stuck as never before. Several times it resisted every effort to open it, and when at last it gave way I had a distinct feeling that some colossal, unseen shape had suddenly released it—a shape that soared away on nonmaterial but audibly beating wings. When I found the horrible drawing I felt that it was not precisely where I had left it. Applying the key in the other book, I soon saw that the latter was no instant guide to the secret. It was only a clue—a clue to a secret too black to be left lightly guarded. It would take hours—perhaps days—to extract the awful message.

Shall I live long enough to learn the secret? The shadowy black arms and paws haunt my vision more and more now, and seem even more titanic than at first. Nor am I ever long free from those vague, unhuman presences whose nebulous bulk seems too vast for the chambers to contain. And now and then the grotesque, evanescent faces and forms, and the mocking portrait-shapes, troop before me in bewildering confusion.

Truly, there are terrible primal arcana of earth which had better be left unknown and unevoked; dread secrets which have nothing to do with man, and which man may learn only in exchange for peace and sanity; cryptic truths which make the knower evermore an alien among his kind, and cause him to walk alone on earth. Likewise are there dread survivals of things older and more potent than man; things that have blasphemously straggled down through the aeons to ages never meant for them; monstrous entities that have lain sleeping endlessly in incredible crypts and remote caverns, outside the laws of reason and causation, and ready to be waked by such blasphemers as shall know their dark forbidden signs and furtive passwords.

April 24

Studied the picture and the key all day in the attic. At sunset I heard strange sounds, of a sort not encountered before and seeming to come from far away. Listening, I realised that they must flow from that queer abrupt hill with the circle of standing stones, which lies behind the village and some distance north of the house. I had heard that there was a path from the house leading up that hill to the primal cromlech, and had suspected that at certain seasons the van der Heyls had much occasion to use it; but the whole matter had hitherto lain latent in my consciousness. The present sounds consisted of a shrill piping intermingled with a peculiar and hideous sort of hissing or whistling—a bizarre, alien kind of music, like nothing which the annals of earth describe. It was very faint, and soon faded, but the matter has set me thinking. It is toward the hill that the long, northerly "ell" with the secret chute, and the locked brick vault under it, extend. Can there be any connexion which has so far eluded me?

April 25

I have made a peculiar and disturbing discovery about the nature of my imprisonment. Drawn toward the hill by a sinister fascination, I found the briers giving way before me, *but in that direction only*. There is a ruined gate, and beneath the bushes the traces of the old path no doubt exist. The briers extend part way up and all around the hill, though the summit with the standing stones bears only a curious growth of moss and stunted grass. I climbed the hill and spent several hours there, noticing a strange wind which seems always to sweep around the forbidding monoliths and which sometimes seems to whisper in an oddly articulate though darkly cryptic fashion.

These stones, both in colour and in texture, resemble nothing I have seen elsewhere. They are neither brown nor grey, but rather of a dirty yellow merging into an evil green and having a suggestion of chameleon-like variability. Their texture is queerly like that of a scaled serpent, and is inexplicably nauseous to the touch—being as cold and clammy as the skin of a toad or other reptile. Near the central menhir is a singular stone-rimmed hollow which I cannot explain, but which may possibly form the entrance to a long-choked well or tunnel. When I sought to descend the hill at points away from the house I found the briers intercepting me as before, though the path toward the house was easily retraceable.

April 26

Up on the hill again this evening, and found that windy whispering much more distinct. The almost angry humming came close to actual speech—of a vague sibilant sort—and reminded me of the strange piping chant I had heard from afar. After sunset there came a curious flash of premature summer lightning on the northern horizon, followed almost at once by a queer detonation high in the fading sky. Something about this phenomenon disturbed me greatly, and I could not escape the impression that the noise ended in a kind of unhuman hissing speech which trailed off into guttural cosmic laughter. Is my mind tottering at last, or has my unwarranted curiosity evoked unheard-of horrors from the twilight spaces? The Sabbat is close at hand now. What will be the end?

April 27

At last my dreams are to be realised! Whether or not my life or spirit or body will be claimed, I shall enter the gateway! Progress in deciphering those crucial hieroglyphs in the picture has been slow, but this afternoon I hit upon the final clue. By evening I knew their meaning—and that meaning can apply in only one way to the things I have encountered in this house.

There is beneath this house—sepulchred I know not where—an ancient forgotten One who will shew me the gateway I would enter, and give me the lost signs and words I shall need. How long It has lain buried here—forgotten save by those who reared the stones on the hill, and by those who later sought out this place and built this house—I cannot conjecture. It was in search of this Thing, beyond question, that Hendrik van der Heyl came to New-Netherland in 1638. Men of this earth know It not, save in the secret whispers of the fear-shaken few who have found or inherited the key. No human eye has even yet glimpsed It—unless, perhaps, the vanished wizards of this house delved farther than has been guessed.

With knowledge of the symbols came likewise a mastery of the Seven Lost Signs of Terror—and a tacit recognition of the hideous and unutterable Words of Fear. All that remains for me to accomplish is the Chant which will transfigure that Forgotten One who is Guardian of the Ancient Gateway. I marvel much at the Chant. It is composed of strange and repellent gutturals and disturbing sibilants resembling no language I have ever encountered—even in the blackest chapters of the *Livre d'Eibon*. When I visited the hill at sunset I tried to read it aloud, but evoked in response only a vague, sinister rumbling on the far horizon, and a thin cloud of elemental dust that writhed and whirled like some evil living thing. Perhaps I do not pronounce the alien syllables correctly, or perhaps it is only on the Sabbat—that hellish Sabbat for which the Powers in this house are without question holding me—that the great Transfiguration can occur.

Had an odd spell of fright this morning. I thought for a moment that I recalled where I had seen that baffling name of Sleght before, and the prospect of realisation filled me with unutterable horror.

April 28

Today dark ominous clouds have hovered intermittently over the circle on the hill. I have noticed such clouds several times before, but their contours and arrangements now hold a fresh significance. They are snake-like and fantastic, and curiously like the evil shadow-shapes I have seen in the house. They float in a circle around the primal cromlech—revolving repeatedly as though endowed with a sinister life and purpose. I could swear, too, that they give forth an angry murmuring. After some fifteen minutes they sail slowly away, ever to the eastward, like the units of a straggling battalion. Are they indeed those dread Ones whom Solomon knew of old—those giant black beings whose number is legion and whose tread doth shake the earth?

I have been rehearsing the Chant that will transfigure the Nameless Thing, yet strange fears assail me even when I utter the syllables under my breath. Piecing all evidence together, I have now discovered that the only way to It is through the locked cellar vault. That vault was built with a hellish purpose, and must cover the hidden burrow leading to the Immemorial Lair. What guardians live endlessly within, flourishing from century to century on an unknown nourishment, only the mad may conjecture. The warlocks of this house, who called them out of inner earth, have known them only too well, as the shocking portraits and memories of the place reveal.

What troubles me most is the limited nature of the Chant. It evokes the Nameless One, yet provides no method for the control of That Which is evoked. There are, of course, the general signs and gestures, but whether they will prove effective toward such an One remains to be seen. Still, the rewards are great enough to justify any danger—and I could not retreat if I would, since an unknown force plainly urges me on.

I have discovered one more obstacle. Since the locked cellar vault must be traversed, the key to that place must be found. The lock is infinitely too strong for forcing. That the key is somewhere hereabouts cannot be doubted, but the time before the Sabbat is very short. I must search diligently and thoroughly. It will take courage to unlock that iron door, for what prisoned horrors may not lurk within?

Later

I have been shunning the cellar for the past day or two, but late this afternoon I again descended to those forbidding precincts. At first all was silent, but within five minutes the menacing padding and muttering began once more beyond the iron door. This time it was loud and more terrifying than on any previous occasion, and I likewise recognised the slithering that bespoke some monstrous sea-beast—now swifter and nervously intensified, as if the thing were striving to force its way through the portal to where I stood.

As the pacing grew louder, more restless, and more sinister, there began to pound through it those hellish and unidentifiable reverberations which I had heard on my second visit to the cellar—those muffled reverberations which seemed to echo from far horizons like distant thunder. Now, however, their volume was magnified an hundredfold, and their timbre freighted with new and terrifying implications. I can compare the sound to nothing more aptly than to the roar of some dread monster of the vanished saurian age, when primal horrors roamed the earth, and Valusia's serpent-men laid the foundation-stones of evil magic. To such a roar—but swelled to deafening heights reached by no known organic throat—was this shocking sound akin. Dare I unlock the door and face the onslaught of what lies beyond?

April 29

The key to the vault is found. I came upon it this noon in the little locked room—buried beneath rubbish in a drawer of the ancient desk, as if some belated effort to conceal it had been made. It was wrapped in a crumbling newspaper dated Oct. 31, 1872; but there was an inner wrapping of dried skin—evidently the hide of some unknown reptile—which bore a Low Latin message in the same crabbed writing as that of the notebooks I found. As I had thought, the lock and key were vastly older than the vault. Old Claes van der Heyl had them ready for something he or his descendants meant to do—and how much older than he they were I could not estimate. Deciphering the Latin message, I trembled in a fresh access of clutching terror and nameless awe.

"The secrets of the monstrous primal Ones," ran the crabbed text, "whose cryptic words relate the hidden things that were before man; the things no one of earth should learn, lest peace be forever forfeited; shall by me never suffer revelation. To Yian-Ho, that lost and forbidden city of countless aeons whose place may not be told, I have been in the veritable flesh of this body, as none other among the living has been. Therein have I found, and thence have I borne away, that knowledge which I would gladly lose, though I may not. I have learnt to bridge a gap that should not be bridged, and must call out of the earth That Which should not be waked or called. And what is sent to follow me will not sleep till I or those after me have found and done what is to be found and done.

"That which I have awaked and borne away with me, I may not part with again. So is it written in the Book of Hidden Things. That which I have willed to be has twined its dreadful shape around me, and—if I live not to do the bidding—around those children born and unborn who shall come after me, until the bidding be done. Strange may be their joinings, and awful the aid they may summon till the end be reached. Into lands unknown and dim must the seeking go, and a house must be built for the outer Guardians.

"This is the key to that lock which was given me in the dreadful, aeon-old, and forbidden city of Yian-Ho; the lock which I or mine must place upon the vestibule of That Which is to be found. And may the Lords of Yaddith succour me—or him—who must set that lock in place or turn the key thereof."

Such was the message—a message which, once I had read it, I seemed to have known before. Now, as I write these words, the key is before me. I gaze on it with mixed dread and longing, and cannot find words to describe its aspect. It is of the same unknown, subtly greenish frosted metal as the lock; a metal best compared to brass tarnished with verdigris. Its design is alien and fantastic, and the coffin-shaped end of the ponderous bulk leaves no doubt of the lock it was meant to fit. The handle roughly forms a strange, non-human image, whose exact outlines and identity cannot now be traced. Upon holding it for any length of time I seem to feel an alien, anomalous *life* in the cold metal—a quickening or pulsing too feeble for ordinary recognition. Below the eidolon is graven a faint, aeon-worn legend in those blasphemous, Chinese-like hieroglyphs I have come to know so well. I can make out only the beginning—the words "my vengeance lurks"—before the text fades to indistinctness. There is some fatality in this timely finding of the key—*for tomorrow night comes the hellish Sabbat*. But strangely enough, amidst all this hideous expectancy, that question of the Sleght name bothers me more and more. Why should I dread to find it linked with the van der Heyls?

Walpurgis-Eve—April 30
The time has come. I waked last night to see the sky glowing with a lurid greenish radiance—that same morbid green which I have seen in the eyes and skin of certain portraits here, on the shocking lock and key, on the monstrous menhirs of the hill, and in a thousand other recesses of my consciousness. There were strident whispers in the air—sibilant whistlings like those of the wind around that dreadful cromlech. Something spoke to me out of the frore aether of space, and it said, "The hour falls." It is an omen, and I laugh at my own fears. Have I not the dread words and the Seven Lost Signs of Terror—the power coercive of any Dweller in the cosmos or in the unknown darkened spaces? I will no longer hesitate.

The heavens are very dark, as if a terrific storm were coming on—a storm even greater than that of the night when I reached here, nearly a fortnight ago. From the village—less than a mile away—I hear a queer and unwonted babbling. It is as I thought—these poor degraded idiots are within the secret, and keep the awful Sabbat on the hill. Here in the house the shadows gather densely. In the darkness the key before me almost glows with a greenish light of its own. I have not yet been to the cellar. It is better that I wait, lest the sound of that muttering and padding—those slitherings and muffled reverberations—unnerve me before I can unlock the fateful door.

Of what I shall encounter, and what I must do, I have only the most *general* idea. Shall I find my task in the vault itself, or must I burrow deeper into the nighted heart of our planet? There are things I do not yet understand—or at least, prefer not to understand—despite a dreadful, increasing, and inexplicable sense of bygone familiarity with this fearsome house. That chute, for instance, leading down from the little locked room. But I think I know why the wing with the vault extends toward the hill.

6 p.m.

Looking out the north windows, I can see a group of villagers on the hill. They seem unaware of the lowering sky, and are digging near the great central menhir. It occurs to me that they are working on that stone-rimmed hollow place which looks like a long-choked tunnel entrance. What is to come? How much of the olden Sabbat rites have these people retained? That key glows horribly—it is not imagination. Dare I use it as it must be used? Another matter has greatly disturbed me. Glancing nervously through a book in the library I came upon an ampler form of the name that has teased my memory so sorely: Trintje, wife of Adriaen Sleght. The *Adriaen* leads me to the very brink of recollection.

Midnight

Horror is unleashed, but I must not weaken. The storm has broken with pandaemoniac fury, and lightning has struck the hill three times, yet the hybrid, malformed villagers are gathering within the cromlech. I can see them in the almost constant flashes. The great standing stones loom up shockingly, and have a dull green luminosity that reveals them even when the lightning is not there. The peals of thunder are deafening, and every one seems to be horribly *answered* from some indeterminate direction. As I write, the creatures on the hill have begun to chant and howl and scream in a degraded, half-simian version of the ancient ritual. Rain pours down like a flood, yet they leap and emit sounds in a kind of diabolic ecstasy.

"*Iä! Shub-Niggurath! The Goat with a Thousand Young!*"

But the worst thing is within the house. Even at this height, I have begun to hear sounds from the cellar. *It is the padding and muttering and slithering and muffled reverberations within the vault. . . .*

Memories come and go. That name of Adriaen Sleght pounds oddly at my consciousness. Dirck van der Heyl's son-in-law—his child old Dirck's granddaughter and Abaddon Corey's great-grand-daughter. . . .

Later

Merciful God! *At last I know where I saw that name.* I know, and am transfixed with horror. All is lost. . . .

The key has begun to feel warm as my left hand nervously clutches it. At times that vague quickening or pulsing is so distinct that I can almost feel the living metal move. It came from Yian-Ho for a terrible purpose, and to me—who all too late know the thin stream of van der Heyl blood that trickles down through the Sleghts into my own lineage—has descended the hideous task of fulfilling that purpose. . . .

My courage and curiosity wane. I know the horror that lies beyond that iron door. What if Claes van der Heyl was my ancestor—need I expiate his nameless sin? *I will not—I swear I will not!* . . .

[*Writing here grows indistinct*]

Too late—cannot help self—black paws materialise—am dragged away toward the cellar. . . .

Two Black Bottles

Not all of the few remaining inhabitants of Daalbergen, that dismal little village in the Ramapo Mountains, believe that my uncle, old Dominie Vanderhoof, is really dead. Some of them believe he is suspended somewhere between heaven and hell because of the old sexton's curse. If it had not been for that old magician, he might still be preaching in the little damp church across the moor.

After what has happened to me in Daalbergen, I can almost share the opinion of the villagers. I am not sure that my uncle is dead, but I am very sure that he is not alive upon this earth. There is no doubt that the old sexton buried him once, but he is not in that grave now. I can almost feel him behind me as I write, impelling me to tell the truth about those strange happenings in Daalbergen so many years ago.

It was the fourth day of October when I arrived at Daalbergen in answer to a summons. The letter was from a former member of my uncle's congregation, who wrote that the old man had passed away and that there should be some small estate which I, as his only living relative, might inherit. Having reached the secluded little hamlet by a wearying series of changes on branch railways, I found my way to the grocery store of Mark Haines, writer of the letter, and he, leading me into a stuffy back room, told me a peculiar tale concerning Dominie Vanderhoof's death.

"Y' should be careful, Hoffman," Haines told me, "when y' meet that old sexton, Abel Foster. He's in league with the devil, sure's you're alive. 'Twa'n't two weeks ago Sam Pryor, when he passed the old graveyard, heared him mumblin' t' the dead there. 'Twa'n't right he should talk that way—an' Sam does vow that there was a voice answered him—a kind o' half-voice, hollow and muffled-like, as though it come out o' th' ground. There's others, too, as could tell y' about seein' him standin' afore old Dominie Slott's grave— that one right agin' the church wall—a-wringin' his hands an' a-talkin' t' th' moss on th' tombstone as though it was the old Dominie himself."

Old Foster, Haines said, had come to Daalbergen about ten years before, and had been immediately engaged by Vanderhoof to take care of the damp stone church at which most of the villagers worshipped. No one but Vanderhoof seemed to like him, for his presence brought a suggestion almost of the uncanny. He would sometimes stand by the door when the people came to church, and the men would coldly return his servile bow while the women brushed past in haste, holding their skirts aside to avoid touching him. He could be seen on week days cutting the grass in the cemetery and tending the flowers around the graves, now and then crooning and muttering to himself. And few failed to notice the particular attention he paid to the grave of the Reverend Guilliam Slott, first pastor of the church in 1701.

It was not long after Foster's establishment as a village fixture that disaster began to lower. First came the failure of the mountain mine where most of the men worked. The vein of iron had given out, and many of the people moved away to better localities, while those who had large holdings of land in the vicinity took to farming and managed to wrest a meager living from the rocky hillsides. Then came the disturbances in the church. It was whispered about that the Reverend Johannes Vanderhoof had made a compact with the devil, and was preaching his word in the house of God. His sermons had become weird and grotesque—redolent with sinister things which the ignorant people of Daalbergen did not understand. He transported them back over ages of fear and superstition to regions of hideous, unseen spirits, and peopled their fancy with night-haunting ghouls. One by one the congregation dwindled, while the elders and deacons vainly pleaded with Vanderhoof to change the subject of his sermons. Though the old man continually promised to comply, he seemed to be enthralled by some higher power which forced him to do its will.

A giant in stature, Johannes Vanderhoof was known to be weak and timid at heart, yet even when threatened with expulsion he continued his eerie sermons, until scarcely a handful of people remained to listen to him on Sunday morning. Because of weak finances, it was found impossible to call a new pastor, and before long not one of the villagers dared venture near the church or the parsonage which adjoined it. Everywhere there was fear of those spectral wraiths with whom Vanderhoof was apparently in league.

My uncle, Mark Haines told me, had continued to live in the parsonage because there was no one with sufficient courage to tell him to move out of it. No one ever saw him again, but lights were visible in the parsonage at night, and were even glimpsed in the church from time to time. It was whispered about the town that Vanderhoof preached regularly in the church every Sunday morning, unaware that his congregation was no longer there to listen. He had only the old sexton, who lived in the basement of the church, to take care of him, and Foster made a weekly visit to what remained of the business section of the village to buy provisions. He no longer bowed servilely to everyone he met, but instead seemed to harbor a demoniac and ill-concealed hatred. He spoke to no one except as was necessary to make his purchases, and glanced from left to right out of evil-filled eyes as he walked the street with his cane tapping the uneven pavements. Bent and shriveled with extreme age, his presence could actually be felt by anyone near him, so powerful was that personality which, said the townspeople, had made Vanderhoof accept the devil as his master. No person in Daalbergen doubted that Abel Foster was at the bottom of all the town's ill luck, but not a one dared lift a finger against him, or could even approach him without a tremor of fear. His name, as well as Vanderhoof's, was never mentioned aloud. Whenever the matter of the church across the moor was discussed, it was in whispers; and if the conversation chanced to be nocturnal, the whisperers would keep glancing over their shoulders to make sure that nothing shapeless or sinister crept out of the darkness to bear witness to their words.

The churchyard continued to be kept just as green and beautiful as when the church was in use, and the flowers near the graves in the cemetery were tended just as carefully as in times gone by. The old sexton could occasionally be seen working there, as if still being paid for his services, and those who dared venture near said that he maintained a continual conversation with the devil and with those spirits which lurked within the graveyard walls.

One morning, Haines went on to say, Foster was seen digging a grave where the steeple of the church throws its shadow in the afternoon, before the sun goes down behind the mountain and puts the entire village in semi-twilight. Later, the church bell, silent for months, tolled solemnly for a half-hour. And at sundown those who were watching from a distance saw Foster bring a coffin from the parsonage on a wheelbarrow, dump it into the grave with slender ceremony, and replace the earth in the hole.

The sexton came to the village the next morning, ahead of his usual weekly schedule, and in much better spirits than was customary. He seemed willing to talk, remarking that Vanderhoof had died the day before, and that he had buried his body beside that of Dominie Slott near the church wall. He smiled from time to time, and rubbed his hands in an untimely and unaccountable glee. It was apparent that he took a perverse and diabolic delight in Vanderhoof's death. The villagers were conscious of an added uncanniness in his presence, and avoided him as much as they could. With Vanderhoof gone they felt more insecure than ever, for the old sexton was now free to cast his worst spells over the town from the church across the moor. Muttering something in a tongue which no one understood, Foster made his way back along the road over the swamp.

It was then, it seems, that Mark Haines remembered having heard Dominie Vanderhoof speak of me as his nephew. Haines accordingly sent for me, in the hope that I might know something which would clear up the mystery of my uncle's last years. I assured my summoner, however, that I knew nothing about my uncle or his past, except that my mother had mentioned him as a man of gigantic physique but with little courage or power of will.

Having heard all that Haines had to tell me, I lowered the front legs of my chair to the floor and looked at my watch. It was late afternoon.

"How far is it out to the church?" I inquired. "Think I can make it before sunset?"

"Sure, lad, y' ain't goin' out there t'night! Not t' that place!" The old man trembled noticeably in every limb and half rose from his chair, stretching out a lean, detaining hand. "Why, it's plumb foolishness!" he exclaimed.

I laughed aside his fears and informed him that, come what may, I was determined to see the old sexton that evening and get the whole matter over as soon as possible. I did not intend to accept the superstitions of ignorant country folk as truth, for I was convinced that all I had just heard was merely a chain of events which the over-imaginative people of Daalbergen had happened to link with their ill-luck. I felt no sense of fear or horror whatever.

Seeing that I was determined to reach my uncle's house before nightfall, Haines ushered me out of his office and reluctantly gave me the few required directions, pleading from time to time that I change my mind. He shook my hand when I left, as though he never expected to see me again.

"Take keer that old devil, Foster, don't git ye!" he warned, again and again. "I wouldn't go near him after dark fer love n'r money. No siree!" He re-entered his store, solemnly shaking his head, while I set out along a road leading to the outskirts of the town.

I had walked barely two minutes before I sighted the moor of which Haines had spoken. The road, flanked by a whitewashed fence, passed over the great swamp, which was overgrown with clumps of underbrush dipping down into the dank, slimy ooze. An odor of deadness and decay filled the air, and even in the sunlit afternoon little wisps of vapor could be seen rising from the unhealthful spot.

On the opposite side of the moor I turned sharply to the left, as I had been directed, branching from the main road. There were several houses in the vicinity, I noticed; houses which were scarcely more than huts, reflecting the extreme poverty of their owners. The road here passed under the drooping branches of enormous willows which almost completely shut out the rays of the sun. The miasmal odor of the swamp was still in my nostrils, and the air was damp and chilly. I hurried my pace to get out of that dismal tunnel as soon as possible.

Presently I found myself in the light again. The sun, now hanging like a red ball upon the crest of the mountain, was beginning to dip low, and there, some distance ahead of me, bathed in its bloody iridescence, stood the lonely church. I began to sense that uncanniness which Haines had mentioned; that feeling of dread which made all Daalbergen shun the place. The squat, stone hulk of the church itself, with its blunt steeple, seemed like an idol to which the tombstones that surrounded it bowed down and worshipped, each with an arched top like the shoulders of a kneeling person, while over the whole assemblage the dingy, gray parsonage hovered like a wraith.

I had slowed my pace a trifle as I took in the scene. The sun was disappearing behind the mountain very rapidly now, and the damp air chilled me. Turning my coat collar up about my neck, I plodded on. Something caught my eye as I glanced up again. In the shadow of the church wall was something white—a thing which seemed to have no definite shape. Straining my eyes as I came nearer, I saw that it was a cross of new timber, surmounting a mound of freshly turned earth. The discovery sent a new chill through me. I realized that this must be my uncle's grave, but something told me that it was not like the other graves near it. It did not seem like a *dead* grave. In some intangible way it appeared to be *living,* if a grave can be said to live. Very close to it, I saw as I came nearer, was another grave; an old mound with a crumbling stone about it. Dominie Slott's tomb, I thought, remembering Haines's story.

There was no sign of life anywhere about the place. In the semi-twilight I climbed the low knoll upon which the parsonage stood, and hammered upon the door. There was no answer. I skirted the house and peered into the windows. The whole place seemed deserted.

The lowering mountains had made night fall with disarming suddenness the minute the sun was fully hidden. I realized that I could see scarcely more than a few feet ahead of me. Feeling my way carefully, I rounded a corner of the house and paused, wondering what to do next.

Everything was quiet. There was not a breath of wind, nor were there even the usual noises made by animals in their nocturnal ramblings. All dread had been forgotten for a time, but in the presence of that sepulchral calm my apprehensions returned. I imagined the air peopled with ghastly spirits that pressed around me, making the air almost unbreathable. I wondered, for the hundredth time, where the old sexton might be.

As I stood there, half expecting some sinister demon to creep from the shadows, I noticed two lighted windows glaring from the belfry of the church. I then remembered what Haines had told me about Foster's living in the basement of the building. Advancing cautiously through the blackness, I found a side door of the church ajar.

The interior had a musty and mildewed odor. Everything I touched was covered with a cold, clammy moisture. I struck a match and began to explore, to discover, if I could, how to get into the belfry. Suddenly I stopped in my tracks.

A snatch of song, loud and obscene, sung in a voice that was guttural and thick with drink, came from above me. The match burned my fingers, and I dropped it. Two pin-points of light pierced the darkness of the farther wall of the church, and below them, to one side, I could see a door outlined where light filtered through its cracks. The song stopped as abruptly as it had commenced, and there was absolute silence again. My heart was thumping and blood racing through my temples. Had I not been petrified with fear, I should have fled immediately.

Not caring to light another match, I felt my way among the pews until I stood in front of the door. So deep was the feeling of depression which had come over me that I felt as though I were acting in a dream. My actions were almost involuntary.

The door was locked, as I found when I turned the knob. I hammered upon it for some time, but there was no answer. The silence was as complete as before. Feeling around the edge of the door, I found the hinges, removed the pins from them, and allowed the door to fall toward me. Dim light flooded down a steep flight of steps. There was a sickening odor of whisky. I could now hear someone stirring in the belfry room above. Venturing a low halloo, I thought I heard a groan in reply, and cautiously climbed the stairs.

My first glance into that unhallowed place was indeed startling. Strewn about the little room were old and dusty books and manuscripts—strange things that bespoke almost unbelievable age. On rows of shelves which reached to the ceiling were horrible things in glass jars and bottles—snakes and lizards and bats. Dust and mold and cobwebs encrusted everything. In the center, behind a table upon which was a lighted candle, a nearly empty bottle of whisky, and a glass, was a motionless figure with a thin, scrawny, wrinkled face and wild eyes that stared blankly through me. I recognized Abel Foster, the old sexton, in an instant. He did not move or speak as I came slowly and fearfully toward him.

"Mr. Foster?" I asked, trembling with unaccountable fear when I heard my voice echo within the close confines of the room. There was no reply, and no movement from the figure behind the table. I wondered if he had not drunk himself to insensibility, and went behind the table to shake him.

At the mere touch of my arm upon his shoulder, the strange old man started from his chair as though terrified. His eyes, still having in them that same blank stare, were fixed upon me. Swinging his arms like flails, he backed away.

"Don't!" he screamed. "Don't touch me! Go back—go back!"

I saw that he was both drunk and struck with some kind of a

nameless terror. Using a soothing tone, I told him who I was and why I had come. He seemed to understand vaguely and sank back into his chair, sitting limp and motionless.

"I thought ye was him," he mumbled. "I thought ye was him come back fer it. He's been a-tryin' t' get out—a-tryin' t' get out sence I put him in there." His voice again rose to a scream and he clutched his chair. "Maybe he's got out now! Maybe he's out!"

I looked about, half expecting to see some spectral shape coming up the stairs.

"Maybe who's out?" I inquired.

"Vanderhoof!" he shrieked. "Th' cross over his grave keeps fallin' down in th' night! Every morning the earth is loose, and gets harder t' pat down. He'll come out an' I won't be able t' do nothin'."

Forcing him back into the chair, I seated myself on a box near him. He was trembling in mortal terror, with the saliva dripping from the corners of his mouth. From time to time I felt that sense of horror which Haines had described when he told me of the old sexton. Truly, there was something uncanny about the man. His head had now sunk forward upon his breast, and he seemed calmer, mumbling to himself.

I quietly arose and opened a window to let out the fumes of whisky and the musty odor of dead things. Light from a dim moon, just risen, made objects below barely visible. I could just see Dominie Vanderhoof's grave from my position in the belfry, and blinked my eyes as I gazed at it. That cross *was* tilted! I remembered that it had been vertical an hour ago. Fear took possession of me again. I turned quickly. Foster sat in his chair watching me. His glance was saner than before.

"So ye're Vanderhoof's nephew," he mumbled in a nasal tone. "Waal, ye might's well know it all. He'll be back arter me afore long, he will—jus' as soon as he can get out o' that there grave. Ye might's well know all about it now."

His terror appeared to have left him. He seemed resigned to some horrible fate which he expected any minute. His head dropped down upon his chest again, and he went on muttering in that nasal monotone.

"Ye see all them there books and papers? Waal, they was once Dominie Slott's—Dominie Slott, who was here years ago. All them things is got t' do with magic—black magic that th' old Dominie knew afore he come t' this country. They used t' burn 'em an' boil 'em in oil fer knowin' that over there, they did. But old Slott knew, and he didn't go fer t' tell nobody. No sir, old Slott used to preach here generations ago, an' he used to come up here an' study them books, an' use all them dead things in jars, an' pronounce magic curses an' things, but he didn't let nobody know it. No, nobody knowed it but Dominie Slott an' me."

"You?" I ejaculated, leaning across the table toward him.

"That is, me after I learned it." His face showed lines of trickery as he answered me. "I found all this stuff here when I come t' be church sexton, an' I used t' read it when I wa'n't at work. An' I soon got t' know all about it."

The old man droned on, while I listened, spellbound. He told about learning the difficult formulae of demonology, so that, by means of incantations, he could cast spells over human beings. He had performed horrible occult rites of his hellish creed, calling down anathema upon the town and its inhabitants. Crazed by his desires, he tried to bring the church under his spell, but the power of God was too strong. Finding Johannes Vanderhoof very weak-willed, he bewitched him so that he preached strange and mystic sermons which struck fear into the simple hearts of the country folk. From his position in the belfry room, he said, behind a paint-ing of the temptation of Christ which adorned the rear wall of the church, he would glare at Vanderhoof while he was preaching, through holes which were the eyes of the Devil in the picture. Ter-rified by the uncanny things which were happening in their midst, the congregation left one by one, and Foster was able to do what he pleased with the church and with Vanderhoof.

"But what did you do with him?" I asked in a hollow voice as the old sexton paused in his confession. He burst into a cackle of laughter, throwing back his head in drunken glee.

"I took his soul!" he howled in a tone that set me trembling. "I took his soul and put it in a bottle—in a little black bottle! And I buried him! But he ain't got his soul, an' he cain't go neither t' heaven n'r hell! But he's a-comin' back after it. He's a-tryin' t' get out o' his grave now. I can hear him pushin' his way up through the ground, he's that strong!"

As the old man had proceeded with his story, I had become more and more convinced that he must be telling me the truth, and not merely gibbering in drunkenness. Every detail fitted what Haines had told me. Fear was growing upon me by degrees. With the old wizard now shouting with demoniac laughter, I was tempted to bolt down the narrow stairway and leave that accursed neighbor-hood. To calm myself, I rose and again looked out of the window. My eyes nearly started from their sockets when I saw that the cross above Vanderhoof's grave had fallen perceptibly since I had last looked at it. It was now tilted to an angle of forty-five degrees!

"Can't we dig up Vanderhoof and restore his soul?" I asked almost breathlessly, feeling that something must be done in a hurry. The old man rose from his chair in terror.

"No, no, no!" he screamed. "He'd kill me! I've fergot th' formula, an' if he gets out he'll be alive, without a soul. He'd kill us both!"

"Where is the bottle that contains his soul?" I asked, advancing threateningly toward him. I felt that some ghastly thing was about to happen, which I must do all in my power to prevent.

"I won't tell ye, ye young whelp!" he snarled. I felt, rather than saw, a queer light in his eyes as he backed into a corner. "An' don't ye touch me, either, or ye'll wish ye hadn't!"

I moved a step forward, noticing that on a low stool behind him there were two black bottles. Foster muttered some peculiar words in a low, singsong voice. Everything began to turn gray before my eyes, and something within me seemed to be dragged upward, trying to get out at my throat. I felt my knees become weak.

Lurching forward, I caught the old sexton by the throat, and with my free arm reached for the bottles on the stool. But the old man fell backward, striking the stool with his foot, and one bottle fell to the floor as I snatched the other. There was a flash of blue flame, and a sulfurous smell filled the room. From the little heap of broken glass a white vapor rose and followed the draft out the window.

"Curse ye, ye rascal!" sounded a voice that seemed faint and far away. Foster, whom I had released when the bottle broke, was crouching against the wall, looking smaller and more shriveled than before. His face was slowly turning greenish-black.

"Curse ye!" said the voice again, hardly sounding as though it came from his lips. "I'm done fer! That one in there was mine! *Dominie Slott took it out two hundred years ago!*"

He slid slowly toward the floor, gazing at me with hatred in eyes that were rapidly dimming. His flesh changed from white to black, and then to yellow. I saw with horror that his body seemed to be crumbling away and his clothing falling into limp folds.

The bottle in my hand was growing warm. I glanced at it, fearfully. It glowed with a faint phosphorescence. Stiff with fright, I set it upon the table, but could not keep my eyes from it. There was an ominous moment of silence as its glow became brighter, and then there came distinctly to my ears the sound of sliding earth. Gasping for breath, I looked out of the window. The moon was now well up in the sky, and by its light I could see that the fresh cross above Vanderhoof's grave had completely fallen. Once again there came the sound of trickling gravel, and no longer able to control myself, I stumbled down the stairs and found my way out of doors. Falling now and then as I raced over the uneven ground, I ran on in abject terror. When I had reached the foot of the knoll, at the entrance to that gloomy tunnel beneath the willows, I heard a horrible roar behind me. Turning, I glanced back toward the church. Its wall reflected the light of the moon, and silhouetted against it was a gigantic, loathsome, black shadow climbing from my uncle's grave and floundering gruesomely toward the church.

I told my story to a group of villagers in Haines's store the next morning. They looked from one to the other with little smiles during my tale, I noticed, but when I suggested that they accompany me to the spot, gave various excuses for not caring to go. Though there seemed to be a limit to their credulity, they cared to run no risks. I informed them that I would go alone, though I must confess that the project did not appeal to me.

As I left the store, one old man with a long, white beard hurried after me and caught my arm.

"I'll go wi' ye, lad," he said. "It do seem that I once heard my gran'pap tell o' su'thin' o' the sort concernin' old Dominie Slott. A queer old man I've heared he were, but Vanderhoof's been worse."

Dominie Vanderhoof's grave was open and deserted when we arrived. Of course it could have been grave-robbers, the two of us agreed, and yet. . . . In the belfry the bottle which I had left upon the table was gone, though the fragments of the broken one were found on the floor. And upon the heap of yellow dust and crumpled clothing that had once been Abel Foster were certain immense footprints.

After glancing at some of the books and papers strewn about the belfry room, we carried them down the stairs and burned them, as something unclean and unholy. With a spade which we found in the church basement we filled in the grave of Johannes Vanderhoof, and, as an afterthought, flung the fallen cross upon the flames.

Old wives say that now, when the moon is full, there walks about the churchyard a gigantic and bewildered figure clutching a bottle and seeking some unremembered goal.